ABOUT THE ILLUSTRATIONS

The illustrations accompanying the stories on pages 5–141 are Scandinavian engravings, originally carved on stones during the Viking Age, a period of Scandinavian expansion and sea domination that began around the eighth century and lasted into the eleventh. Some picture stones depict scenes from daily life; others contain mythological imagery.

The runes accompanying the stories on pages 147–299 are taken from Icelandic grimoires—magician's handbooks. The special characters were inscribed on barrel-lids, cheese blocks, and the scrota of *nábrókarstafur*, breeches made from the skin of dead men. The purpose of such charms were varied, from ensuring victory in wrestling matches to raising the dead from their graves. Some symbols are associated with incantations; one lockbreaking spell, meant to be spoken through a mouthful of a corpse's stomach-fat, reads:

I blow into the lock 'til its cylinder rattles and roars,
while hissing a bellyfat whistle.
May the fiend's foul breath blow fierce into the keyhole;
may the trolls tear it open;
may Puck's partisan imps pull it apart.
Bend back the bolt, all ye devil's urchins;
spring the shackle, all ye scoundrel spirits.

We are writing this copyright page from Albuquerque, New Mexico, on November 2, because we were hoping to contribute some manpower to this state, which was seen as winnable by the good guys in this terrifying and also extremely terrifying and did we mention completely fucking terrifying election. So last night we hung reminder pamphlets on the doorknobs of registered voters, and today we canvassed one particular blue-collar neighborhood, making sure that everyone who could vote walked the three blocks to the Wells Community Center to do that. We were partnered with a young man who shook our hand and said his name was Joey, and in the same breath, he said he'd just come back from Iraq. Really? we said. Yes, he said, "I'm in the Navy, was in Iraq and Kuwait for thirteen months." The guy looked about twelve. He said he was nineteen; he'd enlisted a week after high school. He was short, freckled, a little pudgy, and as he explained his situation, many others in the volunteer line asked to shake his hand and then did so. So we headed out in our rented Kia—not a good car; Thrifty is not such a good company—and once in the neighborhood, started the door-to-door knocking. Other facts about this young man named Joey: his sister and father are also in the Navy. His sister is 21 and his father is 47. All have made 20-year commitments to the service. All returned from Iraq about three weeks ago, and upon their return, were given orders to return to the war on November 18. While walking the neighborhood, we had many questions for Joey. For example: Q: Who is that on your T-shirt? A: That is Tupac. Q: Who do you fellow servicepersons favor, Kerry or Bush? A: The Navy and Air Force are more for Kerry, while the Army and Marines are more for Bush. Q: Even though he dodged the draft? A: Go figure. Q: You were sort of smitten with that girl named Amber, weren't you? A: Holy shit, yeah—she was cute! This had happened a few minutes before, when we knocked on the door of a young woman of 19, who had registered but who our records showed had not yet voted. Joey introduced himself the usual way: "Hello, I'm Joey and I just got back from Iraq." Amber was incredulous. "Did you kill anyone?" she asked. (She really did; it was her first question.) Then Joey actually said this: "Well, I'm not supposed to tell you this, because it's classified, but yeah, I killed people. Maybe twenty or thirty." He said this very much in the way one might describe having had some corns removed. Amber's eyes popped. Then Joey urged her to vote. She said this: "Well, a friend of mine said that votes from people like me aren't counted. My friend says that only rich people's votes matter." Now our eyes popped. Or ears popped. We talked her down from this belief and left her house confident that we'd convinced her to take part in our democracy. Were we confused about what Joey had said about killing Iraqis, given an hour before, he'd told us that he hadn't really stepped off his ship and/or base, and that he was a warehouse technician? Yes, we were confused, and we were also trying—quietly but firmly—to prevent Joey from using the voter roll to jot down Amber's address and phone number. Anyhoo, as the sun went down, it became very cold in New Mexico, dropping from about 60 to 40 in a few minutes. And though we were cautiously excited about our side's prospects, over the next hour, we began to have a very strange and intangible sense of— what was the word? Was the word doom? It was a strange feeling, correlating more or less directly with the onset of darkness and the plumetting temperature. And indeed now, at 3 a.m., in this Albuquerque as the networks continue to draw maps and await concessions, the night is black and the air ever-colder. The only upshot is that fairly soon, and at least for a short while, things will be quiet. We will be able to take a breath, for a moment, and brace ourselves for the next beheading. STAFF OF 826 VALENCIA: Nínive Calegari, Tracy Barreiro, Alvaro Villanueva, Susan Tu, Erin Neeley, Anna Ura. STAFF OF 826NYC: Scott Seeley, Joan Kim, Ted Thompson, Sam Potts, Max Fenton, Liz Coen, Tracy Majka. MCSWYS INTERNS & VOLUNTEERS: Mac Barnett, Karan Mahajan, Rachel Swaby, Claire Caleshu, Shannon DeJong, Angela Petrella, Katie Wudel, David Downs, Kari Hancock, Mike Blair, Kelly Jeanne Tate, Sarah Chihaya, Miles Clark, Terry Leker, Gabe Hudson, Matt Derby, Howie Wyman, Jordan Bass, Alice Kim, George Slavik, David Kramer, Josh Martin. COPY EDITORS: Gideon Lewis-Kraus, Chris Gage. THANKS TO: Birna Anna Björnsdóttir. CONTRIBUTING EDITORS: Sean Wilsey, Lawrence Weschler. WEBSITE EDITOR: John Warner. ASSISTANT WEBSITE EDITOR: Ed Page. BUSINESS MAN: Dave Kneebone. BUSINESS WOMAN: Heidi Meredith. MANAGING EDITOR: Eli Horowitz. PRESIDENT: Barb Bersche. EDITOR: Dave Eggers.

TITLE . . . . AUTHOR . . . . PAGE

A PRECURSOR OF THE CINEMA . . *Steven Millhauser* 5

LIE DOWN AND DIE . . . . *Seth Fried* 35

I UNDERSTAND . . . . *Roddy Doyle* 39

HELLO, CHARLES . . . . *Jimmy Chen* 67

COUNTING UNDERWATER . . . . . . *Kiara Brinkman* 71

ASUNCIÓN . . . . *Roy Kesey* 95

SALES . . . . *Judy Budnitz* 103

MIDNIGHT . . . . *Eric Hanson* 121

MANIFESTO . . . . *Padgett Powell* 127

ORPHANS . . . . *Benjamin Rosenbaum* 137

INTRODUCTION . . . . *Birna Anna Björnsdóttir* . . . 143

FRIDRIK AND THE EEJIT . . . . *Sjón* 147

SEVEN STORIES . . . . *Gyrðir Elíasson* 171

MY ROOM . . . . *Bragi Ólafsson* 191

UNINVITED . . . . *Einar Már Guðmundsson* . . . 197

AMERICA . . . . *Hallgrímur Helgason* 231

A RUSH OF WINGS . . . . *Þórarinn Eldjárn* 237

A ROOM UNDERGROUND . . . . . . *Guðbergur Bergsson* 243

NERVE CITY . . . . *Birna Anna Björnsdóttir,* . . . 275
Oddný Sturludóttir, and
Silja Hauksdóttir

INTERFERENCE . . . . *Andri Snær Magnason* 283

A PRECURSOR
OF THE CINEMA

by STEVEN MILLHAUSER

EVERY GREAT INVENTION is preceded by a rich history of error. Those false paths, wrong turns, and dead ends, those branchings and veerings, those wild swerves and delirious wanderings—how can they fail to entice the attention of the historian, who sees in error itself a promise of revelation? We need a taxonomy of the precursor, an esthetics of the not-quite-yet. Before the cinema, that inevitable invention of the mid-1890s, the nineteenth century gave birth to a host of brilliant toys, spectacles, and entertainments, all of which produced vivid and startling illusions of motion. It's a seductive prehistory, which divides into two lines of descent. The true line is said to be the series of rapidly presented sequential drawings that create an illusion of motion based on the optical phenomenon known as persistence of vision (Plateau's Phenakistoscope, Horner's Zoetrope, Reynaud's Praxinoscope); the false line produces effects of motion based on visual illusions of another kind (Daguerre's Diorama, with its semitransparent painted screens and shifting lights; sophisticated magic-lantern shows with double projectors and overlapping views). But here and there we find experiments in motion that are less readily explained, ambiguous experiments that invite the historian to follow obscure, questionable, and at times heretical paths. It is in this twilit realm that the work of Harlan Crane (1844–1888?) leads its enigmatic life, before sinking into a neglect from which it has never recovered.

Harlan Crane has been called a minor illustrator, an inventor, a genius, a charlatan. He is perhaps all and none of these things. So little is known of his first twenty-nine years that he seems almost to have been born at the age of thirty, a tall, reserved man in a porkpie hat, sucking on a pipe with a meerschaum bowl. We know that he was born in Brooklyn, in the commercial district near the Fulton Ferry; many years later he told W.C. Curtis that from his bedroom window he had a distant view of the church steeples and waterfront buildings of Manhattan, which seemed to him a picture that he might step into one day. His father was a haberdasher who liked to spend Sundays in the country with oil paints and an easel. When Harlan was thirteen or fourteen, the Cranes moved across the river to Manhattan. Nothing more is known of his adolescence.

We do know, from records discovered in 1954, that Crane studied drawing in his early twenties at Cooper Union and the National Academy of Design (1866–1868). His first illustrations for *Harper's Weekly*—"Selling Hot Corn," "The Street Sweeper," "Fire Engine at the Bowery Theater," "Unloading Flour at Coenties Slip"—date from 1869; the engravings are entirely conventional, without any hint of what was to come. It is of course possible that the original drawings (since lost) contained subtleties of line and tone not captured by the crude wood engravings of the day, but unfortunately nothing remains except the hastily executed and poorly printed woodcuts themselves. There is evidence, in the correspondence of friends, to suggest that Crane became interested in photography at this time. In the summer of 1870 or 1871 he set up against one wall of his walk-up studio a long table that became a kind of laboratory, where he is known to have conducted experiments on the properties of paint. During this period he also worked on a number of small inventions: a doll with a mechanical beating heart; an adaptation of the kaleidoscope that he called the Phantasmatrope, in which the turning cylinder contained a strip of colored sequential drawings that gave the illusion of a ceaselessly repeated motion (a boy tossing up and catching a blue ball, a girl in a red dress skipping rope); and a machine that he called the Vivograph, intended to help amateurs draw perfect still lifes every time by the simple manipulation of fourteen knobs and levers. As it turned out, the Vivograph produced drawings that resembled the scrawls of an angry child, the Phantasmatrope, though patented, was never put on the market because of a defect in the shutter mechanism that was essential for masking each phase of motion, and the beating hearts of his dolls kept suddenly dying. At about this time he began to paint in oils and to take up with several artists who later became part of the Verisimilist movement. In 1873 he is known to have worked on a group of paintings clearly influenced by his photographic studies: the Photographic Print series, which consisted of several blank canvases that were said to fill gradually with painted scenes. By the age of thirty, Harlan Crane seems to have settled into the career of a diligent and negligible magazine illustrator, while in his spare time he painted in oils, printed photographs on albumen paper, and performed chemical experiments on his laboratory table, but the overwhelming impression he gives is one of restlessness, of not knowing what it is, exactly, that he wants to do with his life.

Crane first drew attention in 1874, when he showed four paintings at the Verisimilist Exhibition held in an abandoned warehouse on the East River. The Verisimilists (Linton Burgis, Thomas E. Avery, Walter Henry Hart, W.C. Curtis, Octavius Ward, and Arthur Romney Ropes) were a group of young painters who celebrated the precision of photography and rejected all effects of a dreamy, suggestive, or symbolic kind. In this there was nothing new; what set them apart from other realist schools was their fanatically meticulous concern for minuscule detail. In a Verisimilist canvas it was possible to distinguish every chain stitch on an embroidered satin fan, every curling grain in an open package of Caporal tobacco, every colored kernel and strand of silk on an ear of Indian corn hanging from a slanted nail on the cracked and weather-worn door of a barn. But their special delight was in details so marvelously minute that they could be seen only with the aid of a magnifying glass. Through the lens the viewer would discover hidden minutiae—the legs of a tiny white spider half hidden in the velvet folds of a curtain, a few breadcrumbs lying in the shadow cast by a china plate's rim. Arthur Romney Ropes claimed that his work could not be appreciated without such a glass, which he distributed free of charge to visitors at his studio. Although the Verisimilists tended to favor the still life (a briarwood pipe lying on its side next to three burnt matches, one of which was broken, and a folded newspaper with readable print; a slightly uneven stack of lovingly rendered silver coins rising up beside a wad of folded five-dollar bills and a pair of reading glasses lying on three loose playing cards), they ventured occasionally into the realm of the portrait and the landscape, where they painstakingly painted every individual hair on a gentleman's beard or a lady's muff, every lobe and branching vein on every leaf of every sycamore and oak. The newspaper reviews of the exhibition commended the paintings for illusionistic effects of a remarkable kind, while agreeing that as works of art they had been harmed by the baleful influence of photography, but the four works (no longer extant) of Harlan Crane seemed to interest or irritate them in a new way.

From half a dozen newspaper reports, from a letter by Linton Burgis to his sister, and from a handful of scattered entries in journals and diaries, we can reconstruct the paintings sufficiently to understand the perplexing impressions they caused, though many details remain unrecoverable.

Still Life with Fly appears to have been a conventional painting of a dish of fruit on a table: three apples, a yellow pear, and a bunch of red grapes in a bronze dish with repoussé rim, beside which lay a woman's slender tan-colored kid glove with one slightly curling fingertip and a scattering of envelopes with sharply rendered stamps and postmarks. On the side of one of the red-and-green apples rested a beautifully precise fly. Again and again we hear of the shimmering green-ish wings, the six legs with distinct femurs, tibias, and tarsi, each with its prickly hairs, the brick-red compound eyes. Viewers agreed that the lifelike fly, with its licorice-colored abdomen showing through the silken transparence of the wings, was the triumph of the composition; what bewildered several observers was the moment when the fly darted sudden-ly through the paint and landed on an apple two inches away. The entire flight was said to have lasted no more than half a second. Two newspapers denied any movement whatever, and it remains uncertain whether the fly returned to its original apple during visiting hours, but the movement of the painted fly from apple to apple was witnessed by more than one viewer over the course of the next three weeks and is described tanta-lizingly in a letter of Linton Burgis to his sister Emily as "a very pretty simulacrum of flight."

Waves appears to have been a conventional seascape, proba-bly sketched during a brief trip to the southern shore of Long Island in the autumn of 1873. It showed a long line of waves breaking unevenly on a sandy shore beneath a melancholy sky. What drew the attention of viewers was an unusual effect: the waves could be clearly seen to fall, move up along the shore, and withdraw—an eerily silent, living image of relentlessly falling waves, under a cheerless evening sky.

The third painting, *Pygmalion*, showed the sculptor in Greek costume standing back with an expression of wonder-ment as he clutched his chisel and stared at the beautiful marble statue. Observers reported that, as they looked at the painting, the statue turned her head slowly to one side, moved her wrists, and breathed in a way that caused her naked breasts to rise and fall, before she returned to the immobility of paint.

The Séance showed eight people and a medium seated in a circle of wooden chairs, in a darkened room illuminated only by candles. The medium was a stern woman with heavy-lidded eyes, a fringed shawl covering her upper arms, and tendrils of dark hair on her forehead. Rings glittered on her plump fingers. As the viewer observed the painting, the eight faces gradually turned upward, and a dim form could be seen hovering in the darkness of the room, above or behind the head of the medium.

What are we to make of these striking effects, which seem to anticipate, in a limited way, the illusions of motion perfected by Edison and the Lumière brothers in the mid-1890s? Such motions were observed in no other of the more than three hundred Verisimilist paintings, and they inspired a number of curious explanations. The "trick" paintings, as they came to be called, were said to depend on carefully planned lighting arrangements, as in the old Diorama invented by Daguerre and in more recent magic-lantern shows, where a wagon might seem to move across a landscape (though its wheels did not turn). What this explanation failed to explain was where the lights were concealed, why no one mentioned any change in light, and how, precisely, the complex motions were produced. Another theory claimed that behind the paintings lay concealed systems of springs and gears, which caused parts of the picture to move. Such reasoning might explain how a mechanical fly, attached to the surface of a painting, could be made to move from one location to another, but we have the testimony of several viewers that the fly in Crane's still life was smooth to the touch, and in any case the clockwork theory cannot explain phenomena such as the falling and retreating waves or the suddenly appearing ghostly form. It is true that Daguerre, in a late version of his Diorama, created an illusion of moving water by the turning of a piece of silver lace on a wheel, but Daguerre's effects were created in a darkened theater, with a long distance between seated viewers and a painted semitransparent screen measuring some seventy by fifty feet, and cannot be compared with a small canvas hanging six inches from a viewer's eyes in a well-lit room.

A more compelling theory for the historian of the cinema is that Harlan Crane might have been making use of a concealed magic lantern (or a projector of his own invention) adapted to display a swift series of sequential drawings, each one illuminated for an instant and then abolished before being replaced by the next. Unfortunately there is no evidence whatever of beams of light, no one saw a tell-tale flicker, and we have no way of knowing whether the motions repeated themselves in exactly the same way each time.

The entire issue is further obscured by Crane's own bizarre claim to a reporter, at the time of the exhibition, that he had invented what he called "animate paint"—a paint chemically treated in such a way that individual particles were capable of small motions. This claim—the first sign of the future showman—led to a number of experiments performed by chemists hired by the Society for the Advancement of the Arts, where at the end of the year an exhibition of third-rate paintings took place. As visitors passed from picture to picture, the oils suddenly began to drip down onto the frames, leaving behind melting avenues, wobbly violinists, and dissolving plums. The grotesque story does not end here. In 1875 a manufacturer of children's toys placed on the market a product called Animate Paint, which consisted of a flat wooden box containing a box of brightly colored metal tubes, half a dozen slender brushes, a manual of instruction, and twenty-five sheets of specially prepared paper. On the advice of a friend, Crane filed suit; the case was decided against him, but the product was withdrawn after the parents of children with Animate Paint sets discovered that a simple stroke of chrome yellow or crimson lake suddenly took on a life of its own, streaking across the page and dripping brightly onto eiderdown comforters, English-weave rugs, and polished mahogany tables.

An immediate result of the controversy surrounding Crane's four paintings was his expulsion from the Verisimilist group, which claimed that his optical experiments detracted from the aim of the movement: to reveal the world with ultraphotographic precision. We may be forgiven for wondering whether the expulsion served a more practical purpose, namely, to remove from the group a member who was receiving far too much attention. In any case, it may be argued that Crane's four paintings, far from betraying the aim of the Verisimilists, carried that aim to its logical conclusion. For if the intention of verisimilism was to go beyond the photograph in its attempt to "reveal" the world, isn't the leap into motion a further step in the same direction? The conventional Verisimilist wave distorts the real wave by its lack of motion; Crane's breaking wave is the true Verisimilist wave, released from the falsifying rigidity of paint.

Little is known of Crane's life during the three years following the Exhibition of 1874. We know from W.C. Curtis, the one Verisimilist who remained a friend, that Crane shut himself up all day in his studio, with its glimpse of the distant roof of the Fulton Fish Market and a thicket of masts on the East River, and refused to show his work to anyone. Once, stopping by in the evening, Curtis noticed an empty easel and several large canvases turned against the wall. "It struck me forcibly," Curtis recorded in his diary, "that I was not permitted to witness his struggles." Exactly what those struggles were, we have no way of knowing. We do know that a diminishing number of his undistinguished woodcut engravings continued to appear in *Harper's Weekly*, as well as in *Appleton's Journal* and several other publications, and that for a time he earned a small income by tinting portrait photographs. "On a long table at one side of the studio," Curtis noted on one occasion, "I observed a wet cell, a number of beakers, several tubes of paint, and two vessels filled with powders." It remains unclear what kinds of experiment Crane was conducting, although the theme of chemical experimentation raises the old question of paint with unusual properties.

In 1875 or 1876 he began to frequent the studio of Robert Allen Lowe, a leading member of a loose-knit group of painters who called themselves Transgressives and welcomed Crane as an offender of Verisimilist pieties. Crane began taking his evening meals at the Black Rose, an ale house patronized by members of the group. According to Lowe, in a letter to Samuel Hope (a painter of still lifes who later joined the Transgressives), Crane ate quickly, without seeming to notice what was on his plate, spoke very little, and smoked a big-bowled meerschaum pipe with a richly stained rim, a cherry-wood stem, and a black rubber bit as he tilted back precariously in his chair and hooked one foot around a table leg. He wore a soft porkpie hat far back on his head and followed the conversation intently behind thick clouds of smoke.

The Transgressive movement began with a handful of disaffected Verisimilists who felt that the realist program of verisimilism did not go far enough. Led by Robert Allen Lowe, a painter known for his spectacularly detailed paintings of dead pheasants, bunches of asparagus, and gleaming magnifying glasses lying on top of newspapers with suddenly magnified print, the Transgressives argued that Verisimilist painting was hampered by its craven obedience to the picture frame, which did nothing but draw attention to the artifice of the painted world it enclosed. Instead of calling for the abolishment of the frame, in the manner of trompe l'oeil art, Lowe insisted that the frame be treated as a transition or "threshold" between the painting proper and the world outside the painting. Thus in a work of 1875, *Three Pears*, a meticulous still life showing three green pears on a wooden table sharply lit by sunlight streaming through a window, the long shadows of the pears stretch across the tabletop and onto the vine-carved picture frame itself. This modest painting led to an outburst of violations and disruptions by Lowe and other members of the group, and their work made its way into the Brewery Show of 1877.

The Transgressive Exhibition—better known as the Brewery Show, since the paintings were housed in an abandoned brewery on Twelfth Avenue near the meat-packing district—received a good deal of unfavorable critical attention, although it proved quite popular with the general public, who were attracted by the novelty and playfulness of the paintings. One well-known work, *The Window*, showed a life-sized casement window in a country house. Real ivy grew on the picture frame. *The Writing Desk*, by Robert Allen Lowe, showed part of a roll-top desk in close-up detail: two rows of pigeon holes and a small, partly open door with a wooden knob. In the pigeon holes one saw carefully painted envelopes, a large brass key, folded letters, a pince-nez, and a coil of string, part of which hung carelessly down over the frame. Viewers discovered that one of the pigeon holes was a real space containing a real envelope addressed to Robert Allen Lowe, while the small door, composed of actual wood, protruded from the picture surface and opened to reveal a stoneware ink bottle from which a quill pen emerged at a slant. Several people reached for the string, which proved to be a painted image. *Grapes*, a large canvas by Samuel Hope, showed an exquisitely painted bunch of purple grapes from which real grapes emerged to rest in a silver bowl on a table beneath the painting. After the first day, a number of paintings had to be roped off, to prevent the public from pawing them to pieces.

In this atmosphere of playfulness, extravagance, and illusionist wit, the paintings of Harlan Crane attracted no unusual attention, although we sometimes hear of a "disturbing" or "uncanny" effect. He displayed three paintings. *Still Life with Fly #2* showed an orange from which the rind had been partially peeled away in a long spiral, half a sliced peach with the gleaming pit rising above the flat plane of its sliced flesh, the hollow, jaggedly broken shell of an almond beside half an almond and some crumbs, and an ivory-handled fruit knife. To the side of the peach clung a vertical fly, its wings depicted against the peach-skin, its head and front legs rising above the exposed flesh of the peach. An iridescent drop of water, which seemed about to fall, clung to the peach-skin beside the fly. A number of viewers claimed that the fly suddenly left the canvas, circled above their heads, and landed on the upper right-hand corner of the frame before returning to the peach beside the glistening, motionless drop. Several viewers apparently swatted at the fly as it flew beside them, but felt nothing.

A second painting, *Young Woman*, is the only known instance of a portrait in the oeuvre of Harlan Crane. The painting showed a girl of eighteen or nineteen, wearing a white dress and a straw bonnet with a cream-colored ostrich plume, standing in a bower of white and red roses with sun and leaf-shadow stippling her face. In one hand she held a partly open letter; a torn envelope lay at her feet. She stood facing the viewer, with an expression of troubled yearning. Her free hand reached forward as if to grasp at something or someone. Despite its Verisimilist attention to detail—the intricate straw weave of the bonnet, the individual thorns on the trellis of roses—the painting looked back to the dreary conventions of narrative art deplored by Verisimilists and Transgressives alike; but what struck more than one viewer was the experience of stepping up close to the painting, in order to study the lifelike details, and feeling the unmistakable sensation of a hand touching a cheek.

The third painting, *The Escape*, hung alone in a small dusky niche or alcove. It depicted a gaunt man slumped in the shadows of a stone cell. From an unseen window a ray of dusty light fell slantwise through the gloom. Viewers reported that, as they examined the dark painting, in the twilit niche, the prisoner stirred and looked about. After a while he began to crawl forward, moving slowly over the hard floor, staring with haunted eyes. Several viewers spoke of a sudden tension in the air; they saw or felt something before or beside them, like a ghost or a wind. In the painting, the man had vanished. One journalist, who returned to observe the painting three days in succession, reported that the "escape" took place three or four times a day, at different hours, and that, if you watched the empty painting closely, you could see the figure gradually reappearing in the paint, in the manner of a photographic image appearing on albumen paper coated with silver nitrate and exposed to sunlight beneath a glass negative.

Although a number of newspapers do not even mention the Crane paintings, others offer familiar and bogus explanations for the motions, while still others take issue with descriptions published in rival papers. Whatever one may think of the matter, it is clear that we are no longer dealing with paintings as works of art, but rather with paintings as *performances*. In this sense the Brewery Show represents the first clear step in Harlan Crane's career as an inventor-showman, situated in a questionable realm between the old world of painting and the new world of moving images.

It is also worth noting that, with the exception of Lowe's *Writing Desk*, Transgressive paintings are not trompe l'oeil. The trompe l'oeil painting means to deceive, and only then to undeceive; but the real ivy and the real grapes immediately present themselves as actual objects disruptively continuing the painted representation. Harlan Crane's animate paintings are more unsettling still, for they move back and forth deliberately between representation and deception, and have the general effect of radically destabilizing the painting—for if a painted fly may at any moment suddenly enter the room, might not the painted knife slip from the painted table and cut the viewer's hand?

After their brief moment of notoriety in 1877, the Transgressives went their separate ways. Samuel Hope, Winthrop White, and C.W.E. Palmer returned to the painting of conventional still lifes; Robert Allen Lowe ventured with great success into the world of children's-book illustration; and John Frederick Hill devoted his remaining years to large, profitable paintings of very white nudes on very red sofas, destined to be hung above rows of darkly glistening bottles in smoky saloons.

Crane now entered a long period of reclusion, which only in retrospect appears the inevitable preparation for his transformation into the showman of 1883. It is more reasonable to imagine these years as ones of restlessness, of dissatisfaction, of doubt and questioning and a sense of impediment. Such a view is supported by the few glimpses we have of him, in the correspondence of acquaintances and in the diary of W.C. Curtis. We know that in the summer of 1878 he took a series of photographs of picnickers on the Hudson River, from which he made half a dozen charcoal sketches that he later destroyed. Not long afterward, he attempted and abandoned several small inventions, including a self-cleaning brush: through its hollow core ran a thin rubber tube filled with a turpentine-based solvent released by pressing a button. For a brief time he took up with Eliphalet Hale and the Sons of Truth, a band of painters who were opposed to the sentimental and falsely noble in art and insisted on portraying subjects of a deliberately vile or repellent kind, such as steaming horse droppings, dead rats torn open by crows, blood-soaked sheets, scrupulously detailed pools of vomit, rotting vegetables, and suppurating sores. Crane was indifferent to the paintings, but he liked Hale, a soft-spoken God-fearing man who believed fervently in the beauty of all created things.

Meanwhile Crane continued to take photographs, switching in the early 1880s from wet-collodion plates to the new dry-gelatin process in order to achieve sharper definition of detail. He also began trying his hand at serial photography. At one period he took scores of photographs of an unknown woman in a chemise with a fallen shoulder strap as she turned her face and body very slightly each time. He tested many kinds of printing paper, which he coated with varying proportions of egg white, potassium iodide, and potassium bromide, before sensitizing the prepared paper in a solution of silver nitrate. He told W.C. Curtis that he hated the "horrible fixity" of the photographic image and wished to disrupt it from within. In 1881 or 1882 we find him experimenting with a crude form of projector: to an old magic lantern he attached a large, revolving glass disk of his own invention on which transparent positives were arranged in phase. One evening, to the astonishment of Curtis, he displayed for several seconds on a wall of his studio the Third Avenue El with a train moving jerkily across.

But Crane did not pursue this method of bringing photographs to life, which others would carry to completion. Despite his interest in photography, he considered it inferior to painting. After attending a photographic exhibition with W.C. Curtis, he declared: "Painting is dead," but a week later at an oyster bar he remarked that photography was a "disappointment" and couldn't compare with paint when it came to capturing the textures of things. What is striking in the career of Harlan Crane is that more than once he seemed to be in the direct line of invention and experimentation that led to the cinema of Edison and the Lumières, and that each time he turned deliberately away. It was as if he were following a parallel line of discovery, searching for an illusion of motion based not on serial photographs and perforated strips of celluloid, but on different principles altogether.

The Phantoptic Theater opened on October 4, 1883. People purchased tickets at the door, passed through a foyer illuminated by brass gas-lamps on the walls, and made their way toward an arched opening half-concealed by a thick crimson curtain hung on gold rings. The curtain, the arch, and the rings turned out to be images painted on the wall; the actual entrance was through a second, less convincing curtain that opened into a small theater with a high ceiling, worn redplush seats for some three hundred people, a cut-glass chandelier, and a raised stage with a black velvet curtain. Between the audience and the stage stood a piano. Newspaper reports differ in certain details, but the performance appears to have begun by the emergence from a side door of a man in evening dress and gleaming black shoes who strode to the piano bench, flung out his tails, sat grandly down, threw back his head, and began to play a waltz described variously as "lively" and "melancholy." The hissing gas-jets in the chandelier grew quiet and faint as the footlights were turned up. Slowly the black curtain rose. It revealed an immense oil painting that took up the entire rear wall of the stage and was framed on three sides by a polished dark wood carved with vine leaves and bunches of grapes.

The painting showed a ballroom filled with dancers: women with roses and ropes of pearls in their high-piled hair, heavily flounced ball-gowns that swept along the floor, and tight-corseted bosoms pressing against low-cut necklines trimmed with lace; men with beards and monocles, tight-waisted tailcoats, and very straight backs. A hearth with a fire was visible in one wall, high windows hung with dark-blue velvet curtains in another. As the audience watched and the pianist played his lively, melancholy waltz, the figures in the painting began to dance. Here the newspaper accounts differ. Some say the figures began to waltz suddenly, others report that first one pair of dancers began to move and then another—but it is clear to everyone that the figures are moving in a lifelike manner, made all the more convincing by the waltz music welling up from the piano. Other movements were also observed: the flames in the fireplace leaped and fell, a man leaning his elbow on the mantelpiece removed his monocle and replaced it in his eye, and a woman with yellow and pink roses in her hair fanned herself with a black silk fan.

The audience, exhilarated by the spectacle of the waltzing figures, soon began to notice a second phenomenon. Some of the dancers appeared to emerge from the ballroom onto the stage, where they continued waltzing. The stage, separated from the first row of seats by the piano and a narrow passage-way, gradually seemed to become an extension of the ballroom. But the optical effect was unsettling because the dancers on the stage were seen against a ballroom that was itself perceived as a flat perspective painting—a painted surface with laws of its own. After no more than a minute or two the dancers returned to the painting, where for several minutes they continued to turn in the picture until the last notes of the waltz died away. Gradually—or suddenly, according to one journalist—the figures became immobile. In the auditorium, the gaslights in the chandelier were turned up.

From a door at stage-left emerged Harlan Crane, dressed in black evening clothes and a silk top hat that glistened as if wet in the glare of the gas-jets. He stepped to the front of the stage and bowed once to enthusiastic applause, sweeping his hat across his body. He rose to wait out the shouts and cheers. Holding up a hand, he invited the audience onto the stage to examine his painting, asking only that they refrain from touching it. He then turned on his heel and strode out of sight.

An assistant came onto the stage, carrying a long red-velvet rope. He suspended the rope between two wooden posts at both ends of the painting, some three feet from its surface.

Members of the audience climbed both sets of side steps onto the stage, where they gathered behind the velvet rope and examined the vast canvas. Sometimes they bent forward over the rope to study the painting more closely through a lorgnette or monocle. In this second phase of the show, the theater may be said to have withdrawn certain of its features and transformed itself into an art museum—one that contained a single painting. The evidence we have suggests that it was in fact an oil painting, with visible brushstrokes, rather than a screen or other surface onto which an image had been cast.

There were three showings daily: at two o'clock, four o'clock, and eight o'clock. Crane, who was present at every performance, never varied his routine, so that one wit said it wasn't Harlan Crane at all, but a mechanical figure, like Kempelen's Chess Player, fitted out with one of Edison's talking machines.

Contemporary accounts speculate lavishly about the secret of the motions, some seeing the Phantoptic Theater as a development of the old Diorama, others arguing that it was done with a specially adapted magic lantern that projected serial images of dancers onto a motionless background. But the motions of the Diorama were nothing like those of the Phantoptic Theater, for Daguerre's effects, produced by artful manipulation of light, were limited to extremely simple illusions, such as lava or masses of snow rushing down the side of a mountain; and the theory of serial projection, while anticipating later advances in the development of the cinema, cannot explain the emergence of the dancers onto the stage. For their part, the dancers on stage were variously explained as real actors appearing from behind a curtain, as images projected onto "invisible" screens, and as optical illusions produced by "hidden lenses" that the writer does not bother to describe. In truth, the riddle of Crane's *Ballroom* illusions has never been solved. What strikes the student of cinema is the peculiar position assumed by Crane and his theater with respect to the history of the illusion of motion. For if in one respect the Phantoptic Theater shares the late-nineteenth-century fascination with the science of moving images, in another it looks back, far back, to a dim, primitive world in which painted images are magical visions infused with the breath of life. Crane's refusal to abandon painting and embrace the new technology of serial photographs, his insistence on creating illusions of motion that cannot be accounted for in the new way, make him a minor, quirky, exasperating, and finally puzzling figure in the pre-history of the cinema, who seizes our attention precisely because he created a riddling world of motion entirely his own.

For a while the daily shows of the Phantoptic Theater continued to draw enthusiastic audiences, even as the press turned its gaze in other directions. By the end of the year, attendance had begun to decline; and by the middle of January the theater rarely held more than a few dozen people, crowded expectantly into the front rows.

We have several glimpses of Crane during this period. In the diary of W.C. Curtis we hear that Crane is hard at work on a new painting for his theater, though he refuses to reveal anything about it; sometimes he complains of "difficulties." One evening in December, Curtis notes with surprise the presence of a youngish woman at the studio, with auburn hair and a "plain, intelligent" face, whom he recognizes as the woman in the chemise. Crane introduced her first as Annie, then as Miss Merrow; she lowered her eyes and quickly disappeared behind a folding screen that stood in one corner of the studio. After this, Curtis saw her now and then on evening visits, when she invariably retreated behind the screen. Crane never spoke of her. Curtis remarks on his friend's "secretive" nature, speculates that she is his mistress, and drops the subject.

One evening at an ale house, Crane suddenly began to speak of his admiration for Thomas Edison. Unfolding a newspaper, he pointed to an interview in which the inventor insisted on the importance of "chance" in his discoveries. Crane read several passages aloud, then folded the paper and looked up at Curtis. "A methodical man who believes in chance. Now what does that sound like to you, Curtis?" Curtis thought for a moment before replying: "A gambler." Crane, looking startled and then pleased, gave a laugh and a shake of the head. "I hadn't thought of that. Yes, a gambler." "And you were thinking—" "Oh, nothing, nothing—do you have any matches, Curtis, I never seem to—but a methodical man, who believes in chance—tell me, Curtis, have you ever heard a better definition of an artist?"

Not until March of 1884 was a new piece announced. The opening took place at eight o'clock in the evening. The black velvet curtain rose to reveal *Picnic on the Hudson*, a monumental painting that showed groups of picnickers sitting in sun-checked green shade between high trees. Sunlight glowed in sudden bursts: on the corner of a white cloth spread on the grass, on a bunch of red grapes in a silver dish, on the lace sleeve of a lavender dress, on the blue-green river in the background, where sunlit portions of a two-stacked steamer were visible through the trees. As the pianist played a medley of American melodies ("Aura Lee," "Sweet Genevieve," "Carry Me Back to Old Virginny," "I'll Take You Home Again, Kathleen"), *Picnic on the Hudson* began to show signs of life: the second of the steamer's smokestacks emerged fully from behind the trunk of an oak, a squirrel moved along a branch, the hand of a picnicker held out a glistening crystal glass, into which, from the mouth of a wine bottle, poured a ruby-colored liquid. A small boy in boots and breeches and a feathered hat strolled into view, holding in one hand a red rubber ball. A young woman, wearing a straw poke bonnet trimmed with purple and gold pansies, slowly smiled. The several groups of men and women seated on the grass seemed to feel a great sense of peacefulness, in the warm shade, under the trees, on a summer afternoon beside the Hudson. A number of viewers later said that the painting created in them a feeling of deep repose.

As the picnickers relaxed on the riverbank, one of them, a mustached young man in a bowler hat who had been gazing toward the river, turned his head lazily in the direction of the audience and abruptly stopped. The woman in the straw bonnet, following his gaze, turned and stared. And now all the faces of the people in the painting turned to look toward the viewers, many of whom later spoke of feeling, at that moment, a sensation of desire or yearning. Someone in the audience rose and slowly climbed the steps to the stage; others soon followed. Once on the stage, they walked up and down along the painting, admiring its Verisimilist accuracy of detail—the brown silk stitching on the back of a woman's white kid glove, the webbed feet and overlapping feather-tips of a tiny seagull sitting on the railing of the steamer, the minuscule fibers visible in the torn corner of a folded newspaper on the grass. Contemporary reports are unclear about what happened next, but it appears that a man, reaching out to feel the canvas, experienced in his fingertips a sensation of melting or dissolving, before he stepped into the painting. Those who entered the painting later reported a "dreamlike feeling" or "a sense of great happiness," but were less clear about the physical act of entry. Most spoke of some kind of barrier that immediately gave way; several felt hard canvas and paint. One woman, a Mrs. Amelia Hartman, said that it reminded her of immersing herself in the ocean, but an ocean whose water was dry. Inside the painting, the figures watched them but did not speak. The mingling seems to have lasted from about ten minutes to half an hour, before the visitors experienced what one described as a "darkening" and another as "stepping into deep shade." The deep shade soon revealed itself to be a corridor lit by dimmed gas-jets, which led to a door that opened into the side of the auditorium.

When all the members of the audience had returned to their seats, the pianist drove his music to a crescendo, threw back his head with a great agitation of hair, struck three ringing chords, and stopped. The figures in the painting resumed their original poses. Slowly the curtain came down. Harlan Crane walked briskly out onto the apron, bowed once, and strode off. The showing was over.

Newspaper reviews outdid themselves in their attempts to explain the new range of effects produced by Crane in *Picnic on the Hudson*. The *New York News* proposed a hollow space behind the painting, with actors and a stage set; the picture, an ingenious deception, was nothing but a diaphanous screen that separated the actors from the stage. The proposed solution fails to mention the hardness of the canvas, as reported by many members of the audience, and in any case it cannot explain why no one ever detected anything resembling a "diaphanous screen," or how the mysterious screen vanished to permit entry. Other explanations are equally unsatisfactory: one columnist described the barrier as an artificially produced "mist" or "vapor" onto which magic lantern slides were projected, and another suggested that the audience, once it reached the stage, had inhaled an opiate sprayed into the atmosphere and had experienced a shared hallucination.

These explanations, far from revealing the secret of Crane's art, obscured it behind translucent, fluttering veils of language, which themselves were seductive and served only to sharpen the public's curiosity and desire.

Picnic on the Hudson was shown to a packed house every evening at eight o'clock, while *The Ballroom* continued to be displayed daily to diminishing audiences. By early summer, when evening attendance at the Phantoptic Theater showed signs of falling off, a rumor began to circulate that Crane had already started a new work, which would usher in an age of wonder; and it was said that if you listened closely, in the theater, you could hear the artist-showman moving about in the basement, pushing things out of the way, hammering, preparing.

A single anecdote survives from this period. In a dockside restaurant with a view of the Brooklyn ferry across the river, Crane told W.C. Curtis that as a child he had thought he would grow up to be a ferryboat captain. "I like rivers," he said. "I thought I'd travel a lot." Curtis, a well-traveled man who had spent three years in Europe in his twenties, urged Crane to go abroad with him, to Paris and Munich and Venice. Crane appeared to consider it. "Not far enough," he then said. Curtis had also spent six months in China; he immediately began to sing the praises of the Orient. Crane gave "an odd little laugh" and, with a shrug of one shoulder, remarked, "Still not far enough." Then he lit up his pipe and ordered another dish of Blue Point oysters.

We know very little about *Terra Incognita*, which was shown only a single time (February 6, 1885). From the foyer of the Phantoptic Theater, visitors were led down a flight of steps into a dark room illuminated by a few low-burning gas-jets in glass lanterns suspended from the ceiling. Gradually the viewers became aware of a painting rising up on all sides—a continuous twelve-foot-high canvas that stretched flat along all four walls and curved at the wall junctures.

The vast, enclosing composition seemed at first to be painted entirely black, but slowly other colors became visible, deep browns and blackish reds, while vague shapes began to emerge. Here the evidence becomes confused. Some claimed that the painting represented a dark cavern with rocks and ledges. Others spoke of a dark sea. All witnesses agreed that they gradually became aware of shadowy figures, who seemed to float up from the depths of the painting and to move closer to the surface. A woman screamed—it isn't clear when—and was harshly hushed. At some point several figures appeared to pass from the surface into the dark and crowded room. Precisely what took place from then on remains uncertain. One woman later spoke of a sensation of cold on the back of her neck; another described a soft pressure on her upper arm. Others, men and women, reported "a sensation of being rubbed up against, as by a cat," or of being touched on the face or bosom or leg. Not all impressions were gentle. Here and there, hats were knocked off, shawls pulled away, hands and elbows seized. One witness said, "I felt as though a great wind had blown through me, and I was possessed by a feeling of sweetness and despair." Someone screamed again. After a third scream, things happened very quickly: a woman burst into tears, people began pushing their way to the stairs, there were cries and shouts and violent shoving. A bearded man fell against the canvas. A young woman in a blue felt hat trimmed with dark red roses sank slowly to the floor.

The commotion was heard by a janitor sweeping the aisles of the upper theater. He came down to check and immediately ran outside for a policeman, who hurried over and appeared at the top of the stairs with a lantern and a nightstick to witness a scene of dangerous panic. People were sobbing and pushing forward, tearing at one another's bodies, trampling the fallen woman. The policeman was unable to fight his way down. Shrill blows of his whistle brought three more policemen with lanterns, who helped the terrified crowd up the narrow stairway. When it was all over, seven people were hospitalized; the young woman on the floor later died of injuries to the face and head. The painting had been damaged in many places; one portion of canvas showed a ragged hole the size of a fist. On the floor lay broken fans and crushed top hats, torn ostrich plumes, a scattering of dark red rose petals, a mauve glove, an uncoiled chignon with one unraveled ribbon, a cracked monocle at the end of a black silk cord.

Regrettably, newspaper accounts concentrated more on the panic than on the painting. There were the usual attempts at tracing the motions of the figures to hidden magic lanterns, even though not a single visitor reported a beam of light in the darkened, gas-lit room. The penetration of the figures into the room was explained either as a theatrical stunt performed by concealed actors or a delusion stimulated by the heightened anxiety of a crowd in the dark. In truth, we simply cannot explain the reported effects by means of the scant evidence that has come down to us. It is worth noting that no one has ever duplicated the motions produced in the Phantoptic Theater. On strictly objective grounds, we cannot rule out the possibility that Crane's figures in *Terra Incognita* really did what they appeared to do, that is, emerge from the paint and enter the room, perhaps as a result of some chemical discovery no longer recoverable.

By order of the mayor, Crane's theater was closed. Three weeks later, when he attempted to open a second theater, city authorities intervened. Meanwhile the parents of the trampled woman sued Crane for inciting a riot. Although he was exonerated, the judge issued a stern warning. Crane never returned to public life.

In his cramped studio and in neighborhood chophouses we catch glimpses of him over the next few years: a thin-lipped, quiet man, with a clean-shaven face and brooding eyes. He is never without his big-bowled meerschaum with its cherrywood stem and its chewed rubber bit. W.C. Curtis speaks of his melancholy, his long silences. Was he bitter over the closing of his theater, over his brief notoriety that failed to develop into lasting fame? Only once does he complain to Curtis: he regrets, he says, that his "invention" has never been recognized. When he is mentioned in the papers now and then, it is not as an artist or an inventor but as the former proprietor of the Phantoptic Theater.

He is often tired. Curtis notes that Crane is always alone in the evenings when he visits; we hear no further mention of Annie Merrow, who vanishes from the record. For a time Crane returns to his old invention, the Phantasmatrope, attempting to solve the problem of the shutter but abruptly losing interest. He no longer takes photographs. He spends less and less time in his studio and instead passes long hours in coffee shops and cheap restaurants, reading newspapers slowly and smoking his pipe. He refuses to attend art exhibitions. He likes to stroll past the East River piers and ferry slips, to linger before the windows of the sailmakers' shops on South Street. Now and then, in order to pay the rent, he takes a job that he quits after a few weeks: a toy salesman in a department store, a sandwich-board man advertising a new lunchroom. One day he sells his camera for a dollar. He takes long walks into distant neighborhoods, sits on benches at the water's edge, a lean man beside wavering lines of smoke. He appears to subsist on apples and roasted chestnuts bought in the street, on cheap meals in ale houses and oyster bars. He likes to watch the traffic on the East River: three-masted barks, old paddlewheel towboats and the new screw-propelled tugs, steamboats with funnels and masts.

Suddenly—the word belongs to W.C. Curtis—Crane returns to his studio and shuts himself up day after day. He refuses to speak of his work. At ale houses and night cafés he picks at his food, looks restlessly about, knocks out his pipe on the table and packs in fresh tobacco with slow taps of his fingertip. Curtis can scarcely see him behind clouds of smoke. "It's like the old days," Curtis notes in his diary, adding ruefully, "without the joy."

One evening, while Crane is raising to his mouth a glass of dark ale, he pauses in mid-air, as if a thought has crossed his mind, and mentions to Curtis that a few hours ago he rented a room in an old office building on Chambers Street, a few blocks from City Hall Park. Curtis starts to ask a question but thinks better of it. The next day a flurry of hand-lettered signs on yellow paper appears on hoardings and lampposts, announcing a new exhibition on November 1, 1888.

In the small room with its two dust-streaked windows and its roll-top desk, a single painting was on display. Only W.C. Curtis and four of Curtis's friends attended. Crane stood leaning against the opposite wall, between the two windows, smoking away at his pipe. Curtis describes the painting as roughly four feet by five feet, in a plain, varnished frame. A small piece of white paper, affixed to the wall beside it, bore the words SWAN SONG.

The painting depicted Crane's studio, captured with Verisimilist fidelity. Crane himself stood before an easel, with his long legs and a buttoned-up threadbare jacket, gripping his palette and a clutch of brushes in one hand and reaching out with a long, fine-tipped brush in the other as he held his head back and stared at the canvas "with a look of ferocity." The walls of the studio were thickly covered with framed and unframed paintings and pencil-and-chalk sketches by Crane, many of which Curtis recognized from Crane's Verisimilist and Transgressive periods. There were also a number of paintings Curtis had never seen before, which he either passes over in silence or describes with disappointing briskness ("another pipe-and-mug still life," "a rural scene"). On the floor stood piles of unframed canvases, stacked six deep against the walls. One such painting, near a corner, showed an arm protruding from the surface and grasping the leg of a chair. The painting on the easel, half finished, appeared to be a preliminary study for *Picnic on the Hudson*; a number of seated figures had been roughly sketched but not painted in, and in another place a woman's right arm, which had been finished at a different angle, showed through the paint as a ghostly arm without a hand. The studio also included a zinc washstand, the corner of a cast-iron heating stove, and part of a thick table, on which stood one of Crane's magic lanterns and a scattering of yellowed and curling photographs showing a young woman in a chemise, with one strap slipping from a shoulder and her head turned at many different angles.

From everything we know of it, *Swan Song* would have been at home in the old Verisimilist Exhibition of 1874. Curtis notes the barely visible tail of a mouse between two stacked canvases, as well as a scattering of pipe ashes on a windowsill. As he and his friends stood before the painting, wondering what was new and different about it, they heard behind them the word "Gentlemen." In truth they had almost forgotten Crane. Now they turned to see him standing against the wall between the two windows, with his pipe in his hand. Smoke floated about him. Curtis was struck by his friend's bony, melancholy face. Weak light came through the dusty windows on both sides of Crane, who seemed to be standing in the dimmest part of the room. "Thank you," he said quietly, "for—" And here he raised his arm in a graceful gesture that seemed to include the painting, the visitors, and the occasion itself. Without completing his sentence, he thrust his pipe back in his mouth and narrowed his eyes behind drifts of bluish smoke.

It is unclear exactly what happened next. Someone appears to have exclaimed. Curtis, turning back to the painting, became aware of a motion or "agitation" in the canvas. As he watched, standing about a foot from the picture, the paintings in the studio began to fade away. Those that hung on the wall and those that stood in stacks on the floor grew paler and paler, the painting on the easel and the photographs on the table began to fade, and Crane himself, with his palette and brush, seemed to be turning into a ghost.

Soon nothing was left in the painting but a cluttered studio hung with white canvases, framed and unframed. Blank canvases were stacked six deep against the walls. The mouse's tail, Curtis says, showed distinctly against the whiteness of the empty canvas.

"What the devil!" someone cried. Curtis turned around. In the real room, Crane himself was no longer there.

The door, Curtis noticed, was partly open. He and two of his friends immediately left the rented office and took a four-wheeler to Crane's studio. There they found the door unlocked. Inside, everything was exactly as in the painting: the easel with its blank canvas, the empty rectangles on the walls, the table with its scattering of blank printing paper, the stacks of white canvas standing about, even the ashes on the windowsill. When Curtis looked more closely, he had the uneasy sensation that a mouse's tail had just darted out of sight behind a canvas. Curtis felt he had stepped into a painting. It struck him that Crane had anticipated this moment, and he had an odd impulse to tip his hat to his old friend. It may have been the pale November light, or the "premonition of dread" that came over him then, but he was suddenly seized by a sense of insubstantiality, as if at any moment he might begin to fade away. With a backward glance, like a man pursued, he fled the empty studio.

Crane was never seen again. Not a single painting or sketch has survived. At best we can clumsily resurrect them through careless newspaper accounts and the descriptions, at times detailed, in the diary of W.C. Curtis. Of his other work, nothing remains except some eighty engravings in the pages of contemporary magazines—mediocre woodblock reproductions in no way different from the hurried hackwork of the time. Based on this work alone—his visible oeuvre—Harlan Crane deserves no more than a footnote in the history of late-nineteenth-century American magazine illustration. It is his vanished work that lays claim to our attention.

He teases us, this man who is neither one thing nor another, who swerves away from the history of painting in the direction of the cinema, while creating a lost medium that has no name. If I call him a precursor, it is because he is part of the broad impulse in the last quarter of the nineteenth century to make pictures move—to enact for mass audiences, through modern technology, an ancient mystery. In this sense it is tempting to think of him as a figure who looks both ways: toward the future, when the inventions of Edison and the Lumières will soon be born, and toward the remote past, when paintings were ambiguously alive, in a half-forgotten world of magic and dream. But finally it would be a mistake to abandon him here, in a shadow-place between a vanished world and a world not yet come into being. Rather, his work represents a turn, a dislocation, a bold error, a venture into a possible future that somehow failed to take place. One might say that history, in the person of Harlan Crane, had a wayward and forbidden thought. And if, after all, that unborn future should one day burst forth? Then Harlan Crane might prove to be a precursor in a more exact sense. For even now there are signs of boredom with the old illusions of cinema, a longing for new astonishments. In research laboratories in universities across the country, in film studios in New York and California, we hear of radical advances in multidimensional imaging, of mobile vivigrams, of a modern cinema that banishes the old-fashioned screen in order to permit audiences to mingle freely with brilliantly realistic illusions. The time may be near when the image will be released from its ancient bondage to cave wall and frame and screen, and a new race of beings will walk the earth. On that day the history of the cinema will have to be rewritten, and Harlan Crane will take his place as a prophet. For us, in the meantime, he must remain what he was to his contemporaries: a twilight man, a riddle. If we have summoned him here from the perfection of his self-erasure, it is because his lost work draws us toward unfamiliar and alluring realms, where history seems to hesitate for a moment, in order to contemplate an alternative, before striding on.

The diary of W.C. Curtis, published in 1898, makes one last reference to Harlan Crane. In the summer of 1896 Curtis, traveling in Vienna, visited the Kunsthistorisches Museum, where a still life (by A. Muntz) reminded him of his old friend. "The pipe was so like his," Curtis writes, "that it cast me back to the days of our old friendship." But rather than devoting a single sentence to the days of his old friendship, Curtis describes the painting instead: the stained meerschaum bowl, the cherrywood stem, the black rubber bit, even the tarnished brass ring at the upper end of the bowl, which we hear about for the first time. The pipe rests on its side, next to a pewter-lidded beer stein decorated with the figure of a hunting dog in relief. Bits of ash, fallen from the bowl, lie scattered on the plain wooden tabletop. In the bowl glows a small ember. A thin curl of smoke rises over the rim.

LIE DOWN AND DIE

by SETH FRIED

MY FATHER WAS shot and killed the day after I was born. He was in St. Louis, Missouri, at the time and I am forced to assume that things did not go well for him there. I am forced to assume a great deal about my father: that he was tall, that he shaved against the grain, or that his death was tragic and undeserved—and while I have never been one to give in to superstitions, I am also forced to assume that somehow he knew he would never live long enough to see me alive.

For instance, he took me to a baseball game when I was still in the womb. There is a photograph of my mother leaning back uncomfortably in Tiger Stadium, a baseball cap propped at a careful angle on her stomach. This seems, to me, the act of a man who had serious doubts concerning his ability to survive the nine months it would take for his son to be born.

My mother never explained why my father had been shot or by whom, which even as a child I regarded as strange—a strangeness which was complicated by the fact that when I was thirteen years old my mother was abducted on an unannounced, impromptu trip to Niagara Falls and was never seen again.

My family was full of stories like that: dubious suicides, sudden disappearances, the police always suspecting foul play. An uncle would vanish only to be found mangled in farm equipment miles away from home, a cousin would run away, turning up weeks later with her wrists slit in the cargo hull of a ship bound for South America. It was as if our family tree had been written in invisible ink, names and branches disappearing as quickly as they were written.

Even things that were attached to our family by the simple means of possession seemed doomed; pets would burst into flames, appliances, fresh out of the box, would eerily fail to work.

I remember watching my Aunt Loyola one summer afternoon as she plugged a brand-new blender into the wall of her cream-colored kitchen and held down the button marked pulse. She listened intently to the unnatural whirrs and clicks as the blades refused to spin and then, suddenly, as if the hum of the blender's failing was the sound that marked all our dooms, she burst into tears.

Six months later she was struck and killed by a rust-colored Buick in the parking lot of Blessed Sacrament Church after Saturday night mass.

These deaths, of course, were difficult to grow up around and to this day when I leave my apartment it is not without a certain amount of consternation. I see vans with tinted windows, crop threshers and wood chippers placed inexplicably in the middle of busy streets; there are suspicious sounds, angry-looking strangers, reckless people everywhere, all bent toward some yet-unknown harm—and at these times, when I see the moment coming, streetlights flickering out the second I step under them, the moment of my certain, untimely death, I tend to think of my mother and father in terms of fate and possibilities.

I think about the possibility of a foul ball hitting my mother in the stomach that day at Tiger Stadium and the subsequent miscarriage. I think about my father dodging the bullet meant for him in St. Louis and beating his assailant within an inch of his life. I think about my mother going over the Falls in a barrel, narrowly escaping abduction and explaining her story to rescuers after being fished out of the foaming waters and pried out of the barrel; I see her, standing on the deck of a stunned ferry, damp and breathless.

My mind drifts and the moment passes and then I'm never dead—and all at once the idea that the world is a history of sad and preposterous deaths seems almost comforting.

What happens after that can be different. Sometimes afterward the moon looks big or there's the faraway sound of a train or I might hear a dog bark or locusts so loud it hurts.

I UNDERSTAND

by RODDY DOYLE

CHAPTER ONE

THIS MORNING, I stand at the bus stop. I have been in this city three months. I begin to understand the accent. I already know the language. How do you do? Is this the next bus to Westminster? I have brought my schoolroom English with me. There is no Westminster in this city but I know what to say when the next bus goes past without stopping.

—Fuck that.

People smile. One man nods at me.

—Good man, bud, he says. —Making the effort.

I smile.

I understand. This word, *bud*. It is a friendly word. But I cannot say Bud to this man. I cannot call him Bud. A man like me can never call an Irish man Bud. But I can say, Fuck that. The expletive is for the bus, the rain, the economy, life. I am not insulting the bus driver or my fellow bus-stop waiters. I understand. My children will learn to call other children Bud. They will be Irish. They will have the accent. If I am still here. And if I have children.

It is spring. I like it now. It is bright when I stand at the bus stop. It is warm by the time I finish my first job. Early morning is the best time. It is quiet. There are not many people on the footpaths. I do not have to look away. Eyes do not stare hard at me. Some people smile. We are up early together. Many are like me. I am not resented.

I polish floors in a big department store. I like pushing the buffer over the wooden floor. I am used to hard work but every machine and tool has its own pain. With the buffer, it was in my arms. It was like riding an electric horse. My arms shook for a long time after I finished. I felt the buffer every time I closed my eyes. I heard it. Now, I like it. I control it. It is my horse now and I am the cowboy. This morning, I push the buffer too far. The flex becomes tight and the plug jumps out of the socket. I have to walk across the big floor to insert the plug. It is a correct time to say Fuck that. But I do not say it. I am alone.

I like this job. I like the department store when it is empty. I like that I am finished very early. I wear my suit to the store and I change into my work clothes in one of the changing rooms. I carry my work clothes in a bag that I found in my room. It is a bag for Aston Villa. It is not a very good team, I think, but the bag is good. It is grand. I understand. How are you? Grand. How's the head? Grand. That's a great day. It is grand.

One time, the supervisor was outside the changing room when I came out.

—Make sure you don't help yourself to any of the clothes, she said.

I saw her face as she looked at me. She was sorry for what she had said. She looked away. She is nice. She is grand. She leaves me alone.

Every month, the window models are changed. This

morning is a change day. Pretty women and men with white hair are taking out old models and putting in new ones. The new ones have no heads. I wait to see them put heads on the models, on top of the summer clothes, but they do not. One day, perhaps, I will understand.

I change into my suit and I go home. Today, I walk because it is nice and I save some money. It is warm. I walk on the sunny sides. It is not a time to worry. I eat and I go to bed for a time. The room is empty. My three friends are gone, at their works. Sometimes I sleep. Sometimes the bad dreams do not come. Most times I lie awake. There is always some noise. I do not mind. I am never alone in this house. I do not know how many people live here.

I get up in the afternoon and I watch our television. I like the programs in which American men and women shout at each other and the audience shouts at them. It is grand. I also like MTV, when there are girls and good music. They are also grand. Today, I watch pictures of people, happy in Baghdad. A man hits a picture of Saddam with his shoe. He does this many times.

I get dressed for my second job. I do not wear my suit. I do not like my second job but it is there that my story starts.

CHAPTER TWO

My second job takes me to the place called Temple Bar. I walk because the bus is too slow when other people are going home from work. The streets are busy but I am safe. It is early and, now, it is spring and daylight.

Temple Bar is famous. It is the center of culture in Dublin and Ireland. But many drunk people walk down the streets, shouting and singing with very bad voices. Men and even women lie on the pavements. I understand. These are stag and hen people, from England. Kevin, my Irish friend, explained. One of these people will soon be married, so they come to Temple Bar to fall on the street and urinate in their trousers or show their big breasts to each other and laugh. Kevin told me that they are English people but I do not think that this is right. I think that many of them are Irish. Alright, bud? What are you fucking looking at? But Kevin wants me to believe that these drunk people are English. I do not know why, but Kevin is my friend, so I do not tell him that, in my opinion, many of them are Irish.

Here, I am a baby. I am only three months old. My life started when I arrived. My boss shows me the plug. He holds it up.

—Plug, he says.

He puts the plug into the plug-hole. He takes it out and he puts it in again.

—Understand? he says.

I understand. He turns on the hot water.

—Hot.

He turns on the cold water.

—Cold. Understand?

I understand. He points at some pots and trays. He points at me.

—Clean.

I understand. He smiles. He pats my shoulder.

All night, I clean. I am in a corner of the big kitchen, behind a white wall. There is a radio that I can listen to when the restaurant is not very noisy. This night, the chefs joke about the man in Belfast called Stakeknife. The door to the alley is open, always, but I am very hot.

—How come you get all the easy jobs?

I look up. It is Kevin, my friend.

—Fuck that, I say.

He laughs.

Food is a good thing about this job. It is not the food that is left on the plates. It is real, new food. I stop work for a half hour and I sit at a table and eat with other people who work here. This is how I met Kevin. He is a waiter.

—It's not fair, he says, this night, when he sees my wet

and dirty T-shirt. —You should be a waiter instead of having to scrub those fucking pots and pans.

I shrug. I do not speak. I do not want to be a waiter, but I do not want to hurt his feelings, because he is a waiter. Also, I cannot work in public. All my work must be in secret, because I am not supposed to work. Kevin knows this. This is why he says that it is not fair. I think.

The door to the alley is near my corner, and it is always open. Fresh air comes through the open door but I would like to perspire and lock the door, always. But, even then, it must be opened sometimes. I must take out the bags of rubbish, old chicken wings and french fries and wet napkins. I must take them out to the skip.

And, really, this is the start of my story. This night, I carry a bag outside to the alley. I lift the lid of the skip, I drop in the bag, I turn to go back.

—There you are.

He is in front of me, and the door is behind him.

—Hello, I say.

—Polite, he says.

I understand. This is sarcasm.

—Did you think about that thing we were talking about? he says.

—Yes, I say.

—Good. And?

—Please, I say, —I do not wish to do it.

He sighs. He hits me before he speaks.

—Not so good.

I am on the ground, against the skip. He kicks me.

I must explain. The story starts two weeks before, when this man first grabbed my shoulder as I dropped a bag into the skip. He spoke before I could see his face.

—Gotcha, gotcha.

He told me my name, he told me my address, he told me that I had no right to work here and that I would be deported. I turned. He was not a policeman.

—But, he said, —I think I can help you.

He went. Three times since, he has spoken to me.

Now, this night, I stand up. He hits me again. I understand. I cannot fight this man. I cannot defend myself.

CHAPTER THREE

I am alone again in the alley behind the restaurant. The man has gone. I check my clothes. I am no dirtier than I was before I came out here. I check my face. I take my hand away. There is no blood.

He will be back. Not here. But it will be tonight. I know exactly what this man is doing. I am no stranger to his tactics. I go back into the restaurant. I work until there is no more work to do and it is time to go home. Every night, this is the time I do not like. Tonight, I know, it will be worse.

I walk with Kevin to the corner of Fleet Street and Westmoreland Street. He has his bicycle.

—Are you alright? he asks.

—Yes, I say.

—You're quiet.

—I am tired.

—Me too, knackered. Seeyeh.

—See you.

I will buy a bicycle. But, tonight, I must walk. It is later than midnight. There are no buses. I walk across the bridge. I walk along O'Connell Street. I do not look at people as they come towards me. I cross to the path that goes up the center of the street. It is wider and quieter. And, I think, safer. But never safe. It is a very long, famous street. I do not like it. All corners are dangerous.

This night no one stares or spits at me. No words are thrown at my back. No one pushes against me. Once or twice, I look behind. I expect to see the man. He is not there. This, too, I expect. It is his plan. Then I think that I will not go home. I will hide. But this is a decision that he would expect of me. He is watching. I keep walking. I do not look behind.

The last streets to my house are narrow and dark. Cars pass one at a time, and sometimes none at all, as I walk to my street. I walk towards a parked car. It is a jeep, made by Honda.

A cigarette lands on the footpath.

—I'm giving them up.

He is alone.

—D'you smoke, yourself?

—No, I do not.

—Four years I was off them. Can you believe that?

But he is not alone. Two more men are behind me and beside me. They hold my arms.

—In you get.

A hand pushes my head down, and protects my head as I am pushed into the backseat. I am in the middle, packed between these two big men. They are not very young.

The driver does not drive. We go to nowhere.

—Have you had a re-think? he says.

—Excuse me? I say, although I understand his words.

—Have you thought about what I said?

—Yes.

He does not look back and he does not look in the rearview mirror.

—And?

—Please, I say. —Please, tell me more about my duties.

The men beside me laugh. They do not hit me.

—Duties? says the driver. —Fair enough. That's easily done. You go to another place, here in Ireland, sometimes just Dublin. You deliver a package, or pick one up. You come back without the package, or with it. Now and again. How's that?

I cannot shrug. There is not room. I do not ask what the packages will contain. The question, I think, might result in violence. And I do not intend to deliver the packages.

—Do you have a driver's license? he says.

—No.

—Doesn't matter. You'll be getting the train.

The men laugh.

—All pals, says the driver. —We'll take you home.

It is a very short distance. The men at my sides talk to each other.

—So the doctor, says one man, —the specialist. He said, Put your fuckin' finger on that.

—Were you not out?

—Out where?

—Knocked out.

—No.

The driver turns the last corner and stops at my house. He opens his door and gets out.

—There's a 99 percent success rate, says the man at my left.

—Well, the wife's brother died on the table last year.

—But he was probably bad before he went in.

—That's true.

The big man at my left gets out. I follow him. The driver hits me before I straighten, as I get out. The other man is right behind me. He also hits me. The driver tries to grab my hair but it is too short. He pulls my shoulder.

—None of this is racially motivated. Understand?

I nod. I understand.

—Grateful?

I nod.

—Good man. And, come here. There'll be a few euros in it for you.

—Thank you.

—No problem, he says. —And, by the way, I know your days off.

There are no more blows. I am alone on the footpath. I watch the jeep turn the corner.

CHAPTER FOUR

My next day off is Sunday. But I know that, in fact, the man in the jeep will decide. My next day off will be any day he wants it to be.

I must wait. I must decide.

It rains this morning. I do not like the rain but I like what it does. It makes people rush; it makes them concentrate on their feet. It is a good time for walking.

I must think.

I can run.

I can run again.

I am very tired. The buffer controls me this morning. I follow it across the floor.

I will not run. I decided that I would not run again when I came to Ireland, and I will not change my mind. I ran away from my home and my country. I ran away from London. Now, I will not run.

It still rains.

But what will I do? What is my plan?

I stand at the service entrance behind the department store. The lane is one puddle.

I wait for the plan to unfold in my mind. I look, but the lane is empty. Perhaps the man in the jeep does not know about my early-day life. I do not believe this. The plan stays folded and hidden.

—God, what a country.

The supervisor has opened the door. She stands beside me. She looks at the water. She judges its depth.

—What made you come to this feckin' place?

Then she looks at me.

—Sorry.

I understand: she sees famine, flies, drought, huge, starving bellies.

—I like this, I say.

—You don't.

—Please, I say. —I do.

—Why? she asks.

I do not want to make her uncomfortable. But I tell her.

—It is safer when it rains.

—Oh.

I have not told the men who share my room. They have their own stories, and I do not want to bring trouble to them. I do not know what to tell them.

She has not moved yet. She looks at the rain.

—Busy? she says.

—Excuse me?

—Are you busy these days?

I shrug. I do not wish to tell her about my other work.

—Have you time for a coffee? she says.

I am stupid this morning. At first, I do not understand. Then I look at her.

—Please, I say. —With you?

Her face is very red. She is not beautiful. She laughs.

—Well, yes, she says. —If it's not too much bloody trouble.

She is, I think, ten years older than I.

—Forget it, she says.

—No, I say. —I mean. Yes.

—You're sure?

—Yes.

—Come on.

She tries to run through the rain but her legs are very stiff and her shoes are not for running. She stops after few steps and walks instead. I walk beside her. We go down a lane and then it is Grafton Street. I look behind me; I see no one. We enter the café called Bewley's.

She will not allow me to hold the tray. Nor will she allow me to pay for two cups of coffee and one doughnut. She chooses the table. People stare, others look quickly away. I stand until she sits. She takes the cups off the tray. I sit.

—Thank you.

She puts the doughnut in front of me. I feel foolish. Does

she think I am her son? I did not ask for this doughnut. But I am hungry.

—People smell when it's been raining. Did you ever notice?

—Yes, I say.

Again, I feel foolish. Is she referring to me?

She lifts her cup. She smiles.

—Well. Cheers.

—Yes, I say.

I lift my cup but I do not smile. The coffee is good but I wish I was outside, under the rain. I think she is trying to be kind—I am not sure—but I wish I was outside, going home. It would be simpler.

—Any regrets? she says.

—Excuse me?

—D'you ever wish you'd stayed at home?

She tries to smile.

—No, I say.

I do not tell her that I would almost certainly be dead if I had stayed at home.

—I like it here, I say.

It is the answer they want to hear.

—God, she says. —I don't like it much and I'm *from* here.

I look behind, and at the queue at the counters.

—Am I that uninteresting? she says.

I look at her.

—Excuse me?

—Am I boring you?

—No.

—What's wrong?

—Please, I say. —Nothing.

—What's wrong?

I do not want this. I do not want her questions. So I smile.

—Fuck that, I say.

But she does not laugh. She cries. I do not understand. And now I see the man in the jeep. He is here, of course, without the jeep, but the keys are in his hand. He walks towards me. I hear the keys.

CHAPTER FIVE

The man stops at our table. He picks up the remaining piece of my doughnut.

—Tomorrow, he says.

He looks at the supervisor.

—Breaking your heart, love, is he?

She looks shocked. He laughs. He turns, and his car key scrapes my head. He goes.

She no longer cries but her face is very white, and pink—stained by anger and embarrassment.

—I am sorry, I say.

—Who was that? she said.

—Please, I say. —A friend.

—He was no friend, she says.

I look at her.

—Sure he wasn't?

—No, I say. —He is not a friend.

—What is he then?

—I do not know.

I stand up now. I must go.

—Thank you, I say. —Goodbye.

I am grateful to her, but I do not want to be grateful. It is a feeling that I cannot trust. I have been grateful before. Gratitude unlocks the door that should, perhaps, stay locked.

—Fine, she says.

She is angry. She does not look at me now.

—Goodbye, I say, again.

I go.

I go home. My three friends are gone, at their works. I lie on the bed. I do not sleep. I watch our television. American men and women shout at each other. The audience shouts at them. On the programme called *Big Brother*, a man washes his clothes. He is not very good at this. His friends sleep. I watch them.

I understand. I will see the man before tomorrow. He must let me see that the decision is not mine. I must know that there is no choice. I will see his violence tonight. I know this.

I know this and, yet, I am still hungry. I might die but I want a sandwich. I was hungry some minutes after I watched my father die. The hunger was welcome; there was no guilt. It made me move; it made me think.

I want a sandwich and I make a sandwich. In this house the choice is mine, as is the cheese. The bread, I borrow. I eat, and watch the *Big Brother* people sit.

It is time to go.

It rains. I walk. A drunk woman falls in front of me. I do not stop. She is very young. Her friend sits down beside her, in the water.

I walk through the restaurant. There are not so many customers. I go to the back door. I look out. There is no one there. I shake the rain from my jacket. I hang it up. I fill the sink. I start.

I welcome the heat of the water. I welcome the pleasure, and the effort that the work demands. I scrub at the fear. I search for it. The work is good. I am alert and useful. I have knives beside me, and in the water. I can think, and I cannot be surprised.

—Great weather.

It is Kevin. He is very wet.

—Fuck that, I say.

—I have a new one for you, he says. —Ready?

—Yes.

I take my hands from the water.

—Me bollix, he says. —Repeat.

—My—

—No. Me.

—Me. Bollix.

—Together.

—Me bollix.

—Excellent, says Kevin. —Top man.

He dries his hair with a tea-towel.

—Please, what does it mean?

—My balls.

—Thank you.

—You're welcome. I'm meeting some people after. Want to come?

I answer immediately.

—No. Thank you.

He sees my face; he sees something I feel.

—Sure?

—Perhaps, I say.

—Good.

He puts the tea-towel on my shoulder.

—Later, he says.

—Me bollix, I say.

—Excellent.

I resume the washing. The restaurant starts to fill. I am glad of this. I am very occupied. There is an argument between the manager and one of the chefs—the radio is too loud. A pigeon walks into the kitchen. I go out quickly to the skip with full bags, but there is no one waiting for me. It is a good night, but now it is over. I take a knife. I put it in my pocket.

—Are you coming? says Kevin.

—Yes, I say.

I do not want to bring trouble to Kevin, but I do not want to go home the expected way, at the expected time.

—Excellent, says Kevin.

Outside, it rains. The street is quiet. I walk with Kevin. He pushes his bicycle. We hurry.

We go to a pub.

—It is not closed? I ask.

—No, said Kevin. —It opens late. It's not really a pub.

I do not understand.

—More a club.

Still, I do not understand. I have not been to many pubs. The men at the door stand back, and we enter. It is very hot inside, the music is very loud, and it is James Brown.

I talk; I shout.

—James Brown.

Kevin smiles.

—You know him?

Now I smile.

And I see her.

CHAPTER SIX

I see her, my supervisor, but she is not among Kevin's friends. She is standing at a different table, with other people. She sees me. She nods. I nod.

I am introduced to Kevin's friends. The music is loud. I do not hear names. There are five people, three women, two men. All shake my hand vigorously; all offer me space at the table. I stand between two of the women.

I look. She is looking at me. She looks away.

Kevin shouts into my ear.

—What are you having?

—Excuse me?

—Drink.

—Please, I say. —A pint of Guinness.

He moves to the bar.

The woman at my left side speaks.

—Guinness, yeah?

—Yes.

—Nice one.

I nod. She nods. I smile. She smiles. She is pretty. Her breasts and teeth impress me. I hope that she will say something else. I can think of nothing to say.

She speaks. It is exciting.

—You work with Kevin, yeah?

She shouts.

—Bollix to it, I say.

I shout.

She laughs.

—Yeah, she says.

She nods. I do not really understand but, looking at her smile at me, I am quite happy.

One Guinness is placed in front of me. A white sleeve holds the glass. I look. It is not Kevin. The man, a barman, nods at the next table. The supervisor is there. She lifts her glass. She has given me this Guinness.

She smiles.

I do not want to touch it.

The other woman speaks.

—You've an admirer, she says.

She is smiling.

So many smiling women.

—You'll hurt her feelings if you don't drink it.

I pick up the Guinness. I smile at the supervisor. I drink. I smile. I look away.

Kevin's friend, the other woman, is no longer looking at me.

No more smiling women. Kevin comes to the table with another Guinness for me. He sees that it is not the first, and is confused.

—What's the story? he says.

His friend, the woman, turns to us.

—He has an admirer, she says. —Amn't I right?

—Fuck that, I say.

I now have two pints of Guinness.

—It's good to be Irish, says Kevin.

She laughs at Kevin, and she smiles at me. I do not know which is more significant, the laughter or the smile.

—What's your name? she asks.

Perhaps the smile. I hope so.

—Tom, I say.

I have many names.

—Oh, she says. —I was expecting something a bit more exotic.

—I apologize, I say.

I smile. She smiles.

—Is Thomas more exotic? I ask.

She laughs.

—Not really.

I like this girl's teeth, very much. I like her smile. I like the sound of her laughter.

I have many names.

—And yours? I say.

—Ailbhe, she says.

—Oh, I say. —I too was expecting something more exotic.

Again, she laughs. Her open mouth is beautiful.

—Please, I say.

I shout.

—Spell this name.

Her mouth is now close to my ear. She spells the name, very, very slowly. If she does this because she thinks that I am stupid, for this time only, I am most grateful.

—Please, I say.

I shout.

—Does this name have a meaning?

Yeah, she says.

She shouts.

—It's Irish for The Slut Who Drinks Too Much At The Weekends.

She sees my shock. I see hers.

—Sorry, she says. —It's an old joke. Friends of mine. We made up silly meanings for our names.

She holds up her glass.

—I'm drinking Ballygowan.

I understand.

—And I'm only a slut now and again.

I think I understand.

—And it is not the weekend, I say.

—Well, yeah, she says.

I am grateful for the Guinness. I can hide behind it as I drink. I can think. I can decide. I like this girl. And I like her sense of humor.

It is a thing that I had forgotten: I, too, have a sense of humor.

I smile. And she smiles.

—Out for the night?

It is the wrong woman who now speaks to me. It is the supervisor.

—Thank you, I say.

—Ah, well, she says.

She shouts.

—This morning was a bit weird, wasn't it?

It was just this morning that we drank coffee in Bewley's? I am surprised. It has been a very long day.

I shrug. I am afraid to speak, but must.

—It was nice, I say. —Thank you.

—Ah, well.

I think that she is drunk.

—That guy, she says. —This morning. He was a bit creepy, wasn't he?

I do not want to talk about the man. I do not want to talk to her about him.

—D'you not think? she says.

I will leave. I must.

—Do you need rescuing?

Ailbhe's mouth is at my ear. She whispers.

—Please, I say. —Yes.

CHAPTER SEVEN

—God, she says. —You came a bit fast-ish.

—Please, I say. —You are very beautiful.

—You're good-looking yourself, she says. —But I'd

planned on making the most of it.

—I—

—Don't say you're sorry. I'm only joking. Will we get into the bed?

I have not seen a bed.

—Yes, I say.

She stands. I stand.

I pick up my shoes. A bus passes. The headlights race across the wall and ceiling. She closes the hall door.

—That's better, she says.

She turns on the light.

I follow her.

I cannot remember her name. This is very strange. I want to run away but I also want to follow this woman. I like her. But, even so, her name has disappeared.

The hall light clicks off suddenly. It is dark but I see and hear her unlock a door.

—You do not live in the entire house? I ask.

—No, she says. —Just this place.

So, we made love in a public hall. Again, I want to run.

The door is open. She turns on the light. I enter. It is the room of a woman. I am glad that I am here.

It is not a big bed. We lie beside each other.

I like this woman. I wish that I could remember her name. She remembers mine.

—Dublin's a bit of a dump, isn't it, Tom?

—Please, I said.

And I remember.

—Avril.

—Who the fuck is Avril?

—You are not Avril?

—No, Tim, I'm not Avril.

She sits up.

—But call me whatever you like.

She leans down and whispers into my ear.

—Avril.

I like this woman.

I wake up.

I know where I am, but I am surprised. I slept. This was not my plan. The man with the jeep expects to meet me this morning. But I am here; I am not at home. I look at the curtains. There is strong daylight at its edges. I am not at the department store, at work.

She is beside me, asleep, this woman who's name, I am sure, is almost Avril.

I get out of the bed.

She wakes.

—Get back in here, you.

Please, I say. —I must go. To work.

—You work nights, she says.

—I have two jobs, I say.

—Poor you, she says.

She notices that I hesitate. She sees me fumble with my shoelaces.

—Give work a miss, she says.

I would like to do this, very much. I would like to take off my clothes and stay. I would like to touch this woman's warm skin and stay close to it.

But I cannot do this. The man might know where I am. He might be outside, waiting. He is not a patient man.

My laces are tied. I stand up.

—Goodbye, I say. —Thank you.

I open the door.

—Ailbhe, she says.

—That is your name? Ailbhe.

—That's it, she says. —See if you can remember it till tonight.

—I will remember, I say.

—We'll see, she says.

—My bollix.

It rains and, this morning, I do not like it. I am too far away to walk, so I must wait for a bus. I see no jeeps, parked or coming towards me. But I think that I am being watched. I want to move, to run away, but I wait.

The bus is very slow. It is full, so I must stand. I cannot see through the windows because of the condensation. But I do not need to see to know: the bus is not moving. I will be late. I will be late.

I am very late.

The service door behind the department store is locked.

I knock and wait. I try to hear approaching feet. I knock.

A hand is on my shoulder. A hard hand, grabbing, pushing me to the door.

—The very man.

The door opens as my head hits it. My face falls into the supervisor's jacket.

I get free and see her face. She is looking at the man and she is angry. She does not seem to be surprised.

—Go away, she says.

—I was just talking to Thomas, he says. —Wasn't I, Thomas?

He looks at me. He smiles.

—Yes, I say.

—He's doing a bit of work for me, he says.

He smiles at her.

—You know yourself. No questions asked. No visas needed.

He winks.

—I told you once, she says. —Go away and leave him alone.

And she stands between me and the man. The door is narrow. I cannot pass her. I do not try.

—And what if I don't? he says. —Will you call the Guards?

He laughs, and winks again.

—No, she says. —I'll do better than that.

He stops laughing.

CHAPTER EIGHT

The supervisor stares at the man. He tries to understand her. I can see it in his face: this woman must be taken seriously. And I can see him fight this fact. He would like to hit her. But he is worried. He is no longer sure.

I am ashamed. The woman stands between me and the man—he continues to look at her. And I do not feel safe. For now, he cannot reach me. But she cannot stand in front of me forever, for more than five minutes. And I do not want her to stand there. I am not a child. I am not a man who will hide behind a woman. Or another man. I will not hide.

—Please, I say. —Please.

I realize now; I understand. I say *please* too often. The word is not often understood in this country. I am not weak.

—You must leave me alone, I say.

They look at me, the man and the woman. She turns. He already looks my way. They both look pleased, surprised, uncertain. They wonder: Is he talking to me? They had forgotten, perhaps, that I am there.

The man moves. She blocks his path.

Again, I say it.

—You must leave me alone.

She knows. I am talking to her. He knows. I am talking to him. She looks puzzled, then angry. He steps back. He knows that he will get me soon.

—I'm trying to help, she says.

—Yes, I say. —Thank you.

—He's dangerous, she says.

—Yes.

He is dangerous and he is a fool.

—I know his type, she says.

I nod. I also know his type. I have been running from his type for too many years. I will not run now. I will do this myself.

He is a fool because he has not seen me. He has not bothered to look. He sees a man he can frighten and exploit, and he is certain that he can do this. The men who made me fight when I was a boy, they too saw fear and vulnerability. They made me do what they wanted me to do; they made me destroy and kill, for ten years. I am no longer a boy. This man frightens me but I, too, am a man. I know what a hard man is in the language of this city. Tough, ruthless, respected, feared. This man looks at me and sees none of these qualities. He sees nothing. He is a fool.

The supervisor shrugs.

—Sure? she says.

She is a good woman.

—Yes, I say.

Her mobile phone is in her hand. She holds it up.

—I can make a call, she says. —That's all I'd need.

—No, I say. —Thank you.

She shrugs again.

—You know best. I suppose.

—Yes, I say.

She steps aside. He doesn't move. She walks behind me. He doesn't move. She walks away. He doesn't move. He stays in the alley. I am in the department-store corridor. The door begins to close. I stop it.

He speaks.

—Come on out here till we have a chat.

I step out. I let go of the door. I hear it close behind me; I hear it click, shut, locked. I do not look back.

—So, he says. —What's the story?

It is not a question. It is not a real question. An answer does not interest him. I see men to my right. They have entered the alley; they were there already. Two men. I have seen them before. They were with him the night he forced me into his Honda jeep. I do not look at these men. I concentrate on the important man.

—So, he says, again.

Still, it still rains.

—You're a bit of a messer, he says. —Aren't you?

—No, I say. —I am not.

He looks at me.

Carefully. For the first time.

Too late.

—Right, he says.

It is as if he shakes himself, as if he has just now woken up.

He must take control.

But I will not be controlled.

I walk away.

I walk. Past his colleagues. They move, prepared to grab, to hit—unsure. I walk. I do not look back.

I will walk away from here. Because I have decided to.

If he shouts I will hear but I will not listen.

If they grab my shoulders I will feel their hands but I will ignore them. I will feel their blows but I will not stop or turn around. I will fall forward and refuse to look.

If he shoots me I will die. I will be gone. He will gain nothing. He knows this. Now.

He understands.

—Hey! Hey!

I walk away.

CHAPTER NINE

I walk out of the alley. To a narrow street that is always dark. I do not look behind. I do not hurry. I hear no one behind me. I do not think that I am followed.

I am now on Grafton Street. I am not a fool. I do not think that the crowds will bring me safety. If the man wishes to injure me, if he thinks that he must, he will.

I walk.

If he decides to hurt me, or kill me, because I have humiliated him in front of his colleagues, he will wait. He will not do it here. There are too many people, and too many security cameras. If he wants to teach me, and others, a lesson, he might do it here: Nowhere is safe—*do as we say*.

I do not think that he will attack me here. Perhaps he knows: he can teach me nothing.

I am a fit man and I enjoy walking. Just as well—as they say here. I must walk all day.

Fuck that.

I know that I am smiling. It is strange. I did not know that I was going to. It is good. To find the smile, to feel it.

I pass a man who is standing on a crate. He is painted blue and staying very still. When somebody puts money into the bucket in front of him, he moves suddenly. Perhaps I will do that. I will paint myself blue. I will disappear.

—Fuck that.

A man looks at me, and looks away.

I am the blue man who says Fuck that.

I must walk. All this day.

I cannot sit. I cannot stop. I cannot go home. I must be free. I must keep walking.

I walk. I walk all day. Through Temple Bar. Along the river, past tourists and heroin addicts, strangely sitting together. Past the Halfpenny Bridge and O'Connell Bridge. Past the Custom House and the statues of the starving Irish people. I walk to the Point Depot. Across the bridge—the rain has stopped, the clouds are low—I walk past the toll booths, to Sandymount. No cars slow down, no car door slams behind me. I am alone.

I walk on the wet sand. I see men in the distance, digging holes in the sand. They dig for worms, I think. They look as if they stand on the sea. It is very beautiful here. The ocean, the low mountains, the wind.

It is becoming dark when I cross the tracks at the station called Sydney Parade.

I will go to work. I will not let them stop me. I will go to work. I will buy a bicycle. I will buy a mobile phone. I am staying. I will not paint myself blue. I will not disappear.

It is dark now. It is dangerous. Cars approach, and pass.

I walk the distance to Temple Bar. I walk through crowds

and along parts of the streets that are empty. I pass men alone and women in laughing groups.

I am, again, on Grafton Street, where my wandering started this morning. I walk past the blue man. It seems that he has not moved.

I arrive at Temple Bar. A drunk man steps into my way. His friends are behind him. His shoulder brushes mine.

—Sorry, bud.

I make sure that there is no strong contact. I walk through his friends. I do not step off the pavement. I do not increase my pace.

I reach the restaurant at the same time as Kevin. I wait, as he locks his bicycle.

—Did you get a good night's sleep last night? he says.

I understand. This is called slagging.

—Yes, I say. —Thank you.

—Does she snore? he asks.

I surprise myself.

—Only time will tell, I say.

He laughs. I also laugh. I know now what I must do, where I must go. But, first, there is something that I must know.

—Please, I say. —Kevin.

It is later. The restaurant is closed. I cycle Kevin's bicycle; it is mine for tonight.

I remember her corner. I remember her house.

I ring the bell. I wait.

I look behind me. No jeep, no waiting men.

I hear the door. I turn. She is there.

—Well, she says.

—Good evening.

—So, she says. —Do you remember my name?

—Yes, I say.

Kevin told me. I wrote it on my sleeve.

—Yes, I say. –Your name is Ailbhe.

—Ten out of ten, she says. —Enter.

—Please, I say.

I look at the street. I look at her.

—I might be in danger, I say.

—I like the sound of that, she says. —Come in.

HELLO, CHARLES

by JIMMY CHEN

WHERE HWY. 12 MEETS Walgreen's, take a left if you're going east and right if you're going west. Cross the tracks, past the first light, and it's that old white house with too many triangles. Come up the stairs, apartment C, the door will be open. But you know this already, you've done this every week, bringing your daughter's mail over, because when she signed up for all those credit cards and catalogs, she thought she might be living there with you, your wife, and your other daughter, or you, her mother, and sister, respectively. Let's not mention her brother, your son, who carries a softened cardboard box around with all his clothes, driving from town to town.

And those times when you knock and nobody answers, you slip the mail under the door, a crack so wide that the draft blows the mail farther inside. When you see his name on the envelope you remember him, how he was going to be your son-in-law, the situation, and the time you flew over there and drove across the country home with her, your daughter, who was no longer engaged and afraid of the world. You drove most of the way, watching your daughter sleep in the passenger seat, her mouth a tired straight line and her entire life in the backseat. And now you're crouching, balanced on one hand, mounting away from the closed door.

You drive to the house that you live in. The road is a throbbing triangle bumping under the dark blue sky. The yellow lines dive under your truck like silent bullets. It's long after dinner and your other daughter and her mother, your wife, are falling asleep. They have small mouths and scratches for eyes. They don't hear you come in even when they're awake. From your driveway, the house is a slab of warm air and black windows. It's very cold and you can see your breath slowly disappearing, stubborn like a charcoal drawing being erased. You get back into your truck, because your house is no longer yours.

Sometimes you call your daughter on the phone, her voice more ageless than her body, so you imagine her a small girl, when the whole family sang hymns in churches for money. You used to close your eyes to separate your own voice from your wife and children's, to distance yourself from them, so you could hear them together, without you. It was easiest this way to love them fully, without the throttle of your throat messing up the clarity of their voices. It was like you stood in a corner, away from the picture being taken, already holding an empty frame in your hand.

The lights along Hwy. 12 offer nearer constellations, arranged in block letters and familiar logos. You pass them every night, their heavy glow cast on your face like fresh war paint. At the stoplight, in the lane next to you, a young woman looks into the rearview mirror and you wonder whether she's looking at herself or at the cars behind her. Her eyes are lit red by the brake lights in front of her. You wonder if, by chance, your daughter knows her. When the light changes she turns left, moving away from the lights, into the paved forest of this small town.

You crunch up the gravel road, enter the house where your daughter lives. The stairwell is a cracked drum. You try to step lightly, to contain the reverberation, but the boards ache beneath you, cringing under your weight. In a world with only four corners, you have used all of yours up. You are left to face the wide plateau and hang like an exhaled balloon, slowly breathing in. When you knock this time the door is opened. From inside, your daughter says hello, but the voice doesn't match the face in front of you, and I extend my hand.

COUNTING UNDERWATER

by KIARA BRINKMAN

THE BOY HAS asthma. At the playground, his mother has him trained to come over to the bench and rest every twenty minutes or so. He sits on my lap and catches his breath. We don't say anything to each other. I put my hand on his back and I can feel his bird heart beating. I am becoming a little afraid of him.

He wakes me up in the morning by tickling my feet. I rent the spare room and his mother leaves me with him more and more. I think she's depressed or on drugs. I tell the boy I don't like to be tickled. "That's okay," he says and he keeps doing it. "Where's your mom?" I ask. He stops tickling me then and shrugs. He stares at me. I stretch and sit up. For the last few days, he's been out of school on winter vacation. "Let me get ready," I say. He leaves me alone to shower and get dressed.

When I come out, he's eating cereal in front of the television. There's a talk show on. It says "HELPING EACH OTHER GET OVER OUR PHOBIAS" in the lower-left corner of the screen. Four happy clowns with big smiles are dancing in circles around a screaming woman. The screaming woman starts crying and tries to hide under her chair. "You like to watch this?" I ask. "No," the boy says. We look at each other.

"Let's go," I tell him, but he just sits there and stares at the TV. "I can't find my shoes," he says.

I go look in his room and then my room. Finally, I find his shoes in the kitchen, under the table. "In here," I shout and he comes.

Outside, the cold makes the boy's nose run. I carry a few tissues in my pocket for him. If I don't hand him a tissue in time, he wipes his nose on his sleeve. The snot leaves a cloudy white stain there.

It's been raining again. The streets are wet and it smells peppery like pine trees. The cars are all shiny-clean. "Why don't we ever see the rain?" the boy asks. "Good question," I say, because I don't know why it's only been raining in the middle of the night.

The boy follows a little behind me and I keep looking back to make sure he's still there. "What?" he says, each time I turn to check. "Nothing," I say.

In the diner, we sit at the counter because the boy likes the high twisty chairs. I read the want ads in the newspaper and he colors the same picture on the back of the kids' menu. The waitress brings him three fat crayons in a paper cup. Red, green, and blue. The picture is of teenagers on a date, sharing a milkshake with two straws. The boy colors their skin red. I keep asking the waitress to bring more water.

In the newspaper, I circle jobs that look promising, but I've stopped calling about them. The boy's mother doesn't make me pay rent. I don't know if it's because she just forgets or doesn't care or if it's some kind of compensation for leaving me with the boy.

"Are we going to see Charlene today?" the boy asks. Charlene is my mother. He likes to visit her, because she has a big jacuzzi bathtub. He wears his swimming trunks and plays in it like it's a pool. Also, she lets him color on her walls with magic marker. In her bad French accent she calls him "Le Petit Artiste."

I tell him we are going to see her tomorrow afternoon.

"She's funny," the boy says and he smiles, still looking down, coloring the two teenagers.

We go to the aquarium to pass the time. There's a moving walkway that circles around and goes by all the tanks. We ride around in the cool, quiet dark.

"Which is your favorite fish today?" the boy whispers. We whisper inside the aquarium, like it's a movie theater or a library.

Today I say I like the baby shark so we step off the moving walkway to go stand by the shark tank. The baby shark looks just as mean as the big sharks. A sign says "DO NOT TOUCH THE GLASS," but there's nobody watching. We put our hands on the tank, palms pressed flat, and lean in close. The boy rests his forehead against the glass. Our eyes follow the baby shark and it's like disappearing into sleep. A humming sound vibrates out of the tank.

The boy tugs on my coat sleeve. I look at him and he points to the tank with the small, brightly colored fish. I nod and he walks slowly over there. He likes to watch the sparkly rainbow fish that look like tiny, ugly angels with their long, flowing fins. I stay at the shark tank. The baby shark swims low, close to the sand.

A couple hours after the boy goes to sleep, I have to pick him up out of bed and carry him to the bathroom. He is hot and sweaty and heavy. I hold him up under his armpits and stand him in front of the toilet. His legs are limp and his head flops forward. I hold him there and blow cool air onto the back of his neck until he starts to wake up. Then he can stand by himself. "You have to go," I say and I put up the seat. I know now if he doesn't go, he wets the bed and then I have to wash the sheets. I turn on the water to help him and then I leave to give him his privacy.

When he's done, he comes out and holds up his arms for me to pick him up and carry him back to bed.

In the morning I find him in front of the TV. "Enough," I say and I turn it off. He throws his white stuffed bunny at me. I let it hit me in the stomach and bounce off. The bunny lands on its back, staring up at the ceiling. I put my hands on my hips and pretend to be mad. The boy starts laughing. He jumps down off the couch and grabs the bunny by the ear. He flings it at my head. I keep standing there like an angry statue and he's laughing harder now.

Then I start to growl and I become a slow giant. I take big, slow-motion steps toward the boy and he screams. This time, I catch the bunny when he throws it at me. I pretend to take a bite out of it and I throw it back at him.

We are at war, throwing the bunny back and forth. I duck one of his throws and the bunny lands in a potted plant. He picks it up and there's a smudge of dirt on its tummy. The boy stops laughing. He takes the bunny into the kitchen and throws it in the garbage can. Then he falls onto the floor, face-first.

I take the bunny out of the garbage. The smudge is small. I try to rub it out.

"Look," I say. "It's okay."

The boy doesn't move. He has his eyes closed tight.

I take the bunny into the bathroom and clean its tummy in the sink with warm water and hand soap. The dirt smudge comes out. Then I blow-dry the wet spot. The bunny fur takes a long time to dry.

I find the boy still in the kitchen. I think he has fallen asleep, but I'm not sure. I don't want to step too close to him so I slide the bunny across the tile floor in his direction. Then I go.

I notice his mother has come home. She's asleep in her room with the door open. All the lights are on and her radio is playing. She always leaves her radio on, even when she's not home. Right now it's playing that long, long Van Morrison song with something about dominoes in drag.

The boy counts the cars that go by while we wait for the bus. "That one's mine," he says when he sees a car he likes. "That one's yours," he says when an ugly car passes and then he laughs at me. Forty-three cars go by before the bus comes.

"Heat button is jammed—can't turn it off," the driver announces when we get on. He's wearing just a white T-shirt and has his pants rolled up to his knees. We sit down and I try to open our window, but it's stuck shut. The stuffy warmth makes me feel like I'm getting sick. "My back is sweaty," the boy says. "Almost there," I tell him. He leans forward and rests his forehead against the seat in front of us. I tap him on the shoulder when we get to our stop.

We walk two blocks to my mother's house. Outside, the air is cool and wet on our faces and feels like sweat. "Rain?" the boy asks. I shake my head no. This is not really even mist.

My mother leaves the door unlocked for us. I knock once before we go in. She's by the window working on her indoor birdbath and birdhouse. There's a tree that grows close to the house. For months, she's kept the window open, hoping the branches will grow right into the house and lead the birds to her birdbath and birdhouse. So far, it has not worked.

"Hello, hello," she says. "Let's sit and talk."

The boy and I sit down on the reddish-orange couch. My

mother sits in her recliner. She's not wearing socks and her feet are purplish from the cold that comes in through the window. Behind her, the wall looks crazy with the boy's drawings. The drawings are mostly fires and dragons.

"I had a terrible toothache," my mother says.

She likes to put candy bars in the microwave and melt them into a gooey mess before she eats them. I tell her we can call the dentist, but she says it's too late.

"The tooth fell out," she explains. "I woke up this morning and there it was on my pillow. The pain is gone."

She opens her mouth wide and points to a hole in the back.

"Did you bleed?" the boy asks.

My mother shakes her head. "No, I don't think so," she says.

The boy scrunches up his face, confused.

"I'm old and sick," my mother tells him. She points to the walls. "Finish your work," she says.

The boy stands and picks up a brown marker from the coffee table. He steps up on a chair and starts drawing a castle.

"Wonderful," my mother says to him and she claps her hands twice. "My Petit Artiste," she says in her bad French accent.

"Mother," I say. "Maybe you should go to the dentist." She looks out the window and says nothing. I try again. I tell her that she still needs to take care of herself, but she waves her hand at me like I'm being silly.

"Richard Harris has died," my mother says. She uses her newscaster voice.

"I know," I say. I heard about it months ago.

She tells me that she met him once when she was five months pregnant with me. He was on the same airplane. She couldn't see him from where she was sitting because she was way in the back and he was up in the front, of course. But then the plane got diverted due to bad weather and landed somewhere in Wyoming. After they got off the plane, Richard

Harris stopped to talk to my mother. She was bent over at a water fountain, taking a drink. He was wearing a long green coat and blue jeans. He pointed toward the ceiling. My mother looked up to where he was pointing. "Tell me," he said. "Is there a God?" She wiped her mouth to give herself time to think about what to say, but all she could think of was, "I don't know." "Wyoming of all places," said Richard Harris. "I'm stuck in Wyoming." Then he was gone.

"Can you believe?" my mother asks me. She looks out the window at her tree. "Of all the times to be fat," she says.

The boy stops coloring and looks down at her.

"Can I see the tooth?" he asks.

My mother stands and takes it out of her pocket. She holds it in a cupped hand for him to come and look. The boy jumps off his chair and goes over to her. He keeps his hands behind his back while he leans in close to look.

"What do you think?" my mother asks.

"Not very sharp," the boy says.

He goes back to coloring his castle. I look at my watch. We should be going. The sun has sunk down below the clouds and the light comes in now. I can see little flecks of dust floating around us.

At home, the boy's mother is still sleeping with the lights and radio on. There's a man sleeping next to her now with his mouth wide open. I shut their door slowly, quietly.

"We're out of cereal," the boy shouts. I find him sitting in the middle of the kitchen floor, eating the last bowl.

"I'll go down to the store and get some more," I say.

On the news, they say something about record-breaking humidity. We are close to the ocean and used to the damp air, the weatherman says, but this is different.

A lady with wiry, white hair shows how the carpeting in her basement is moist in spots and getting moldy. The wallpaper is peeling off at the bottom. She lifts a loose flap of it with her thick, red fingers. Her fingers look so old. They don't seem to bend anymore.

Gentle showers expected again tonight, the eighteenth in a row.

My brother calls from college to see if he should come for Christmas. I can hear music in the background. "Hang on," he says and steps into some quieter place, probably a bathroom. "Whatever you want," I say. There is a long pause and the phone starts to make little crackling noises. "How's Mom?" he asks.

When I picture my mother, I see the whole kitchen too. She's sitting at the table smoking a cigarette. The smoke curves straight up to the light. She has no socks on and her bare feet are purple on the cold tile floor.

"I think she's expecting you," I say. We're quiet again.

"Okay then," my brother says. "Bye."

"Bye," I say.

I hang up and stand there, staring at the phone.

"I need help," the boy yells from his room. He's working on a five-hundred-piece puzzle of three hot-air balloons floating up in the sky.

The boy finds strands of my hair around the house.

"Look, another one," he says. He thinks there's something wrong with me.

I start brushing my hair more often to test how much comes out.

"Let me do it," the boy says.

First he brushes hard, straight down over my ears until they start to burn. After a while, he pays less attention to what he's doing and he brushes softer. The strokes come farther and farther apart. Then he remembers what he's doing again and he brushes more roughly.

"Not good," he says when he looks at how much hair has come out on the brush.

We're running from the bus stop to my mother's house. It's hard to run because we're laughing like crazy. I have to pee really bad. The boy keeps stopping and trying to pull me the wrong way. He wants to make this last because for once it is me who has to go and not him.

My stomach hurts from laughing. I hold my breath to make myself stop. I have the boy's hand and I'm pulling him behind me. For a few seconds, he's quiet too, trying to catch his breath. The legs of his corduroy pants make a swishing noise. I pull him faster and the sound turns into a hum.

Then the boy starts laughing again. I tell him to stop and that makes it worse. He's hysterical and his eyes are watering. "Please," I say and I jump up and down. That's it then. He lets go of my hand and lies down, his arms up over his head and his legs spread out, like he's making snow angels on the cement. He laughs up at the sky.

"Fine," I say. I leave him there and keep running. My mother's house is half a block away. He knows where to go. "Wait," he shouts. I hear him chasing after me.

I open the door hard and it slams back against the wall. "What in the world," my mother says. The boy comes in behind me, wheezing. "Are you okay?" my mother asks him. He needs his inhaler. I know he has it in his pocket. I push past her.

I don't close the bathroom door all the way behind me and a little white puff-dog follows me in. I don't know where the dog has come from. He must be new. He looks new—all clean and fluffy.

The puff-dog sits on the blue bath mat and watches me pee. He cocks his head to the side like he's listening to the sound of it. "Go away," I say, but he just sits there and stares. I try not to look at him.

When I flush the toilet, he runs. I close the door behind him and take my time coming out. My mother has nice soaps. I try the one shaped like a heart. It smells like peaches and makes me hungry.

The boy and my mother are in the kitchen. The microwave is lit up. It's big and old and makes a buzzing noise while it cooks. I guess she's let him pick out another one of her TV dinners. He always takes his time and finds the one with the best dessert.

"Feel better?" my mother asks me and the boy starts laughing again.

"You got a dog?" I ask her. The microwave starts beeping. She reaches over and pops open the door to make it stop.

"For Christmas," she says.

"Where?" the boy asks. He stands up on his chair. He doesn't like dogs.

"Just a little one," I tell him.

My mother goes to take the dinner out of the microwave. She peels off the plastic covering and the steam rises up. Her gray hair looks shiny and silvery in the bright kitchen light. I watch her open a drawer and take out a fork. She sets the dinner down in front of the boy. He's still standing on the chair, but she pretends not to notice this.

"Hot," she tells him.

The boy squats down and sits like that, with his legs still up on the chair. He blows on the food.

"Why a dog?" I ask her.

"You don't like to celebrate anything," she says without looking at me.

She tells the boy about the time I started crying at the restaurant when she had the waiters come out and sing "Happy Birthday" to me. They put a huge sombrero on my head and everyone was watching and clapping. Afterward, I hid under the table and wouldn't come out for the rest of the meal. I remember my mother was wearing pale-blue high heels.

*   *   *

In the late afternoon, we walk. We go straight toward the beach and then we walk along the edge of the water until one of us gets cold or tired and wants to turn around. It has become a contest. Whoever wants to go back loses.

We stop talking when we're ready to give up. We walk with our shoulders up, heads tucked down, watching our feet. The boy has gotten good. "Okay," I say. "Let's go home." He smiles and we turn around.

It's getting dark when we cut across the beach, back up to the main road. Birds are collecting on the telephone wire. The boy stops to count them. Each time a new bird lands, he starts over. "Impossible," I tell him. "Can we go now?" The air is getting damp and misty.

Then, like there is some kind of secret signal in the sky, the birds all fly away at the same moment. Their wings are loud. We don't move until it's quiet again.

"My thing hurts," the boy says. It's poking up against his pants.

"Sorry," I say.

We keep walking. I tell him to zip up his jacket. He has to stop to do it. I wait while he figures out the zipper.

The sky has gone black. Along the sidewalk, we walk in and out of the circles of streetlamp light.

On Christmas Eve, I take the boy to the pet store to buy him a fish. We are the only people in the store and the woman behind the counter watches us. "Can I help you?" she asks. Her voice is too loud. "Just looking now," I tell her.

I explain to the boy that we can't get the fancy fish because they need to be in warm water, which means they are too hard to take care of. I show him the goldfish and the guppies. "These are okay," I say. The boy likes the white ones with the orange spots.

"We're ready now," I tell the woman. She comes over slowly, carrying a plastic baggy and a green net.

"We want two like this," the boy says and points.

The woman coughs and then lifts the lid of the tank. We move out of her way.

"Excuse me," I say. "Do you have any idea how old these fish are?" I know from experience that fish can be disappointing so I just want to make sure we get young ones that last.

"This is a brand-new batch," she says. Then she dips the bag into the tank and fills it up with water. I have a feeling she's lying to us.

"Just out of curiosity," I say, "how do you know how old the fish are when you get them?"

The boy looks at me like he wants me to please be quiet. I shrug my shoulders at him.

The woman dips the plastic baggy in the tank and fills it with water. Then she dunks the green net in and starts chasing after a fish with it.

"We only get new fish, Miss," she says.

She traps a fish against the side of the tank and lifts it up out of the water. I watch the fish flap in the air, its tiny body shaking the green net. She tips it out into the plastic baggy and dunks the green net in again for another fish.

"The same kind?" she asks the boy, not me.

He nods.

After she gets the second fish, she blows air into the plastic baggy and ties it closed. The fish swim in frantic circles, recovering.

"You need a bowl?" the woman asks.

"Yes," the boy says.

The woman gives careful instructions about how to take care of the fish. Then I pay her and she hands me the fish in the plastic baggy. I don't like holding it so I pass it to the boy. I carry the bowl and the food instead.

The boy holds the baggy out in front of him and stares at the fish while we walk to the bus stop. On the ride home, the boy holds the fish on his lap and they bounce around in the baggy. I close my eyes for the rest of the way home and the boy pulls my arm hard when we get to our stop.

My mother is out on the front steps untangling her wind chime. She's been angry at the wind because her wind chime keeps getting all twisted up and won't make a sound until she goes out and fixes it. She complains that sometimes she has to fix it two or three times a day.

"There you are," she shouts at us. I wave to her. The boy is carrying the poinsettia we bought on the way. The plant's leaves stick up in front of his face so he's having trouble seeing where he's going. I am holding his elbow, guiding him like a blind man.

"Merry Christmas," my mother says as we walk up the steps.

"Here," the boy says and he hands her the plant.

"Oh, it's lovely," she tells him.

The boy smiles at me because I was right. I had told him she would like the plant more if he gave it to her.

I help my mother finish untangling the wind chime. "I'm going crazy," my mother says. "I've untangled this twice already today." She throws her hands up in the air. I tell her to calm down, that it is not so bad.

"I can't stand the quiet," she says.

Inside, my brother's sitting on the reddish-orange couch with his punk-rock girlfriend. The girlfriend is wearing headphones. Her music is turned up so loud I can almost make out the lyrics. Somehow, she is also whistling calmly and knitting something with pretty yellow yarn. Next to her, my brother is reading a thick book, probably a history book about a war. He wants to know about every battle that ever happened. He looks up and nods when we walk in. I take the boy's hand and pull him over to the couch so I can introduce him.

The girlfriend stops knitting and slides her headphones down off her ears. "These your drawings?" she asks the boy and points to the walls.

He nods.

"Right on," she says. She hands him a marker from the table. "Draw somebody getting killed by a dragon."

The boy moves a chair over to the wall, steps up, and starts drawing.

"I need some help in here," my mother shouts from the kitchen. I look at my brother and his girlfriend.

"I'm almost finished knitting these socks," the girlfriend says. "They're for your mother," she whispers. My brother says nothing.

"Fine," I say and I go.

My mother wants me to chop vegetables for the salad.

"Your brother hasn't learned any social skills at school," my mother says.

"No," I say. He has never had very much to say to anybody.

"He doesn't even talk to that girl, his friend," my mother says.

"They seem to be happy," I tell her.

The knife slips on the tomato and I cut my finger.

"Shit," I say.

I put my hurt finger in my mouth and suck on it.

"Let me see," my mother says.

She pulls my finger out of my mouth. The blood has a strong, earthy taste. Something about it is like the smell of freshly cut grass or soil in a wet garden. My mother wraps my finger in a paper towel.

"Hold your finger above your heart," she tells me.

I laugh at her.

"Jesus, Mother," I say. "I'm not bleeding to death."

She ignores me and goes back to cooking.

"Go visit with your brother," she says. "I can do this myself."

In the other room, the boy has drawn a picture of my

brother's girlfriend getting eaten by a dragon.

"Hey," the girlfriend says. The boy turns and smiles at her. My brother looks up from his book, but he doesn't seem to understand the picture.

I sit down on the coffee table in front of the couch, facing the two of them. My brother is scanning the page of his book with his finger, looking for his place. He starts reading again.

"So," I say to the girlfriend. "What are you studying at school?"

"Italian," she says. "I'm moving to Italy."

I nod as if I understand why. I imagine my brother walking around Italy, never learning the language and not having to speak to anybody, his voice getting deep and scratchy, like voices do after long nights of sleep.

"It's good of you to stick around here," the girlfriend says to me in a quiet voice. "Is she getting better?"

I don't say anything. The puff-dog wanders into the room and barks gently, calmly, like he's clearing his throat. His fur has been dyed purple. The boy starts laughing at him.

"What is this?" I ask. The puff-dog comes over and sniffs my leg. I feel sorry for him. The girlfriend looks at me.

"Your mother said I could do it," she tells me. "I was bored."

The boy comes over and stands by me.

"You're not scared anymore?" I ask him.

"He's purple," the boy says. Saying this makes him laugh all over again.

My brother closes his book and stretches. "I'm tired," he says. He puts his head on the girlfriend's shoulder.

I pick up the dog and hold it up in front of him. "Look," I say.

"So," my brother says.

"Fine," I say. I put the dog down and look through the *Reader's Digest*s stacked up next to me on the coffee table. I find the most recent one and go over to my mother's chair by the window to read. She still has the window halfway open for the tree branches and the birds. Her chair is cold and damp and smells like outside.

"What's wrong?" my brother asks me.

"Nothing," I say.

We're quiet then and I'm cold by the window. I cover my lap with my mother's blanket. I can't concentrate on anything in *Reader's Digest*, but I pretend. My mother comes out of the kitchen to tell us it will be a while before dinner. The turkey needs to cook for at least another hour.

"We'll go to the beach," the girlfriend says. "I'll drive."

I don't like how she always knows what to do, how she has these plans.

"Why?" I ask. "It's cold." I decide that later I'm also going to ask her why she wants to go to Italy.

"Don't be a stick in the mud," my mother says.

The girlfriend has a tiny green car. My brother tilts the front seat forward to let us into the back. The boy sits in the middle, between my mother and me. We drive fast and I close my eyes.

The sun is bright when we get there, but outside the car, it's cold and windy. The wind pulls my hair straight back and holds it there, floating up behind me. We just stand by the car, looking out at the ocean. I close my eyes again and lean against my brother. I link my arm in his. The wind keeps blowing around my head. We are quiet. The sound of the wind and the ocean is constant and fades away. There's nothing to hear.

The day after Christmas, the aquarium is busy. We don't like it because it's hard to see and everybody's talking so we can't concentrate.

"Let's just go," the boy says. He starts pulling me to the door.

"I don't want to go home," I tell him. I stop and he pulls harder.

"I want to go swimming," he says. He means in my mother's jacuzzi bathtub. "Not today," I say, because I know my brother's still there.

"Please" the boy says loudly. People look at us.

"Shh," I tell him.

I look around at the people who are looking at us. They stop staring when I stare back at them. I'm not sure, but I think I see a woman I used to work with. I look away fast, but it's too late. She smiles and walks over, carrying a big pink baby girl on her hip.

"How are you?" she asks me.

"Just fine," I say. I smile at her and then look over at the boy.

"Mom," the boy says quickly. "I want to go." He looks down. I look down too. The floor is shiny, black marble.

"I didn't know you had a son," the woman says. Her baby is wiggling and wants to be put down.

"Well," I say. I shrug. The woman is very religious. If she heard ambulance sirens, she'd get down on her knees in the office and pray. I remember the picture on her desk of her baby getting baptized in a long white lacy dress that hung all the way down to the floor.

I like making her think that I am good enough to be a mother too. I smile at her again.

"We're on our way out," I say. "Happy holidays."

Outside, we walk fast. After three blocks the boy asks where we are going.

"I don't know," I say.

I start laughing and then he laughs too. He runs and I chase him to the end of the block. We cross the street together. His breathing is loud and fast. I make him sit down on a bench and rest until he catches his breath.

The boy lies at the bottom of my mother's jacuzzi. I am supposed to be counting, but my mother keeps interrupting.

"Pull him out," she says. "He's dying." The water at the surface ripples and makes his body look rubbery.

For the last two days, he has been grouchy because I would not bring him here. He left notes hidden all over the house saying "I WANT TO GO SWIMING!" He hid the notes where he knew I'd find them: under the milk in the refrigerator, in my shoes, under my pillow, in my book. "Swimming has two m's," I kept telling him, but he'd put his hands over his ears and pretend not to listen.

The boy shoots up out of the water and takes a deep breath.

"Oh, thank God," my mother says.

"Seventy-three," I tell him.

The boy is disappointed. He hits the water with his fist and makes a big splash.

"No more," I tell him. "You're tired."

"It makes my lungs stronger," he says. This is what his doctor told him.

"Well, I'm not going to count for you," I say.

He turns his back to us and starts playing with the plastic deep-sea diver my mother bought for him.

My mother relaxes. She turns and looks at me. I think she's going to say something, but she just stares.

"What is it?" I ask.

"You know you got your red hair from your grandfather's mother. I've told you that, right?" she asks.

"I don't remember," I say. I hate it when she gets serious like this, like she has to hurry up and tell me everything.

"Your grandfather's mother," she pauses, "your great-grandmother had red hair. Your grandfather loved her very much. She died when he was only eleven," she says.

I don't say anything.

"I only have one picture of her from when she was very young, maybe only thirteen or fourteen," she says.

I nod. She gets up and goes to the other room to get the photograph. I watch her leave and then look at the boy. He is holding the plastic diver under water and counting. At two-hundred, he brings the diver up for air.

"The diver's wearing an oxygen mask," I explain, but the boy ignores me.

My mother comes back with the photograph.

"Look at her beautiful hair," my mother says. Her hair is very long and wavy, but you can't see the color because the photograph is black and white. I take the picture from my mother and look at it closer. The girl is wearing a dress that looks gray, thick white stockings, and black lace-up boots. She is standing with her feet pointing outward, one foot slightly in front of the other, like a ballerina.

In the morning, there's a note taped to my door from the boy's mother. She wants to know if I have any rent money. I don't. I get dressed fast. I'm in a hurry. I need to go out for a while by myself. I need to think.

I tell the boy I have some errands I have to do by myself. "You'll be okay," I tell him. He's already dressed to go out-side and I feel bad. His eyebrows go up like he has something to say to me. I wait. He takes off his winter coat and his scarf and throws them at my feet. Then he runs into his room and slams the door. "I hope you die," he screams and I can tell he's crying.

I go. I have a feeling he's going to run away or somehow disappear and I'll never see him again, but I know if I keep walking, the feeling will go away. I walk fast. I think about what to do and I don't know. I don't know where to go so I decide to get my hair cut. I take the bus to a place I noticed in my mother's neighborhood.

The man who cuts my hair is very small and nervous. He talks so fast I have to guess at what he's asking me. He mostly looks confused by my answers so I may be misunderstanding him. I try to relax. "Just a couple inches off, please," I say again. He keeps adjusting his glasses, as if the adjustment helps him to see better. He brushes my hair and sprays it wet. Then he asks me to stand up. He takes two steps back, away from me. "It would help me to be precise if you remain standing," I think he says. I watch him in the mirror. He is at least four inches shorter than I am.

Afterward, I have that feeling again that the boy is going to disappear and I almost make myself go to the aquarium to see if I will miss him and want to go home. Instead I go to the library. I like to lie down between the stacks on the top floor and pretend I'm hiding from someone. Usually I lie there and think of all the good things that might happen to me, but today I fall asleep and don't wake up until someone flicks on the light in my aisle. I sit up. "What?" I ask. "I didn't ask you anything," the teenager says to me. She starts looking for a book. I lie back down and stare up at the ceiling, waiting for her to go. "Are you homeless or something?" she asks. "Jesus," I say. I stand up. The girl rolls her eyes at me and I leave.

It's almost evening now and I'm disappointed so I decide to go somewhere for a drink, because that's what people do. I find an Irish pub that looks cozy and safe. I sit down at the bar and a man a few stools over waves and moves in closer. I don't really care. He buys me a drink and that's fine too. Then he buys two shots for me and two shots for him. We drink them fast. I start to shiver and my eyes won't focus on anything. I try to look at one thing and my eyes jump to something else. "I don't really like to drink," I tell the man.

He puts on his coat and nods. "Let's go eat," he says. My coat is still on. I haven't taken it off. "Hold on," I say. I cover my ears with my hands and press hard. Sound moves away from me. I make myself stare at the picture behind the bar until I can read what it says. The picture is of a very old man. He's fat and tired looking. Underneath him it says, "Only the good die young." I take my hands off my ears. "Okay," I tell the man and I stand up.

I watch the man's feet. His shoes are brown leather and soft-looking. He walks with his toes pointing outward. I try walking like this too. I hold on to the back of his coat and follow him out the door. I start laughing.

Then we are there, inside a restaurant, and he pulls out a chair for me to sit down. He orders tea and soup for both of us. It is very warm inside. We're sitting by a big window. I keep putting my hand on the glass to feel the cold outside. The tea makes me dizzy and sweaty. My face burns. I put my cheek against the cold window and close my eyes.

"You'll be okay," the man says.

I open my eyes and look at him. He sits with his elbows propped up on the table, his hands folded. He holds very still. I think he's humming, but I'm not sure because the restaurant is so loud. Sound seems to be moving slowly through the room. He begins to eat his food and I think I can still hear him humming, even while he chews.

"My name is Daniel," the man says. He starts asking me questions. Not hard questions about my life now, just questions with easy answers. I talk a lot.

I tell him that I am from the part of California where it never snows. During the winter, my brother and I used to sit and watch the Weather Channel, but our part of the map always stayed a warm red or yellow. It drove us crazy. For years at a time, it stayed sunny and warm.

"I'm going to be sick," I tell the man.

He nods and points to the bathroom in the back of the restaurant. "Do you need help?" the man asks, his voice still slow and calm. I wave my hand at him and walk to the bathroom. I take big steps and bump into chairs and waitresses dressed in black. I look back at the man to see if he's watching. He's looking down at his hands, minding his own business.

The bathroom is all cold, white tile. A window is open and the air is cool. I want to crawl outside, but then I cough and I am sick. Afterward, I feel better. I splash water on my face and stand under the open window and let my face dry cold. Someone knocks on the door. "Coming," I say.

I walk back to the table carefully. "I'm going home now," I tell the man. I put my hand on his shoulder for a second and then I go.

The boy is sitting there watching TV when I get home. I go sit next to him.

"It's really late," I tell him. He doesn't look at me or say anything.

On TV, there's a woman counting. She counts to one hundred and then she switches to a different language. Sometimes she pauses to take a drink of water from a paper cup. Her name is Sleepy Jane.

The boy falls asleep with his head resting on the arm of the couch. I curl up on my half of the couch and go to sleep.

It's cold in the morning. The TV is still on and I reach for the remote to turn it off. The boy is standing by the window, watching the rain.

"Good morning," I say.

"The fish are scared," he says. "They're acting funny."

I go to his room to check on them. They are swimming fast at the top of the bowl, their mouths reaching up, biting at the air.

"I think they're hungry," I shout at the boy. He runs in and feeds them.

"How long has it been raining?" I ask him.

"I don't know," the boy says.

The fish calm down.

"They'll be all right," I say.

He carries the bowl with us into the family room and sets it down on the window ledge. I push the couch over to the window so we can sit and watch the rain. The boy asks if he can brush my hair. "Yes," I say. He runs into my room to get the brush, then jumps back onto the couch. I bounce up a little bit when he lands. He starts brushing.

After a while, he brushes more slowly and I sit there, waiting for the next stroke.

The steadiness of the rain makes me tired. I fall asleep on the couch. When the rain gets a little quieter and softer, I wake up and then I doze off again. The boy has set up his car race-track around my feet. He clocks each car with his stopwatch and writes down the times. The yellow car is doing the best.

I yawn and stretch out my legs. The boy looks at me. "Mom got a boyfriend and we're moving," he says.

I look down at my hands on my lap. I keep looking at my hands, but I can't feel them there. I can feel the air around us—cold and very still. I look up and then the boy and I are looking at each other.

"Where are you guys going?" I ask. My voice is cold.

"I don't know," the boy says. He starts chewing on his shirt collar and looks away.

I close my eyes again. It probably won't happen. They won't move. I make myself open my eyes and I watch the boy.

He pushes his yellow car slowly along the racetrack. He keeps chewing on his shirt. I feel bad for him.

"You might like it," I say. "Wherever you go."

He stops pushing his car. "I want to go outside," he says. He walks over to the door and puts on his coat.

"Come on," he tells me.

We walk close together and I try to hold his red, kid-sized umbrella over us both. Our shoes get wet and start to squeak. "Look," the boy says. He points at the ground, at how the rain bounces up off the sidewalk.

We walk all the way to my mother's house.

The door's unlocked and inside my mother's asleep in her chair by the window. The boy and I sit together on the reddish-orange couch, looking at my mother and shivering in our wet clothes.

"I want to go swimming," the boy whispers close to my ear.

"Okay," I say and I nod. He slides off the couch and his shoes squeak as he walks down the hallway to the bathroom. I listen until I can't hear anything except for the loud, rushing sound of the water filling up the tub.

I keep watching my mother in her chair and I remember how a long time ago we took a nap together in this room. We must have been closer then, because it was possible for us to lie down together in a sunny spot on the warm, brown carpet and sleep all afternoon. I know that when I woke up later that day, it was dark and my mother was still sleeping. There was nowhere to go and nothing about to happen next, and I could just stay there with her and wait.

ASUNCIÓN

by ROY KESEY

IT IS A BEAUTIFUL CITY: flowering jacarandas, old yellow street-cars, Sunday afternoons in the plaza rich with heat and bird-song. It is also an excellent city in which to be mugged. By this I mean that on the whole the muggers here are extremely inefficient.

I have been the intended victim of five attempted mug-gings thus far during my three years in Asunción. Though my Spanish is perfect and most of my clothes are made locally, it is clear what I am, even from a distance; muggers note my pale skin and the lack of grace in my straight-backed walk, and they know immediately that I was born elsewhere, in a country where salaries are high and jobs are plentiful, where the streets are swept and the air is clean. Do they resent this? Do they rage at my good fortune? I don't believe they do. I believe their only thought is this: Here is another foreigner, another soft victim.

Blanco—in Spanish it means both "Caucasian" and "target," among other things. But there is a difference between spotting a target and hitting one. I have never been mugged successfully, because I am far stronger than I appear, and because I am not afraid.

They do not like confrontation of any kind, these criminals. When they work in groups it is generally in groups of four, and this is how it will happen: Muggers one and two will start an argument in front of you, hoping to distract your attention; mugger three will push you from behind, and mugger four will tug violently at your purse or briefcase. If you do not let go, they will almost always scatter.

There is of course the slight possibility that instead of scattering they will stand their ground and puff out their chests and demand that you give them what they have tried and failed to rip from your hands; in this case, in general, you have only to puff out your chest as well. If you do, they will most likely slink away—slinking, it is precisely what they do, the slinking of dogs that have been kicked—and you will be left alone, sweaty and victorious.

But of those few who do not run at the first sign of confrontation, there is a small percentage, a very small percentage, who will likewise not slink away once you have puffed out your chest. Instead they will smile. When you meet a mugger such as this, you must swing as hard as you can and you must pray not to miss. If you miss he will pull a knife from his belt, will stab you in the chest, will kill you. That is the only rule.

Of course I detest all muggers, but there is a constant roil inside of me, the struggle between acid and base, perhaps, the latter seeking to neutralize, the former to overwhelm: I was taught as a child to hate the sin and love the sinner. I have never been very successful at this, but now at least I know that it is possible. This last scenario, wherein you are accosted by one of the very, very few muggers who smile and do not run, it is how I met the latest great love of my life.

* * *

I was on my way home from work, striding through the dense summer dusk, the heat at last relenting. A young woman was twenty or thirty yards ahead of me, walking in the same direction. The moment I saw her, I began to speed up.

It was not that I wanted to speak to her, to compliment her eyes or her smile, to undress her slowly and spread her across my bed—I did not desire any of this. I wanted only to be close to her for a moment. This is something I have felt so many times, man or woman or child—it is all the same, the need to be close. Sometimes it is all that one requires.

This was not, I think, the first time I had seen the young woman. That night she was dressed neither poorly nor well, but cleanly: pressed black trousers, smooth white blouse, low black heels that clicked as she walked. She smelled of jasmine and moved through her own quiet music as I closed in.

Then he came from the side, he was slender and lithe, and he went for her purse but she held to it just long enough for me to reach them. I shoved him in the back, and he sprawled; she gaped at me, her mouth ever so slightly open, her purse on the ground at her feet.

I retrieved the purse and set it in her hands. Now she was not watching me. She was watching the mugger who stared up at us from where he lay.

—Just go, I said to her. Go now, go quickly, fly.

She nodded, turned away, turned back. The mugger was getting to his feet. I stepped toward him and he raised both hands. The woman turned away again and started walking, faster and faster, and at last she disappeared around the far corner.

If the mugger had taken off just then, he could have caught her in the space of two or three blocks. Of course I would have followed, would have arrived soon enough. But he did not pursue her, not at all. Instead he squared his shoulders and puffed out his chest.

—Your wallet, he said.

I puffed out my chest as well, and he smiled. It was a beautiful smile. I knew that it was time, time to swing as hard as I could, praying not to miss. As long as I didn't miss, one punch would have been sufficient, I think. But I didn't. I couldn't. His smile was so beautiful.

There was movement, one hand flitting to his belt, still the smile, still I could not swing, the smile, my hands at my sides, but something failed, something caught, he pulled and tugged and his smile waned and finally I was free of him. I set my feet and drew back my fist, something flashed at his belt and I swung, the blow starting in the strength of my legs, surging up through my back and chest, through my shoulder and arm and into my fist, his hand was rising and again the flash as I hit him and he flurried and collapsed face-down across the curb.

I waited for him to rise, but he did not. His body trembled in that low light. There was a more distant movement then, and I looked up, saw the young woman standing at the corner. I motioned, and my motion was unclear even to me, it meant for her to stay or to go, I have no idea.

When she disappeared again I stepped to the mugger and flipped him over, thinking to kick him in the face, to show him that mugging is wrong, that it makes an already hard world still harder. As he slumped onto his back I saw his hand held tightly to his stomach. I saw the blood that bubbled up through his fingers. I saw that what had flashed at his belt was a knife now buried to the hilt in his abdomen.

I bent over him, the knife, his thin chest heaving, his kind and delicate face. One of his eyes was swollen nearly shut, and there were scrapes across his forehead, a gash at one temple. He would not be getting up for some time.

I could have walked away and been done with it, but leaving him there was not possible, not in any real way. He looked up at me and smiled again, that smile. His one open eye was a wonder, long black lashes, a warmth of brown. And at that moment I began to believe he could be taught, to hope he could be saved.

Rafael is his name. I nursed him here in my apartment. We were fortunate that the knife had not pierced his diaphragm, that his internal bleeding was not unmanageable. I set him on my bed, the knife still in place: From films I had learned that if I pulled it out too soon he would bleed too much too fast, would be lost to me.

I fed him only liquids, my own dinner blended until smooth, and I brought him cups of warm herbal tea whenever he complained of thirst. I bathed his scrapes and daubed antiseptic cream on the gash at his temple. I even consulted a pharmacist and bought everything he recommended, the gauze and tape, the antibiotics and painkillers.

I noticed that the ringing of the telephone often disturbed Rafael's rest, so I had it disconnected. And on the morning of the third day, as he lay sleeping, I called a locksmith, who came and put locks on the windows, the interior doors, the kitchen drawers. I try to think only the best of the people I meet, but there is no sense in taking unnecessary risks.

I sat with Rafael each afternoon as heat thickened the air and the city went still. I tried to amuse him with stories of finance and scandal in Brussels and Baghdad, Bombay and Buenos Aires. Always he turned his face away.

Then for nearly a week a fever came and went, came and went; hallucinations took him and he sobbed in Guaraní. When he woke from his frothing fear I asked what he'd seen. He claimed not to remember. Slowly I cured him, and at last he began to reveal himself to me, but his stories came in fragments: the name of a cousin he hadn't seen in years, the title of a book his mother had once read aloud, and then he'd fall silent again.

Through all of this, the fever and shards of past, I eased

the knife out as gently as possible, half an inch per day. Soon the knife threatened to fall of its own accord, and I was unsure what would result if it fell, if the bleeding might resume or additional damage might be done. I braced the knife with damp towels and forbade Rafael to move.

Finally I was able to slip the tip of the blade from his smooth brown hairless skin, and we had a small celebration: champagne, strawberries, candles. Our first kiss. He struggled against it, but not, I think, with much conviction.

A few days later he tried to escape. My downstairs neighbors called me at work to say that it sounded as though some kind of animal was trapped and dying in my apartment, and I came home to find claw marks on the inside of the bedroom door, a broken window, blood smeared along the ledge to where he sat. But the ledge is far too high, the fall too much for anyone who wished to live; as well, the streets below are noisy enough that no distant shout would be heeded. I repaired the window, painted the door, and punched him once, as hard as I could. Then I kissed him, his forehead and cheeks and eyelids, his soft and bloody mouth.

It is difficult to know how much is enough. For a week I kept him bound and gagged in my bedroom. The neighbors complained once or twice of thudding sounds coming through their ceiling, but I calmed them with stories of construction. There is no point in worrying those around you.

The last few days of that week there were no more complaints, and from the depth and gentleness of his gaze each time I entered the bedroom, I came to believe that he now understood. I removed the gag, unbound his feet and hands, massaged his wrists and ankles. I told him of my apartment's many comforts, and promised he would learn them all.

The following day a rasping cough took hold in his chest. I went back to the pharmacist for decongestants and more antibiotics, but the cough grew hollow and deep—bronchitis or pneumonia, I never learned for sure.

It was almost a month before he was healthy again, and in

that time I grew ever more certain I could trust him and his love for me. Sponge bath and hot compress, mentholatum and lemon tea, and bit by bit he told me all I wished to know. His home in Bahía Negra on the bank of the Lateriquique, and the brothers and sisters he'd left there. The fortune he'd come looking for and now knew he'd never find. The garbage he pawed through for food, the bridges under which he slept, the alleys where he laid in wait.

He told me so much, and I could only trust him. When the sickness finally burned itself out, I gave him keys to all the doors of the apartment. He had earned them, I thought. That evening I came home to find him waiting on the living-room sofa. He presented me with gifts: a gold watch and a beautiful leather briefcase. They were stolen, of course, and I beat him unconscious. There is no point in making a hard world still harder.

We had no further problems for the next several days, and on Sunday afternoon I took him to the plaza. It was still very hot, though autumn had begun. We watched the old men sipping their cold tea, the ornate cages at their feet filled with canaries and finches. Rafael begged me to buy him a songbird, and I let him choose. The old man set an unreasonable price, but was not difficult to persuade, and Rafael and I walked slowly home, carrying the cage between us.

Though the canary was a female, Rafael insisted on naming her Teodoro; he cared for her with great tenderness, and of course she sang splendidly. When I returned from work four days ago, I found him leaning over her cage, whistling something pleasantly serene, a folksong of some kind, perhaps in the hope that she would learn it.

I came to stand beside him, asked if the words to the song were in Spanish or Guaraní, and Rafael turned, kissed my mouth, held me. He drew back and something flashed at his belt and this time I was not quick enough. Love slowed me,

I believe. The knife hit me where his knife had hit him on the day we met, or very nearly so. He must have spent hours sharpening the blade, or it would not have slipped in with such grace, such warmth.

I have been lying on the couch since then, drawing the knife out half an inch per day. By the end of next week I will be able to remove it entirely. And how long after that must I wait for full recovery? A month or so, perhaps less.

The pain is only a nuisance; far more troubling is the manner in which Rafael left me. As I slid down the wall he kissed me again, the softest kiss. He drew my wrist to his face and kissed my hand. He stepped over me, and walked to the door. Do you see? Instead of setting Teodoro free, he left her caged, and in so doing surely meant to send me a message. But what does the message mean? There is precisely one way to find out.

Rafael should not be too hard to find. As soon as I am well I will begin my search for him, in the alleys and under the bridges. If he has left Asunción I shall track him, to Esteros or Villarica, to Horqueta or back to Bahía Negra. He may even have left the country: Bolivia, Brazil, Argentina. It will make little difference.

I will find him lying in a hammock beside a slow jungle stream, wild parrots eating guava from his hand; or in a shack above the tree line in the mountains, rain thrashing at the roof; or in a small dirty house on the outskirts of some major city, cinderblock walls, a poster of the Virgin curling up at the corners. I will find him and take him in my arms. I will trace his lips with my fingertips. I will teach him the indefatigable strength of love, the rippling force of forgiveness.

SALES

by JUDY BUDNITZ

MY BROTHER PUTS the new one in the pen out back with the other salesmen. "They just don't ever learn, do they," he says mournfully as he yanks home the latch and notches up one more on the gatepost.

I like to go down there after breakfast, throw my toast crusts over the top. You can hear them scrabbling around, you can see them between the slats. Only a narrow glimpse; none of them are skinny enough yet to be seen fully. But the gaps are wide enough to observe their choice of tie, their sweat-stained button-down shirts, their pinstripe and seersucker and gabardine suits. You can see their priorities at a glance: some have filthy ties and spotlessly shined shoes, others let the dust build up on their toes and keep their ties and pocket-squares clean. Sometimes you can see an eye, sometimes two.

My brother tells me not to, but I like to walk past and

hear their voices hooting out to me. I like to pretend they're calling out for my hot body.

"Set of seventeen knives for the price of twelve! And I'll throw in a free melon-baller!"

"Ma'am, you look like you could use a handy household—"

"And that's just what I'm here to tell you—"

"Just try to look me in the eye and tell me you don't need a—"

"Seven easy payments. Just seven easy payments. That's less than—"

"Hold it in your hand. Lighter than air, I tell you. Just think what—"

"Per day, that's less than the cost of a cup of coffee."

If you squint your ears, you can make it sound like love.

Hands pop out between the slats, holding limp water-stained catalogs, order forms, metal gadgets shaped like squashed dragonflies. They jostle for the spots closest to the fence. I like to keep moving, give them all a chance. They stir up such a cloud of dust you can see it rising above the ten-foot walls. Inside they get hoarse on the grit but never think to close their mouths.

"Last chance—"

"Just between us, I'm willing to make you a special deal—"

"Limited offer—"

"Practically giving it away, don't tell my supervisor—"

"Don't you *want* to cook fast easy low-fat meals for your family? You could be saving lives with this—"

If they all got together and cooperated, stacked up their sample cases in one column, they would be able to climb out. But they are too competitive to think of that. They are sales-men to the core. Occasionally you will see one digging at the base of the fence with an egg beater or a corkscrew decorated with poodles, but he always stops early on for fear of damaging the merchandise.

"If only they used their jaws for digging," my brother always says. He says he'd like to use them to clear the fields.

"Grab one by the heels, get him started, and just push him along, wheelbarrow-style. Better than a lawnmower." Back in the beginning crows gathered on the top of the fence, attracted as they are by anything that glitters. But soon even they got tired of the noise.

The newest one has little triangular eyes deep in pockets of skin, and a mouth that's purplish and fleshy and caved-in like a spoiled fruit. He gets up and brushes off the knees of his pants, first thing, like they all do. Then he looks behind him, takes in the fact that yet another door has been slammed on him. And then he looks around at the others, sizes up the competition, hitches up his trousers. He's got one of those malnourished paunches that hang low and hard against the belt. The others circle him, eyeing his sample case. They're hunched over, defensive postures, ready to spring.

He'll make his pitch, first thing. That's their territory-marker, their plumage, their bellering mating call. If there's two selling competing brands of the same orange-juicer/showerhead-adapter, there will be trouble.

"Get away from there," my sister-in-law calls. "Makes you look cheap and easy."

My sister-in-law likes to stand in windows naked, feeling the sun on the freckled space between her breasts. That is why so many salesmen stop by.

"Why cheap and easy?" I ask her later, when we're sitting on the front veranda in sunglasses and headscarves, watching the afternoon dust storms roll past. Today the waves are tight, dense, low to the ground. They form tubes that last for several minutes before breaking. Far in the distance, you can see teenaged surfers riding them. They wear rubber suits and gas masks. The surfers paint their surfboards the colors of the ocean: green, orange, gold, black. I can see two bobbing up and down on choppy waves. A third has just wiped out, he's skidding across the ground on his knees getting knocked this way and that by stray gusts as the big ones crash over his head. His knees are probably torn up pretty bad by now. We see his surfboard get ripped out of his hands. He lunges for it but it flaps away. Gone. A moment later the wind whips it around behind him and he gets whacked on the head. I bet he's cute.

"You make them think they can score with you," she says.

"But I'm not going to buy anything," I say.

"I mean *emotionally*," Janice says. "They're manipulative because they're insecure. They need to feel loved. It all has to do with their mothers."

"But they don't have mothers," I say.

"Exactly!" she says. Then she talks some more about emotional needs. She always says she doesn't mean to do it, she just happens to walk past the window every day, on her way to getting dressed, and feels like lingering. It's the salesmen who are looking for attention, she says, looking for love, who come to the door longing for some give and take. That's where my brother waits for them.

She says the sun will give us wrinkles, but the dry wind will tighten our pores, so the one will cancel out the other. Janice is younger than me but acts older because she's married and has read two books about how your mind works and is very in touch with her feelings. Her face is not pretty in the grand scheme of things, but relative to those around here she's a stand-out. My brother calls her a hottie at least seven times a day.

Each time I want to tell him, or tell her, that "hot" is not such great praise around here. "Hot isn't it" gets more play than hello. Hot is common as dirt. The salesmen, no matter how hot it gets, keep their jackets on, their ties knotted. By the end of the day all their suits have turned a new darker color from the sweat. I want someone to call me hot.

Janice, her nose is the perfect shape but three sizes too large for her face. Her hair is long and pretty, but grows more from one side than the other, like a wig that's slipped sideways. I could go on. But her neck is like the stalk of a flower, I think, always bending toward you. I don't remember a flower, but I remember that long pliant curve.

The house is set far back from the road. I don't know how the salesmen can see Janice in the window from so far away, but they can. They have a long walk, from the road to the door. They walk with their shoulders back, chests out, even the puny ones, they know they are being watched, the approach is important. The balding ones wear straw boaters, felt fedoras for an old-timey feel. Some let the baldness show, polish their heads, they think it makes them look more reliable. The word for their walk is brisk. Everything is brisk— arms, legs, hair if they have it. Hair parted in the middle, flapping in two brisk wings with every step. The briskness extends down to their fingers and toes, flicking away dust, pinching mustache tips. I know they think about her as they climb the steps: bored lady-of-the-house, alone and in need of company, coming to the door in a hastily thrown-on bathrobe.

It is such a long walk from road to house. If I were more fleet of foot, I'd run out to intercept them, tell them to move on, nothing to see here. My brother tells me to stay out of the way.

"Don't yell at her," Janice says. She says I am to be pitied. Janice says I am sick, I have arrested development. It is very sad, I will be a little child forever and will never taste the illicit fruits of womanhood. I ask her how she knows this. She says she read it in her book.

"Hello? You don't have any of *these*," she says, sticking out her chest. "It means you never will. You'll be an old woman in the body of a little child."

But I'm as tall as she is. I think it's just that I'm built along the lines of my mother, who in the picture I have is flat as a washboard, the effect heightened perhaps by the armor she's wearing, horizontal metal strips stitched together to shield her from the evils in the atmosphere. That's what people thought back then.

Janice just smiles sweetly and says, "You'll see."

I don't believe her. But the more she says it, the more I start to.

I ask my brother if she's right, if I'll never grow up. He doesn't say yes and doesn't say no.

My brother says I should be grateful that I don't have it half as bad as some. He says he's seen them in town, those born with their eyelids stitched together and nothing underneath, or with their faces coming out of their stomachs like a kid's drawing, or our neighbor with fleshy nubbins growing from his gums in place of teeth.

"You should smile more," Janice says. "World of difference." She says I am lucky I have family who love me no matter what I look like.

It's easy for them to say. They've got no visible defects and are happily married. Except my brother gets sunburned bad sometimes when he works outside, to the point of blisters like white worms on his skin. Most of his hair has been burned off his skull by now, there's only a pale corona of fuzz around his head like a dandelion. But that's nothing. They've got each other. They'll bang out some children soon. In the middle of the night I hear them in their room, the furniture getting pushed around by the force of their love and my brother telling Janice all the things he's going to do to her.

People get married now much younger than they used to, or so I'm told. It's because of impatience, I suppose, because of the rules against fornication before marriage, to contain the spread of diseases. Maybe it's turned out to be more than Janice bargained for, but how can she complain? Big empty house, lots of room, fine view of the dust storms, parents gone, only the old-maid sister to get rid of. And my brother's going places, got big plans. Who wouldn't jump at the chance?

At first I thought she did her standing at the window to needle him. But now I wonder if he asked her to do it, right from the start, if it was all a plan. Salesmen-bait. I can't remember which started first, him building the pen or her doing the standing. By now they have it like clockwork: she's in the window right at the hour of midmorning when the air is clearest, and within minutes there's a jaunty step on the veranda, a knock at the door.

Now there are nearly two dozen jawing back in the pen. They'll be kept there until the season cools off. My brother doesn't like to exert himself in the heat.

The newest one—I am sorry about him. I was up in my room and saw him coming up the path and thought, oh no. Maybe because he looked less swaggery than the rest. He came up in a tentative way, scanning the front of the house as if it were a face, as if it had something to tell. He had a clump of brown sticks in his hand—there's a weed here that has round leaves ringed with spikes, people call them flowers but I know the truth—he was carrying them like a present. And he is tall and bony and paunchy but there is something childish about his face. Developmentally arrested? Maybe we have something in common, something we can talk about, given the opportunity.

So I am sorry he is in there with the rest. I go down there in the evening, after the storms, to see how he's faring. It's dark enough that they don't see me and start their pitching. The others are crouched in little huddles, sheltering behind hats and sleeves and sample cases raised above their heads. The new one stands alone. Each time he tries to join a group, they turn their backs and shut him out. I wonder what he's got in his case. Either it's something so junky that the others are snubbing him as an amateur, or else it's so wonderful that they feel threatened and are plotting against him.

None of the others are friends, but there are alliances, business arrangements. They're discussing sales strategy. Intense trading is going on. The toast crusts I tossed this morning have changed hands several times.

The new one doesn't want to dirty up his suit by sitting, so he's leaning up against the fence. I slink up behind him and look at the slice I can see between the slats: hair, neck, collar, seam up the middle of the jacket's back. The boards groan. If he pressed hard, probably, he could break through.

But none of them think that way. The salesmen all think they can talk their way out of anything.

I warned them once about what was coming, I even told them where the nails were loose and the wood rotten. I pulled back a flap and stuck my head through. They were insulted. Have you no faith in our persuasive powers? they all said. We don't need to stoop to base physicality, they said. Won't dirty ourselves with the sweat of manual labor. We will escape by power of elocution alone. And then they tried to sell me skin-brightening cream, hair pomade, chewing gum that cleanses the obscenities from your speech.

A flabby bit of his back pokes between the boards. It wants to be touched. It will be sweaty and gritty, my fingers will taste like salt afterward. He will turn around and see at most half of my face—my face is wide. He will not, I think, see much of my body.

I don't do it. Instead I go back to the house. Janice is mending stockings that have been mended so many times before that now they are all seam. She is using thread I took from one of the salesmen. He said it was a free sample. He said once we tried it we'd want to buy out his whole supply. It is supposed to be invisible. The stockings are supposed to be "nude." I can see everything but Janice says it's just the light in here.

"Janice," I say, "Will I ever—"

"Of course you won't, baby," she says, biting off thread with a nasty clicking of teeth. "No man will ever want you, not the way you look. Men like *mature* women. But don't worry. We'll still love you."

"That wasn't even what I was going to ask."

"Yes it was."

"How do you know?"

"By the lascivious look in your eye," she says. She's sitting on the kitchen table in her underwear, posing and sewing. Apparently she can't get dressed until she repairs the stockings. "I'd just have to take everything off again when I put these back on, so why bother?" she says. I don't know whether she's hoping for my brother to come home, or another salesman. Salesmen eyes on her make her happy. She's not allowed to go near the pen at all.

Her underpants are covered with red kisses. I can't tell whether they're printed on or were made by a mouth and lipstick. I can't see my brother doing that, but who else would? Maybe she made them herself.

"There's nothing wrong with me," I say.

"Denial," she says, smiling sadly.

"You're lying," I say. "Trying to make me feel bad."

"Defense mechanism," she says with the same pitying smile. "Whatever makes you feel better."

I wish she hadn't read that book. It makes her hard to argue with.

"Honey, we need to work on your self-esteem. Then you'll be better able to cope with this problem of yours."

"How do we do that?"

"A makeover," she says in a determinedly cheerful way which means I should leave her alone. She's given me makeovers before. They hurt.

I go up to my room. I have many rooms that I can call mine, it's a big house, there's plenty of space no one wants. Janice is a busy girl. Woman, I should say. She does her busyness downstairs, except when she stands in the window with her nipples close to the glass. There's one room where my brother does his dreaming. The walls are dirty brown but he's painted a white patch on the ceiling. He lies on the floor and falls asleep there, hoping he'll see answers written out on the white cloud.

He's gone most days, but not so far that we can't see him from the veranda. He's flattening the ground, he's building rickety wooden towers. He has a picture from a book, a drawing of a windmill connected to a speedy-looking train on rails. He wants so badly to build it, he has grand plans, but he has no idea how. Even I can see that his towers are no good; each time, before he even gets around to making the fan blades, the windstorms have knocked them to pieces.

I don't know where he thinks he wants to go. What else is there? No one moves except the salesmen, and they keep moving because no one will let them stay anywhere. They are pariahs, no one wants them. That is why they are so belligerent, so full of themselves. Janice says that's a defense mechanism too. Sometimes they come carrying things we need, but most of the time not. They carry diseases, you're not even supposed to touch them. There are signs all along the road, red warning signs with a silhouette of a man with a suitcase and hat, and a big annihilating line through him. My brother says we're doing them a favor by rounding them up.

He hates salesmen, hates being made to want something, the way the salesmen try to make you. "I want to want what I want," he always says. "Don't make me want something I didn't even know I wanted till you dangled it in front of me like a carrot."

"What's a carrot?" I say back. I vaguely recall that it's something yellow and sharp, maybe a sort of shrew with a pointed nose and golden fur. Maybe sort of like Janice.

It's hard to sleep, nights, with the salesmen yammering. They are out there calling to my brother, making offers he can't refuse. They are bargaining with the night clouds, begging them to part and give us a glimpse of the moon they know is still up there. Now or never, no money down, first come first served. My brother doesn't hear; he's busy telling Janice what she can do with her big mouth even though I haven't heard her say a word.

Maybe they dream about selling, maybe they're talking in their sleep.

Next day the dust storms come in tall swells and plumes. The surfers are having a blast, rocketing up and down on the mountains of air. One lags behind, he's wearing a helmet and kneepads. As if those will help him.

Janice says she can see their sexy bods in the rubber suits, even at this distance. "It's all about body language," she says. "But then, you wouldn't know about that."

"I do too."

"You're too young to understand. And always will be, baby."

"You're just saying that. You like to think you're the only real woman on the place. Just give me a few months and I'll catch up."

She pats my hand. "Rationalizing. Bargaining. You're going through the seven stages of grief, honey."

Down in the pen my salesman is looking a bit worse for the wear. Yesterday his hair was doing a poufy pompadour thing, now it's lying in sweaty tangles down to his eyebrows. He's streaming, his white-and-blue striped suit is soaked, sticking wetly to the belly I'm beginning to love so much. His mouth still has a punched-in look. The others rush to the fence and start lipping the minute they see me, but I have yet to hear his voice.

I wait until night, wait till I hear my brother and Janice start up again, then slip back down to the pen. Night is just as hot as day, dark heat like an iron pot. But I know that this means the heat will break soon, it's like a fever that peaks then disappears. And when that happens my brother will go out to the pen and start counting heads. And later the three of us will go through all the sample cases. And fight over them. If there's something that Janice and I both want, all I have to do is talk about our parents and make the sad doggy face and my brother will let me have it.

My salesman—I wonder what's in his case, he guards it so closely. The others open theirs up, flash them around, show off the red plush lining and custom-made compartments. Everything is tattered now, but they don't see it, and they think they can convince you that you don't either.

There is enough dull, reflected light from the clouds for me to see that my salesman is right where I left him, next to the fence. He's trying to sleep curled up on his case, to save his suit, but he's much too big, overflowing on all sides. I stick my arm through and poke him in the leg. The others are murmuring all around. He's quiet but his head comes up. His mouth is a darker bruise in his dark face. I pry off a few boards; it's even easier than I thought. He doesn't help me, but the minute there's an opening he wedges himself into it. He gets stuck, I'm tugging at him and he's puffing in my face. He has that salesman smell of shoe polish and over-worked salivaries. I'm afraid of his skin so I yank on his sleeves, his hair. He looks like a little midget man stuck in the wall: face, foot, abbreviated arms flapping.

Finally we get him through, and he unfolds himself. He slides his case out and we take a walk in a casual fashion. I tell him he is my favorite of all the salesmen, which is not much of a compliment, but maybe he won't think so. It's still fairly dark. I am wearing a baggy nightdress, and I hope he can't see me too well with his little hooded eyes. I am out to prove something, I am not sure what, but it has something to do with Janice.

He opens his mouth for the first time and says, "Are you perchance interested in a little taste of the illicit?"

At first I think this is his way of telling me he wants my hot body, and I feel all hot-excited and cold-scared at the same time, like fever-chills. But then he pats his sample case, and I realize "The Illicit" is the name of some kind of foot powder or floor wax or magazine subscription that will never arrive. And I don't know if I am disappointed or relieved.

I ask to see what's in the case. He holds it away from me and asks if I'm going to tell my brother about him taking his leave. I begin to realize that he's just like the others, making bargains and once-in-a-lifetime deals.

"I might," I say in a mincy way. I sound like Janice. "What's in the case?"

"Something good," he says. And doesn't say anything else, which is highly unusual for a salesman. We're walking through the fields and he starts picking the brown weeds, the ones with spiky round suns at their tips. And he gives them to me in a bunch.

Which makes me want to talk him up more. I ask him about his line of work, and where he's been, and what he thinks of the weather. And he doesn't say much, but the mushy soft mouth opens and closes and I see the little teeth glittering inside like treasure.

I sashay my hips around. Just a little bit. He gave me flowers, after all.

He puts a hand on my shoulder. It is as warm and moist and gritty as I imagined. Just by chance he touches a sort of funny-bone place there. Nerves shoot off it, and I flinch. But still. He touched me. According to Janice, this is how it begins. We'll touch each other in various places and then lie down on the ground somewhere. I look ahead for a patch clear of stones. The sky is turning pink, a sliver of sun is poking up.

I am trying to decide what to touch, his paunchy belly or his squashy face.

"Show me what's in the case," I say again in the Janice voice.

"Let's make a trade," he says, all salesman-like. "I'll show you if you show *me* something."

This is the moment I've been waiting for. "Deal," I say and pull my nightdress over my head so that I feel the hot night wind all over.

"Jumping Jehosaphat!" he says. "What are you doing? Put that back on." His eyes are goggly, face frozen. Janice was right. I'm not hot. I'm off-putting. Downright disgusting. He's horrified, hand to his mouth like he might yark. I drop the nightdress on the ground. He snatches it up and yanks it back down over my head.

"Are you trying to get me killed?" he says, looking at me, then back at the house, me then the house. "Did you hear something?"

I start to cry. I didn't know it was possible to be so ugly people could die just from looking at you.

In these dry climes crying is a noise in your throat. I've never seen a tear. I've heard of people's eyes exploding when they try to squeeze one out.

"Would you be quiet?" he hisses. "Please?"

"You said you wanted me to show you something," I say.

"I wanted you to show me the way to the next town," he says.

"Can I come with you?"

"Of course not," he snorts. "That man will have my head."

I look down at the flowers in my hand and they remind me to feel special. Then suddenly I don't feel special anymore. I remember when I'd seen him do that before.

"You brought some of these for Janice," I say. "When you saw her in the window. You came up to the house looking for *her*."

"She looked—lonely," he says. "A mere gesture," he says. "It didn't mean anything," he says and touches my shoulder again, but all I can think about is that I'm not Janice and never will be, I'll never have kisses on my underpants and the only time a man favors me with flowers is when he's bartering for street directions so he can head up the road and plague more people with his sorry sales pitches.

I know he wishes Janice were here right now. And I wish I were with one of the other salesmen, who might at least try to ornament things with words, paint some sugar fantasies, lie to me, tell me I'm beautiful.

"Which is the way out?"

"That way," I say and point the wrong way, not toward the safety of the road, but toward the horizon where the dust storms are just stirring themselves from sleep. He heads off without another look at me.

"You never even gave me a peek in the case," I say.

He doesn't look back. He must know what a slow runner I am. With that headstart, I'll never catch up.

"Don't you want to…" I call.

"No," he calls back. "Thanks," he says over his shoulder. He keeps going, fast, not brisk, beyond brisk, sloppily running. He's following the line of my finger, heading for the surfers' favorite spot. He should reach it right about the time the swells are highest. With any luck he'll get pounded to pieces.

"Why so glum?" Janice says. She steams my face with a hot towel and we practice deep cleansing breaths.

"Some of the stock busted out last night," my brother says. He doesn't even look at me, he looks at Janice. "They'll be back," he says.

The dust storms are vicious today, solid masses of brown and gray. We can feel the thickness of the air as we watch. Bits of sand scratch against our sunglasses.

"Exfoliating," Janice says.

Later that night some surfers bring my salesman back. Two carry him up to the house laid out on one of their surfboards.

"Don't know what he was thinking," one says.

"Got pretty pounded," says the other.

"Didn't have the right gear or nothing," says a third who's tagging along. He's wearing kneepads, I think he's the one I like to watch.

"We figured he was one of yours," the first says.

"Got the marks and all."

"Bring him around back," my brother says.

Janice is blatantly checking out the smallest surfer, from his greenish dreadlocks to his claw-toed surf booties. How dare she? He's *my* surfer. He's *mine*. "He *is* cute," she says, nudging me.

"Yes," I say. I'm *pretty* sure he is, although it's a little hard to tell since he's still wearing his gas mask. And I can't stop looking at my salesman, the one I tried to help, then tried to hurt by sending him the wrong way. His skin is blasted raw, his hair glittering with silica like diamonds, his nostrils plugged with sand. The eyes are all exposed, the folds of skin completely sheared away.

* * *

The weather breaks a few days later. We have a few clear, cool days before the rains start. My brother assembles his equipment, puts on his face-plate and gloves and heads out to the pen to make a profit. The salesmen see him coming and their voices rise higher than ever. Each year it's like this: the last day is the worst. Like a few dozen auctioneers in the throes of a bidding climax, or a bunch of tone-deaf opera singers shrieking out their deathbed arias. Usually Janice and I go in the house and stick our heads under pillows.

This year she has other ideas. She holds a needle in a candleflame and then pierces my ears with it. Then I add some holes to her lobes, though they're already so perforated it's hard to find a clear space. She likes to wear all her earrings at once. Then when I do find a clear space, I strike some kind of nerve or something, she starts screaming and bleeding sort of badly. "You've got to apply pressure," she keeps saying, but every time I get within three feet of her she starts yowling all over again. We're so distracted we don't even hear the voices outside.

You don't even feel sorry for the salesmen anymore, just annoyed. My brother never even bothered to patch the gaping hole I made in the fence. I guess they all felt it would be beneath them to use it to escape. Except *my* salesman, who might have used it but was too sand-blind to find it again.

Afterward we divvy up the sample cases like we always do. My brother always takes the knife kits, the ones the salesmen like to demonstrate by cutting pennies or tin cans in half. Janice has dibs on the dried-out cosmetics and hosiery. Also the lint brushes and stain removers and superpowerful glues. Also she has this thing for cheese. I take the books and lawn ornaments. And when we get to my salesman's case, I say I want it.

"What's in it?" Janice says.

"Illicit," I say.

My brother gives me a look. He forces it open. It's empty.

"Oh my god," Janice says.

"I don't believe it," my brother says.

"Big oops," Janice says. "We made a mistake."

"What?" I say. "What does it mean?"

"He wasn't the real thing," my brother says.

"A weekend dabbler," Janice says. "A dilettante."

"You mean he was just doing it for fun? But he wasn't even any good at it," I say.

I picture him walking toward the house, empty case in his hand, Janice's breasts winking at him from the window.

"Just doing it for the love of it, I guess," Janice says. And smiles.

"For the love of it?" my brother says.

"See new places, meet new people," Janice says.

My brother just grunts, but his fingers quiver on the red velvet.

I look up from the empty case and see his right eyelid all atwitch. He and Janice exchange a funny look, a panicky, gulpy look, the same look the salesmen get when you press them for details about deliveries that will never come. The room feels tippy suddenly, flat, fake, flimsy as paper. Janice in her apron, my brother in his overalls—who do they think they're kidding? Our world's nothing but a house of cards, twisting and shimmying in the slightest breeze. I could blow it down with a word, a flick of my finger.

I could do it. But I don't. In the silence I say, "Let's open the next one." My brother's shoulder muscles unbunch. He sighs and reaches down another sample case from the stack.

"Are you feeling better?" Janice says kindly, patting my back. "Have you made it through all the seven stages on the road to acceptance?"

"I think so," I say.

But I haven't accepted anything, particularly Janice's explanations. So the next day I go searching for answers on my own. In an old sample case I find a batch of books about teenage development: *Am I Normal?* and *Growing Up Great!*

and *Fun With Puberty*. I sit in my brother's room beneath the white cloud and read them all. Then I read them again to be sure. The books say there's not a darn thing wrong with me. Janice has been lying the whole time. Misinformation. Disinformation. She ought to be arrested for that. Not that there's anyone around to do it.

I lie a long time looking up at the white cloud, listening to the winds filling in the spaces where salesman voices used to be. Out in the field my brother curses as pieces of his tower rain down all around him.

When the next season's salesmen start coming around, he and Janice start it up again, Janice in the window, my brother behind the door. But no one comes. See, there are the salesmen, out on the road; they pause and glance up at the house. But they don't come in—they scurry past, nearly running. The pen stays empty. My brother can't understand it. Janice studies herself in the mirror for hours, wondering, picking at her skin till she bleeds. She thinks she's turning ugly, scaring them away.

But she's wrong. What's happened is I've had enough. I'm fed up with the whole process, Janice prancing around thinking she's hot stuff, the yappy salesmen howling in the yard refusing to save themselves.

It's me making it happen. I've been scratching warnings into the roadside. I've been spreading prickly wire and broken glass across the drive. My brother and Janice have no idea how fast I can run when I want to. I crouch in the dry grass at the roadside and leap out to chase the salesmen away, every one. The salesmen don't know I'm trying to help them, they yell at me that I'm ruining business, standing in the way of the normal flow of commerce. *The customer is always right!* they scream, loud enough to flatten my hair to my head.

MIDNIGHT

by ERIC HANSON

DURING THE REIGN of Stalin, the efficiencies of power reached such a level of refinement that men in gray suits were sent from the Hoover Institution in California to learn how it was done. The information was more gymnastic than encyclopedic, requiring a nimble intelligence.

"Substitute a weathervane for a compass," one of Stalin's gray men told one of Hoover's gray men. "Every day requires a new vocabulary."

"Never drink from the same faucet twice," another said.

"Truth can be cut with a knife to serve two." Multiples. Twins. Doppelgangers. Variations.

"The hand of management must know where every card is inside the deck." To explain this paradigm Stalin loved to tell a story on himself:

He had invited a trade-union official from Wales to dinner inside the Kremlin. After dinner, during which the host ate as freely from the guest's plate as from his own, Stalin took a deck of cards from a drawer in an elaborate lacquered escritoire and another deck from his own pocket. He asked the Welshman, a Mr. Evans, to choose one deck of cards. Mr. Evans chose the deck of cards from the escritoire. Stalin threw the deck of cards he had taken from the escritoire into the fire.

The deck from Stalin's pocket was dog-eared but Stalin shuffled it expertly in his enormous hands. Where would Mr. Evans prefer to play, in the Card Room or in the Gun Room? Mr. Evans chose the Card Room. Stalin nodded agreeably and ushered his guest out of the dining room and down a long mirrored corridor to a set of double doors.

The double doors were exquisitely worked in silver and ebony and emblazoned with two words in large Cyrillic script. "Card. Room," said Stalin, pointing to each door in turn. He smiled and led his guest inside.

Never before in his life had Mr. Evans seen so many guns. In glass cases down the center of the long room, in large Chinese beechwood presses between the windows, in racks crowding the window embrasures, arranged in great pin-wheels on the high, amber-colored walls. The room bristled with every kind of explosive weaponry. It smelled of steel and gun oil.

In the center of the room, beneath a chandelier made out of priceless South American arquebuses, the largest glass gun case of all had been fashioned as a table. Inside it, on the green baize surface, several dozen fancy pistols were arranged in graceful arabesques, punctuated by small powder magazines worked in ivory and jet. By variation, the chair that Stalin held for Mr. Evans to sit on was constructed out of antique crossbows. Both men sat down and Stalin began to shuffle the cards again.

Even in his own story Stalin's dexterity was dazzling. The cards winked in and out of their several piles, were made into fans and collapsing chevaux-de-frise. All the while the absolute ruler of the Soviets grinned excruciatingly. When he was done, the cards had been segregated into seven equal piles. Stalin instructed Mr. Evans to draw a card from the middle of one of the piles, look at it and, without showing it, replace it in the same pile. Mr. Evans did so and Stalin collected all the piles together and shuffled them three times. Then he dealt all of the cards into seven piles again.

All this time he continued to smile contentedly, like someone who has eaten a delicious meal and is anticipating another. This time he turned the topmost card in each pile face up. All seven cards were number cards.

"Is the card you drew one of the cards showing?" he asked. "No," said Mr. Evans. Stalin collected the cards again and shuffled three times and dealt them out again the same way.

He did this again and again, each time asking Mr. Evans if he saw the card he had drawn. Each time Mr. Evans said no.

Stalin never wavered from his suave demeanor. The game went on for some time, well over an hour, and it had been late already when they finished dinner. Finally Stalin collected the cards and set them in the center of the glass table, asking Mr. Evans to cut three times. Mr. Evans did so. From the center pile Stalin pulled the seven of spades and showed it to Mr. Evans.

"This is the card you drew," he said.

Mr. Evans was growing tired of the game and said, "The card I drew was the jack of clubs."

"This is the jack of clubs," said Stalin.

At this point in the story the dictator's eyes always sparkled merrily.

Mr. Evans refused to yield to such an absurdity and said that the card in Stalin's hand was in fact the seven of spades. Even when Stalin held the card in front of his nose Mr. Evans remained calmly adamant.

Stalin pressed a hidden button on the underside of the glass table. Instantly a dozen Cossacks, six feet tall and fully armed, rushed into the room. Mr. Evans didn't move a muscle. In turn, each Cossack was asked to identify the card in

Stalin's hand. Without blinking, and without any visible instruction, each answered that it was the jack of clubs. Stalin looked at Mr. Evans again. Again Mr. Evans reported the evidence of his own eyes.

Stalin unlocked the lid of the display case and lifted it, showering all of the other cards onto the floor. He removed a pistol from the case and held it to Mr. Evans's temple. "Is this not the jack of clubs, Mr. Evans?" "No," came the reply, crisp as the report of a rifle in the icy air outside. With a swift and easy motion, Stalin swung the pistol from his guest's head and fired it into the rapt visage of the nearest of the Cossacks. The Cossack fell dead.

The eleven remaining Cossacks moved not a millimeter. Stalin removed another pistol from the case. Eleven times the same question: eleven times the answer was the same, until all the Cossacks lay dead.

Mr. Evans remained seated. His fleshy face retained its same doughy imperturbability, the black eyes flat and unblinking like currants in a pudding. Stalin went to a small Louis XV desk along the inner wall where there was a telephone. He lifted the black receiver and spoke into it, and shortly five men of various sizes, in tailored suits, appeared. Each of these men was asked the same question, which had become the question of the evening. Each gave the answer that Stalin was seeking. Each time, when Evans disagreed, another pistol was used to the same effect. By now the elegant room resembled an abattoir.

Stalin moved to another table and another telephone. After a few words were spoken into it a section of the gilded wall swung outward to disclose a staircase. A beautiful woman of middle age, expensively dressed, emerged, followed by eight beautiful children of various ages, each dressed in clothes of a nautical description. Each hugged "Uncle" affectionately. Each was asked the same question. Their separate ends followed in a swift mechanical sequence. At the end of this Stalin shrugged, a look of mild perplexity written on his genial face.

Beads of sweat had collected on Mr. Evans's forehead and at the edges of his graying hair.

"This is a silly argument, my friend," said the supreme ruler of all the Russians. "In the grand procession of human history it is but a fly on the nose of the sun, a soap bubble. It is nothing. Please, for the sake of your children, and their children unborn, let us agree at last, so that we may both retire to bed. Look carefully at this card and tell me that it is the jack of clubs that you drew from the deck."

Tears filled Mr. Evans's eyes. He thought of his wife and children, of his parents and of his dear brother who worked as his deputy in the union back in Swansea. He thought of his little garden. At this hour the sun would be smiling on the Penclawdd. In three days he would leave Moscow aboard a train with the rest of his delegation. This evening would be a dream. He was tired. Stalin was right. It was, after all, a silly quarrel. Had it been a test? Was the hero of the party setting him a test to see what kind of material the comrades of the decadent West were made of? Perhaps. But it was late and the evening had ended badly.

After a pause that consumed the last breath of air in the large ornate room, Mr. Evans shrugged his own shoulders and smiled ruefully.

"Comrade," he said. "If you say it is the jack of clubs in your hand, it must, after all, be the jack of clubs, mustn't it? Another time I will remember my glasses."

Stalin laughed, a laugh like an impatient horse, then he wrapped the Welshman in a great warm bear hug, whispering a gruff word in his shell-like ear. And then, with the last weapon in the case, a single-shot derringer, almost a toy, he put a bullet through Mr. Evans's brain.

At the end of his story Stalin was, as always, wreathed in smiles, radiant with charm like a warm July sun, and the gray man from California had no trouble understanding how he had endeared himself to Mr. Roosevelt. He waited for a moral to this beguiling little tale, but none came.

Perhaps that was the lesson from it. A good ruler must hold the questions and the answers in his own hands. He must know every card in the deck, and love each as dearly as his own left testicle. And all disagreements, however large, however small, are silly. In the end, the American realized, they believed the same important thing. To the Absolutist it is always twelve o'clock, straight up. What does it matter if one true believer stands to the right or the left a little? It is the relativists in between who are the enemy.

MANIFESTO

by PADGETT POWELL

THERE'S ABOUT FOURTEEN ounces of this left.

There's hair in it.

It's okay.

If you said "lard-and-hair sandwich" to her, my mother would gag.

Was that a Depression food?

I think it was a joke, but I'm not sure.

I've heard of butter-and-sugar sandwiches. But that would hardly be a Depression meal.

I have no idea what the Depression was, or what the war was, or the wars after that, or before—I don't know anything at all, you get right down to it.

So these codgers have something on us.

Yes they do. That is our cross to bear. Everyone knows shit but us.

Let's make the best of it.

Fuck these codgers.

They come over here with that shit, tell 'em to go eat a lard-and-hair sandwich.

I will.

I wish something would *move* out there.

Where?

Out there. On the broad plain of life.

I *thought* that's where you meant. Me too.

Be nice, some action.

Of some import.

We could say we did something…

With ourself.

Telling a codger who says quite properly we ain't doing shit to eat a lard-and-hair sandwich does not in the long term constitute a life.

No it does not.

Well if a war doesn't break out on you, and you don't stumble into making money, and you can't play ball, and women treat you wrong, or men, and you aren't a movie star, and you don't have any talent, and you aren't smart, etc., what are you, we, supposed to do, exactly?

Live until we die, without any more pondering than a dog, is my guess.

And that is a good guess, but it seems less a guess than the natural conclusion every hapless human being comes to on his witless own. It's a default position. It supports all dufus behavior.

Yes, it even supports "the pursuit of happiness."

Indeed it does.

Today we are becalmed, as we are daily becalmed.

Every day we are becalmed.

Becalmed is our middle name.

My uncle was named Jake Becalmed. His brother was Hansford Becalmed. Their brother was Cuthbert Becalmed.

No one is named Cuthbert Becalmed.

Wait. The fourth brother was Studio Becalmed.

No mother names a son Studio.

This one did.

Is it Italian?

What?

The name *Studio*.

We aren't Italian, is all I can say to that.

So this kid is called Studio, and what happens to him?

Well, he was killed in the war.

I mean what happened to him as a result of his name.

Nothing.

Nobody razzed his ass.

No.

He was Studio, end of chapter.

As far as I know.

Studio Becalmed.

No, their name was not really Becalmed.

That was a joke.

Of sorts.

We aren't very funny, when we joke.

No. Because we are becalmed.

Studio. I like him.

I do too.

Studio Becalmed had one great affair before his brief life was terminated, with the actress Jayne Mansfield.

Who herself was not long-lived.

Indeed not—beheaded on the Chef Menteur—

Yes, in the days when stars went overland in cars instead of in airplanes as they now do.

Anyway, when Studio frolicked with Jayne Mansfield he was like a tiny man lost in the Alps.

I suspect that that is a vulgar reference to her giant bosom?

It is if we let it be. On the other hand what do we know of Studio and his inclinations? He may well have been spiritually lost, not in mountains of flesh as it were but in the blond glow of happiness, or something.

We are safer assuming ourselves vulgar, and maybe Studio too. After all, he was to die in WWII, and men wanting breasts then or otherwise desirous of flesh were not to be discredited as they are today.

Healthy desires today are all clotted up into Healthy Choice.

Yes, and the smart man chooses Not Wanting if he wants to be safe.

Studio, let us say, was the last healthy man.

Why not? I am certain that he was. He was healthy and then he was dead, and Jayne missed him, then died herself, as much of a broken heart as of decapitation.

It's a lovely conceit. Studio lay in the mud, Jayne in the untopped car, forever sundered, or forever together if you can participate in the large fiction of their frolicking together in the final Alps of heaven.

That is a wonderful phrase. I would propose we name us a dog that.

What? Alp?

No. Final Alps of Heaven. They use long names in registry, you know.

I knew that. What would we call the dog?

I think *Final* would be amusing. *Of* would be not bad. *Alp* is out.

Agreed. *Heaven* would require explanations unto the tedious.

We could say we inherited the dog from Studio Becalmed and Jayne Mansfield, that we are the godfathers to their child.

Fifty years after the fact.

Yes.

This has promise. Tell these codgers, don't pet Final Alps of Heaven you asshole, that is the dog of Studio Becalmed and Jayne Mansfield, even you will recall the mountainous breasts she had, *hands off!*

When they look at us as they will, we say, Even if you were gay we would not let you pet that dog. If you were gay of course you would show some respect for that dog. We are having fresh basil pesto for dinner, will you stay?

I bet they won't.

Of course they won't.

Beanie weenies and let them cornhole the dog, they'd stay.

Oh don't be uncharitable. Beanie weenies and we let them play with the dog and they'd stay.

Yes, you are right.

I am always right.

True. Does it get tiring?

Be real. Of course not. Why would it?

It's supposed to.

Yes, and I respect you for playing the straight fool, but really, Constant Rectitude is one of the large peaks in the Final Alps of Heaven.

Let us get another dog and call him that, use his full registered name. Or you could even adapt the name for yourself. Con, Connie, Rex, Tude, Constant Rectitude!

Constant Rectitude, go to your room until your father gets here with his *belt.*

Constant Rectitude took another hiding today for his constant transgressions.

Constant Rectitude and Studio Becalmed have run away to join the circus, but they joined the army instead in error and will die as patriots rather than as syphilitic roustabouts.

Failure is to success as water is to land.

This is the great secular truth.

I believe I will speak this great secular truth to the meddling cocksucking codgers when they come over here telling us we are not shit, rather than get into what kind of sandwich they might eat.

The sandwich advice is too much of a mouthful all around. And Don't pet the dog may not convey the nuance and force we want.

We have failed, yessir, because water is pandemic. Is that too subtle?

Not for me, probably for them.

Fuck them. Are they not the party to whom I am speaking, whom I seek to impress with my meaning and get them off our back and stop begging us for sugary food and stop petting our inherited dog from a man dead fifty years who skied with his nose down the ramp of Mansfield's Alps—are they not whom I seek to have comprehend me and thereby desist in their presuming upon us? Well then fuck them, I will not be clear merely because being clear is my object.

Well put. As well put as any failed man ever put it.

Thank you. Thank you, Constant Rectitude. I would be obliged were I to be henceforth known as Inherent Muddle. These are our new Indian names. I saw two arguably better ones in Poplar North Dakota just off the Ft. Peck Reservation. They were Kills Twice and...

And?

I have forgotten the other name. Also Something Twice, but it was something mundane, not killing, something even faintly ignoble, like Sleeps Twice. I can't recall it.

Failure is to success as water is to land.

I should have written down the names. I was sure I would remember them. They were likable Indians, I presume those brothers, Kills Twice and Forgets Twice or whoever he was.

If we had better *names*, we would be better men, is what we seem to have arrived at.

I'll not argue with that, nor do I know a sane man who would.

When the fucking codgers come over here, just ask them who the hell they are, and when they say their names, just snort!

Snort like a hog inhaling a new potato!

Snort like an armadillo reading a newspaper!

Snort like a man gasping for air in the Alps!

If that school bus goes by here any slower, I'd say it's prowling looking for houses to break in to.

Codger at the wheel?

Codger at every wheel on earth.

I forget where we are.

Me too. I too. What do you mean, exactly?

We are over here, I see that, and all that is over there, and this over hereness and that over thereness is a small part of infinite other relations of hereness and thereness, I see all this, but then I get a bit forgetty, and, just, don't have this particular-in-aggregate setup in my head, and I say something like "I forget where we are." Then I recover, regain my purchase on the system of therenesses, and see the finite hereness of us, but of course by now I realize I have no idea where any of this is, where we are, what we are doing, what we are, in the large picture that makes an aggregate of all the particular systems—

Just shut up.

The driver of that school bus is prowling the streets looking for a stray child to molest. He has the perfect cover. Almost any child on earth will voluntarily enter that bus if the door opens and the monster sweetly proffers a ride.

What is your point?

Was there a time before this, say when Studio Becalmed went to the war, when a school bus itself did not represent the moral depravity of the world?

You had like the Lindbergh baby did you not?

Isn't that different?

I suppose. Why are we now so feckless when we were once arguably heroic, just two generations ago, do you mean?

Precisely what I mean. Two generations ago we would go out there, yank that codger out of that bus, give him a good beating that did not actually put him in the hospital but which decidedly ran him out of town, our object, and the matter would be handled, no legal repercussions, no perverse crimes on our watch, no counseling services involved, no law, nothing but bluebirds and rocks and sticks and good picnics and war when necessary and good heavy phones and not too many of them.

Mayberry.

Yes.

It cannot have been so easy. We are suffering some kind of distortion, I feel certain.

I don't argue that. But do you not agree that we should go out there and beat that pervert off that bus, and that we won't, and that if we won't we submit to the prevailing illness that is here now, whether or not it was there then?

Yes, I agree.

Then Q. E. effing D.

Are we going to be okay?

No. No, we are not.

Okay.

How many of us are there?

There's the two of us, right now. You and me. You and I.

Right now, still all two of us—

Right, we have not become less than two, yet. Still two people here, not yet disintegrated into less than two, albeit we are arguably indistinct from another, so that the proposition that there are two of us may be limited to a kind of biological truth, truth is not the word I want…

I get your meaning, Kemosabe.

The two of us indistinct from each other, in the here here not altogether distinct from the there there, but we are two of us here and okay so far.

But shaky.

Yes, shaky.

Okay. What I want to know is, you know that controversy over butter versus margarine, what I want to know is how did they ever purport to sell something they elected to call *oleo-margarine?* Can you tell me the etiology of a word like that, and even if it is a scientifically honest word why would they not have changed it for palatability as it were? Like a movie star's name? Did you know that Sugar Ray Robinson for example was really named Raymond Cream? Carmen Basilio versus Raymond Cream. Don't put butter on that, here use this oleomargarine. Fix you right up. You are going to have great difficulty tonight with Mr. Cream, Mr. Basilio.

I can't help you with any of this which troubles you. I have my own problems.

Another thing bothering me: what is the song involving a Mr. Bluebird sitting on one's shoulder? I like that song. I can't recover enough of it for it to be of any comfort, but I like it, or think I like it, if there is in fact a song with a Mr. Bluebird witting on one's shoulder.

Did you say witting on one's shoulder?

I meant sitting.

You might have said shitting.

Yes, but I said witting. It's a new song, I like it. I want a bluebird witting on my shoulder.

Don't we all. Imparting the wisdom we lack.

Our problems will soon be over, when this bluebird alights.

I heard Peter Jennings say "passenger manifestoes."

ORPHANS

by BENJAMIN ROSENBAUM

I HAVE BOUGHT the elephant a new green suit. I have bought him a car. I buy him anything he likes.

When I found him, he was naked. He was dusty, from the long road. He had been running, running, in panic and in fear. He did not trumpet. His skin was smooth, not wrinkled like most elephants'. It was the first time I had seen an elephant like that, in the streets of my town. Without the protecting bars of the zoo, without the pity I feel when I sketch the elephants at the zoo. Without indignation at zookeepers and adventurers and hunters. Without shaking my parasol in a zookeeper's face, like a foolish old lady.

He was there in the street, enormous. His skin was shiny, it seemed a color more vivid than gray. An opalescent gray.

I was afraid. The people around me quickened their steps. They were terrified, yet the great web of etiquette and propriety that holds our town steady—like a fly already mummified, and not yet eaten, in a spider's web—kept them from running and screaming, from saying anything. Will we run and scream from an elephant? No, that is what savages do. That is what they were thinking, I know it. Look at our fine hats. Look at our fine automobiles and clothes. Our shoes with spats. We are the masters of all continents. We do not run from elephants.

Yet the matter would not rest there, I knew. I could hardly look at him, because he was so vivid, so great. If I curled myself into a ball, heels against my bottom, arms folded in, head tucked down, I would be no larger than his heart. The elephant did not trumpet, he did not rage. He trudged, each footfall a consequence only of the last. It was the gait of one whom only obstinacy shields from despair. He did not see us. I knew that if he looked up, if he spoke, if he stopped, if he waved his sharp tusks in anything like anger, the thin web of propriety would break. Fear would outrule it. We would run, like naked savages. And then we would shoot him in his great heart, for shaming us.

I felt an unbearable tension; I felt that if I looked at him any longer, something tremendous would happen to me—I would be crushed, I would dissolve into a swarm of butterflies.

I held up my purse as he passed. My dog Henriette was silent on her leash. She did not bark, she did not cower. She accepted the elephant. It gave me courage.

I held up my purse. "Here," I said. "Buy some clothes."

The great feet stopped. The great tusks, white as piano keys—oh, oh, how dare I think of piano keys? I trembled. He regarded me.

"Please," I said, and my throat was tight. "Please." I held out the purse. "They will murder you, otherwise."

The trunk was thick. It had bristles. They brushed against my skin as he took the purse. It was not unpleasant. What ferocious people we were, to make bullets to pierce that great bulk. What masters.

"Thank you," he said. His voice was a low grumble, his accent foreign. "Thank you, madam."

*   *   *

When he came to live with me, I scurried. I had the piano taken out and sold, I was ashamed of its keys. I had the doors widened. He sat in the park while this took place. In his fine black derby hat, his green suit with vest. His enormous shoes with spats. He sat on a bench, and fed the pigeons.

The danger was lessened now. It is one thing for the police to shoot a wild and naked elephant running in the street. A savage, among the boulangeries and bookshops. It is quite another thing to shoot a well-dressed elephant sitting peaceably on a bench, feeding the pigeons, and trying to read the newspaper with the aid of a childrens' illustrated dictionary. It is absurd, and the police here will not do absurd things.

But I wanted him at home, safe within my walls. I brought him when the workmen had just finished the parlor. I stood shyly in the bare space where the piano had been. He came in, stepping gingerly, as if unsure the floor would hold. He gently moved the couch and sat on the floor. He did not meet my eyes. He was as embarrassed as I.

He was learning to walk on his hind legs. He tottered. It was terrifying to watch, like a circus trick. Elephants are not meant to do it. They did not *evolve* to do it, as we *evolved* to do it. We had a million years, in the savannah, to learn to stand. He did it in a month. After that he would not walk in the elephant way, not in the street.

It cost him dearly. He had wrenching pains in his lower back. He used to lie in the small garden behind my house, with its high walls, on the grass and flagstones. I would massage his sore back with a carpet beater, leaning against it, pressing with both hands. "Harder," he would moan, until I would collapse against him, panting. Then he would curl his body around and lift me with his trunk. He would hold me to his chest, and I would be bathed in the deep smell of him, wild and rich. He would laugh in his deep rumble and whisper, "Anyone in the next house would think we were lovers."

My heart would race. I would spread my arms across his chest, placing my cheek on his naked skin.

It is the holy chapter of my life. It is my foretaste of Paradise. When we ate brioches and jam on golden mornings, him sitting in the special chair I had made. I corrected his pronunciation. He drove through the countryside in the car I had made. The whole seat in front was for him. I sat in back. He had a motorist's scarf and goggles. He was dashing.

But then she came.

How could I begrudge her? When I saw how happy he was. He dropped our packages and ran to them, two more naked dirty elephants in the streets of our town. He ran and embraced them. I scrambled for the packages. I could not lift them all. The men in the street glowered at me over their moustaches, as if to say, How many more?

I dragged the packages forward. I am weak, I am old. I looked at the new elephants. One was a cow. That is not my word. That is what they are called. She was a cow. His sister, I thought, his sister. But no, they were cousins. And they marry their cousins, in that savage land.

My house was not big enough for three elephants. My purse was not big enough to clothe three elephants. But I gave, I gave. He brought bales of hay to the courtyard, because she did not like our food. He hovered over her. It took us an hour to convince her to put on shoes, and she never would walk upright.

It was charity, what I did for her, and for the other one, the one in the sailor suit. It had never been charity for him.

The other day I saw that bestial American in the café, the one with the yellow hat. The one with the monkey. I do not like him, but I supposed that we were siblings of a sort. He came to my table, holding a coffee in both hands. I was holding my coffee with both hands. Mine was cold. I had not drunk any. I was staring into it. I was not weeping. I am relatively certain of that. He sat down, unasked.

"Left you, has he? So I hear." I looked up sharply. His eyes were kind.

He drank his coffee in one gulp, and took out his cigar. Henriette cowered at my heels. She despises cigars.

"And after all you spent on him!" the American said, puffing. "Imagine!"

I said nothing.

He leaned forward. "That's why I sold mine to the zoo. They take good care of him, and I see him when I like. We're even going to make a movie with the little fellow!"

I felt as if the people at the other tables were laughing at me. Laughing into their soup. I stood up. I took my parasol and Henriette's leash into my left hand. With my other hand, I threw my coffee in his face.

He was shouting as I walked out.

Today I received a telegram: they have crowned my beloved.

He is King!

He is King!

THE SEASON OF JÓLABÓKAFLÓÐIÐ

INTRODUCTION TO THE ICELANDIC STORIES

by BIRNA ANNA BJÖRNSDÓTTIR

WE SOMETIMES CLAIM that everyone in Iceland is a writer. Sure, it's hyperbole, and as such slightly out of character for a literary tradition long characterized by understatement and restraint. Still, approximately one thousand books are published here each year for a population of about 290,000, one book per 290 persons—no doubt one of many weird per-capita world records we hold.

Into the twentieth century, the generations worked, prayed, and went about their daily lives in buildings made from mud, turf, a few blocks of stone, and the odd stick of wood. Today, little remains of this long history; its tangible elements have melted back into the landscape from which they emerged. Little, that is, except books. Since the medieval times, Icelanders have written far more books than can reasonably be expected from a small peasant population at the edge of the arable world. Popular participation in this literary culture has also been unusual; while the rest of Europe produced its volumes in Latin for learned audiences, Icelanders wrote in the vernacular—producing, among other works, the Icelandic sagas—and literacy was far more widespread than anywhere on the continent.

The most distinguished author to write in Icelandic in the last century was Halldór Laxness, our one Nobel laureate. A giant among his contemporaries, Laxness placed himself squarely in this long tradition of storytelling; upon accepting the Nobel Prize, he paid tribute to the many nameless men and women who "century upon dark century ... sat in their mud huts writing books without so much as asking themselves what their wages would be, what prize or recognition would be theirs. There was no fire in their miserable dwellings at which to warm their stiff fingers as they sat up late at night over their stories. Yet they succeeded in creating not only a literary language which is among the most beautiful and subtlest there is, but a separate literary genre."

So great is the stature of Halldór Laxness that for decades many authors found themselves writing in his shadow. As his presence fades into the distance, however, younger writers have crawled out into the sun. Indeed, Laxness's reputation, along with the long legacy of storytelling, constitutes an invaluable resource for contemporary Icelandic authors.

Like anywhere else, one can't help but stumble across statues of the mighty departed in downtown Reykjavík. The curious thing is that here the poets actually outnumber the politicians. Some even do double duty on their pedestal, as both revered poets *and* respected politicians, for politics and literature have come together in some of Iceland's most renowned figures, historical and contemporary. In the thirteenth century, one of Iceland's most powerful chieftains, Snorri Sturluson (c. 1179–1241), composed Egil's saga, one of the most important works of the Middle Ages, and Snorri's Edda (or the Prose Edda), a manual for poets that is the most extensive source extant on Norse mythology. When Iceland's first minister, Hannes Hafstein, took office in 1904 (after Denmark granted Iceland limited "home-rule"), he had by then already established himself as one of the most beloved poets of his generation. The country's prime minister of the past thirteen years, Davíd Oddsson, is also a writer and published two collections of short stories while in office. And Guðrún Helgadóttir, a member of Althingi, Iceland's parliament, for two decades—and she served as president of Althingi for a number of those years—is also the nation's most beloved children's book writer.

If it sometimes seems as though everyone is a writer in Iceland, it must be noted that most Icelanders juggle several jobs—the only way to run a full-blown state and economy with fewer than 300,000 people, maintaining all the while the illusion of cosmopolitan city life in small-town Reykjavík. The mailman moonlights as a veggie chef, and the DJ teaches kindergarten during the day. Both have a couple of books of poetry out. Of course, there are also professional writers who do nothing but write books—aside, that is, from a little teaching, freelance journalism, wedding singing, copywriting, filmmaking, sales, whatever.

Strange as it may seem, these dedicated writers all publish their books within a month of each other, more or less, during a period commonly known as "the Christmas book flood" (*jólabókaflóðið*). Very nearly the entire crop of fiction each year is published in November and the first week of December, as are the many memoirs. Indeed, this phenomenon structures the working lives of Icelandic authors, synchronizing their creative efforts and their professional moodswings as they all strive to meet the same deadline, after which they fraternize for an unbroken month of book-release parties and make the same round of public readings and interviews, vying for the attention of critics and consumers alike. This seasonal deluge, and the accompanying media hype, is a consequence of the most important social function that books serve in Iceland. Books are the primary currency in the country's gift economy. Without books, Christmas would be something very different.

Everyone gives books and everyone gets books, always the latest releases, hot off the press. Booklovers wait all year long for this exhilarating season, when every newspaper, magazine, radio program, and TV show takes novels and memoirs as cardinal points of reference: the books are new and the news is booked. When the din of the publishers' battles finally dies down and the last critic falls silent—on Christmas Eve—we curl up with our books and read our way through the darkest days of winter.

It is appropriate, then, that this issue is printed and published when the annual book flood is at its apex. Like most issues of *McSweeney's*, it is printed in Reykjavík by Oddi. Though its conception is transatlantic and most of its readers American, its water-birth in the flooded presses of Oddi is quintessentially Icelandic. Its copies meet and greet the latest books of authors featured in the following pages and those of their many colleagues as they all fight their way through the bindery.

FRIDRIK AND THE EEJIT

by SJÓN

THE WORLD OPENS its good eye a crack. A ptarmigan belches. The streams trickle under their glazing of ice, dreaming of the spring when they'll swell to a life-threatening force. Smoke curls up from mounds of snow here and there on the mountainsides—these are their farms.

Everything here is a uniform blue, apart from the glitter of the tops. It is winter in the Dale.

—Hello, I've come to fetch the hemale horse, listen, I'm here to take the freemale porks, oh, er, no, er, you, no, hand over the heehaw forks…

In the yard at Brekka a horse stands beneath a man, and it is the man who is babbling so inanely to himself. He's a big fellow, probably turned forty; there's gray in the pink beard, which hangs untrimmed over his mouth and tumbles from his

---

From *Skugga-Baldur*, a novella.

chin like an ice-bound cataract—yet he is bundled up in clothes like a child all set to spend the day in a snowdrift.

His breeches are hitched right up to his crotch, his coat is far too big or far too small, depending on how you look at it, and his knitted hat is tied so tightly under his chops that he cannot have done it himself. On his hands he wears three pairs of mittens, making it almost impossible for him to hold the reins of the hairy nag on which he sits.

This is the mare Rosa. She champs her bit impatiently. It is her legs that have carried them here. When you look back you can see her hoofprints running from the parsonage at Dalbotn, down over the fields, along the river, across the marshes, up the slopes, to the place where she is now standing, waiting to be relieved of her burden.

Ah, now the man clambers down from her back.

And his true shape is revealed: he is extraordinarily low-kneed, big-bellied, broad-shouldered, and abnormally long-necked, and his left arm is quite a bit shorter than the right. He stamps his feet, beats his arms about himself, shakes his head, and snorts.

The mare flicks her ears.

—Sea-hail porpoise?

The man scrapes the snow from the farm door with his stubby arm:

—Can it be?

He knocks on the door with his good hand and feels the blood rushing to his fist. It's cold. Perhaps he'll be invited inside?

The shadow of a man's head appears in the frost-patterned parlor window, and a moment later the inner door can be heard opening, then the front door is thrust out hard. It clears away the pile that has collected outside overnight, and the cold visitor, retreating before it, falls over backwards, without actually being able to do so.

When he is done falling, he sees that the man he has come to find is standing in the doorway: Fridrik B. Fridjonsson, the herbalist, farmer at Brekka, or the man who owns Abba. The visitor's own name is Halfdan Atlason, "the Rev. Baldur's eejit."

Now he gulps like a fish but says not a word, for before he can recite his piece, Herb-Fridrik invites him to step inside.

And to that the eejit has no other answer than to do as he is asked.

They enter the kitchen.

—Take off your things.

Fridrik squats, opens the belly of the tiled stove, and puts in more kindling. It blazes merrily.

It's warm here, a good place to be.

The eejit bites his thumbs and tugs off his mittens before beginning with trembling hands to struggle with the tight knot on his hat strings. He's in difficulties, but his host frees him from his prison. When Fridrik pulls off his guest's coat a bitter stench is released. Fridrik backs away, nostrils flaring:

—Coffee...

It was always the same with the Dalbotn folk; they sweated coffee. The Rev. Baldur was too mean to give them anything to eat, pumping them instead from morning to night full of soot-black, stewed-to-pulp coffee grounds. Fridrik takes a firm hold of Halfdan's hands; the tremor that shakes them is not a shiver of cold but a nervous disorder— from coffee consumption.

He releases the man's paws and invites him to sit down. Taking a kettle from a peg, he fills it with melted snow and places it on the hotplate on top of the stove. He points to the kettle and says firmly:

—Now, you keep an eye on the water; when the lid moves, come and tell me. I'll be in the parlor nailing down the coffin lid.

The eejit nods and turns his eyes to the kettle. Herb-Fridrik brushes a hand over his shoulders as he leaves the kitchen. After a moment the sound of hammer blows comes from the next room.

The eejit stares at the kettle and stove in turn, but mostly at the stove. It is a widely famed wonder of technology that few have set eyes on. The metal pipe which rises from the stove runs up the wall into the parlor and from there up to the sleeping loft, warming the house, before poking out through the turf-roof and releasing the smoke into the open air. But first and last it is the hand-painted china tiles that enchant: brightly colored flowers sprawl here and there about the body of the stove, nimbler than the eye can follow. Halfdan rocks in his seat as he traces one flower spray, which winds under this one and over that, all the way up to the kettle.

The kettle, yes, just so, he's keeping an eye on it. The water spits as it jumps around between the bottom of the kettle and the glowing hotplate.

Fridrik the herbalist is the man who owns his Abba—that is, Hafdis Jonsdottir, Halfdan's sweetheart. Fridrik and Abba live together, just the two of them, at Brekka—until she marries Halfdan, then she'll come away with him. But where might she be today? He twists his elongated neck to peer over his right shoulder.

In the parlor Fridrik is hammering the last nail into the coffin lid. Halfdan calls in to him:

—I-Hi'm here to fe-fetch the female corpse...

The bleak wording takes Fridrik aback. That's Parson Baldur talking through his manservant. The parsonage servants parroted the priest's mode of speech like a parcel of hens. No doubt one might have called it laughable, had it not been all of a piece, all so ugly and vile.

—I know, Halfdan old chap, I know...

But he is even more shocked by what the eejit says next:

—Whe-here's h-his A-Abba?

The water boils and the kettle lid rattles—it sputters slightly at the rim.

—B-boiling, sniffs Halfdan, and it is the first sound he has uttered since Herb-Fridrik told him that his sweetheart Abba was dead, that she was the female corpse the Reverend had sent him to fetch, and that today the coffin he saw there on the parlor table would be lowered into the ground in the churchyard at Dalbotn. The news so crushed Halfdan's heart that he burst into a long, silent fit of weeping and the tears ran from his eyes and nose, while his ill-made body shook in the chair like a leaf quivering before an autumn gale, not knowing whether it will be torn from the bough that has fostered it all summer long or linger there—and wither; but neither fate is good.

While the man grieved for his sweetheart, Fridrik brought out the tea things: a fine hand-thrown English china pot, two bone-white porcelain cups and saucers, a silver-plate milk jug and sugar bowl, teaspoons, and a strainer made of bamboo leaves. And finally a tea caddy made of planed, oiled oak, marked A.C. PERCH'S THEHANDEL.

He takes the kettle from the hob and pours a little water into the teapot, letting it stand a while so the china warms through. Then he opens the tea caddy, measures four spoonfuls of leaves into the pot, and pours boiling water over them. The heady fragrance of Darjeeling tea fills the kitchen, like the steam that rises from newly plowed earth, and there is also a sweet hint, pregnant with sensuality—with memories of luxury—that only one of them has known: Fridrik B. Fridjonsson, the herbalist from Brekka, in his European clothes; in long trousers and jacket, with a late Byronesque cravat round his neck.

Likewise the scent raises Halfdan's spirits, causing him to forget his sorrow.

—Wh-what's that c-called?

—Tea.

Fridrik pours the tea into the cups and slips the cozy over the English china pot. Halfdan takes his cup in both hands, raises it to his lips, and sips the drink.

—Tea?

It's strange that so good a drop should have such a small name. It should have been called *Illustreret Tidende*; that's the grandest name the eejit knows.

—I-is it Danish?

—No, it's from the mountain Himalaya, which is so high that if you climbed our mountain thirteen times, you still wouldn't have reached the top. Halfway up the slopes of the great mountain is the parish of Darjeeling. And when the birds in Darjeeling break into their dawn chorus, life quickens on the paths that link the tea gardens to the villages. It's the tea-pickers going to their work; they may be poorly dressed, but some have silver rings in their noses.

—I-is it thrushes singing? asks the eejit.

—No, it's the song sparrow, and under its clear song you can hear the tapping of a woodpecker.

—N-no birds I know?

—I expect there are wagtails, answers Fridrik.

Halfdan nods and sips his tea. Meanwhile Fridrik twists up his moustache on the left-hand side and continues his tale.

—At the garden gate they each take their basket and the day's work begins. From then until suppertime the harvesters will pick the topmost leaves from every plant, and their fingertips will be the tea's first staging post on the long journey that may end, for example, in the teapot here at Brekka.

So this morning hour passes.

It is daylight when Fridrik and the eejit Halfdan come out of the farmhouse with the coffin between them. They carry it easily; the dead woman was not large and the coffin is no work of art, knocked together from scraps of timber found around the farm—but it'll do and seems sound enough. The mare Rosa waits out in the yard, sated with hay. The men place the coffin on a sledge, lash it down good and hard, and fasten it either side of the saddle with long spars that lie along the horse's flanks and are tied firmly to the sledge.

After this is done, Fridrik takes an envelope from his jacket. He shows it to Halfdan and says:

—You're to give Reverend Baldur this letter as soon as the funeral is over. If he asks for it before, tell him I forgot to give it to you. Then you're to remember it when he has finished the ceremony.

He pushes the envelope deep into the eejit's pocket, patting the pocket firmly.

—When the funeral's over…

And they say goodbye, the man who owned Abba and her sweetheart—former sweetheart.

Brekka in the Dale, 8th January 1883

Dear Archdeacon Baldur Skuggason,

I enclose the sum of thirty-four crowns. It is payment for the funeral of the woman Hafdis Jonsdottir, and is to cover wages for yourself and six pallbearers, carriage of the coffin from the farm to the church, lying in state, three knells and payment for coffee, sugar, and bread for yourself and the pallbearers, as well as any mourners who may attend.

I do not insist on any singing over the woman, nor any address or recital of ancestry. You are to be guided by your own taste and inclinations, or those of any congregation.

I have seen to the coffin and shroud myself, being familiar with the task from my student days in Copenhagen, as your brother Valdimar can attest.

I hope this now completes our business with regard to Hafdis Jonsdottir's funeral service.

> Your obedient servant,
> *Fridrik B. Fridjonsson*

P.S. Last night I dreamt of a blue vixen. She ran along the screes, heading up the valley. She was as fat as butter, with a pelt of prodigious thickness.

*　*　*

Now the foolish funeral procession lacks for nothing. It sets out from the yard; that is to say, it slides headlong down the slopes, until man, horse, and corpse recover their equilibrium on the riverbank. One could skate along it up the valley, all the way to the church doors at Botn.

Herb-Fridrik goes into the house. He hopes that Halfdan, eejit that he is, won't break open the coffin and peep inside on the way.

On Saturday, April 17, 1868, a great cargo ship ran aground at Onglabrjotsnef on the Reykjanes peninsula, a black-tarred triple-decker with three masts. The third mast had been chopped down, by which means the crew had saved themselves, and the ship was left unmanned, or so it was thought. The splendor of everything aboard this gigantic vessel was such an eye-opener that no one who hadn't seen it for himself would have believed it.

The cabin on the top deck was so large that it could have housed a whole village. It was clear that the cabin had originally been highly decorated, but the gilding and paint had worn off, and all was now squalid inside. Once it had been divided up into smaller compartments but now the bulkheads had been removed and sordid pallets lay scattered hither and thither; it would have resembled a ghost ship, had it not been for the stench of urine. There were no sails, and the remaining tatters and cables were all rotten.

The bowsprit was broken and the figurehead degraded; it had been the image of a queen, but her face and breasts had been hacked away with the sharp point of a knife. Clearly the ship had once, long ago, been the pride of her captain, but had later fallen into the hands of unscrupulous rogues.

It was hard to guess how long the ship had been at sea or when she had met with her fate. There were no logbooks and her name was almost entirely obliterated from bow and stern, though in one place the lettering "…Der Deck…" was visible and in another "V…r ec…," so people guessed she was Dutch in origin.

When this titanic ship ran aground the surf was too rough for putting to sea; any attempt at salvage or rescue was unthinkable. But when an opportunity finally arose, the men of Sudurnes flocked on board and set to in earnest. They broke up the top deck and discovered, to general rejoicing, that the ship was loaded entirely with fish-liver oil. It was stored in barrels of uniform size, stacked in rows, which were so well lashed down that they had to send out to seven parishes for crowbars to free them. This served well.

After three weeks' work the men had unloaded the cargo from the upper deck on to shore; it amounted to nine hundred barrels of fish-liver oil.

Experiments with the oil proved that it was excellent lighting fuel, but it resembled nothing the people knew, either in smell or taste; though perhaps a faint hint of singed human hair accompanied the burning. Malicious tongues in other parts of the country might claim that the oil was plainly "human suet," but they could keep their slander and envy— nothing detracted from the joy of the folk in the southwest over this windfall that the Almighty Lord had brought to their shore so unlooked for, and involving so little effort, loss of life, or expense to themselves.

They now broke open the middle deck, which contained no fewer barrels of oil than the upper; and although the unloading was carried out with manly zeal, they seemed to make no impression. Then, one day, they became aware of life onboard. Something moved in the dark corner by the stern, on the port side, reached by a gangway running between the hull and the triple rows of barrels. There came a sound of sighing and moaning—accompanied by a metallic clanking.

These were uncanny sounds and men were filled with mis-giving. Three stout fellows volunteered to enter the gloom and see what they should see. But just as they were preparing to pounce on the unlooked-for danger, a pathetic creature crept out from under the stack of barrels, and the men very nearly stabbed and crushed it to death with their crowbars, so great was their shock at the sight.

It was an adolescent girl. Her dark hair fell like a wild growth from her head, her skin was swollen and sore with filth; her nakedness was covered by nothing but a torn, stinking sack. There was an iron manacle around her left ankle, which chained her to one of the great ship's timbers, and from her miserable crouch it was not hard to guess what use the crew had made of her. Then there was a bundle that she held in a vicelike grip and would not be parted from.

—Abba…

She said, so emptily that they shuddered, but she could give no further account of herself, despite being questioned. The salvage men realized that she was a simpleton, and some thought she looked as if she was carrying. They brought the girl and bundle ashore and delivered them into the hands of the sheriff's wife. There she was given food and allowed to sleep two nights in a bed before being dressed in fresh clothes and sent to Reykjavik.

The salvage team was still busy on the third Sunday in June when the mail ship Arkturux rounded the cape of Reykjanes. As she passed the wreck of the oil ship, the passengers gathered at the rail to gaze at the colossus that lay stranded in the bay.

The oil porters took a break from their work and waved to the passengers, who waved back blearily, newly emerged from three days' filthy weather north of the Faroes.

Among the passengers was a tall young man. He had a brown-checked woollen blanket round his shoulders, a gray bowler hat on his head, and a long-stemmed pipe in his mouth.

He was Fridrik B. Fridjonsson.

* * *

Herb-Fridrik fills his pipe and contemplates the bundle that sits on the parlor table where the coffin had rested an hour before. It is wrapped in black canvas and tied up with three-ply string—which has held up well despite not having been touched for over seventeen years—and measures some sixteen inches high, twelve inches long, and exactly ten inches wide. Fridrik grasps the bundle firmly, raises it to head height, and shakes it against his ear. The contents are fixed, weight around ten pounds, nothing rattles inside. Any more than it ever has.

Fridrik puts it back on the table and goes into the kitchen. He pokes a match into the stove and carries the flame to his pipe, lighting it with slow, deliberate sucks. The tobacco crackles, he draws the first smoke of the day deep into his lungs, and announces to thin air as he exhales:

—Umph belong Abba.

"Umph" could mean so many things in Abba language: box, chest, casket, ark, or trunk, for example.

Fridrik has long had his suspicions as to what the bundle contains—he has often handled it—but only today will his curiosity be satisfied.

Fridrik crossed paths with Hafdis three days after his arrival in Iceland. He was on his way home from a dinner engagement, a gargantuan coffee-drinking session and singsong at the home of his former tutor, Mr G——. He let his legs decide the route. They swiftly bore him up from Kvosin, out of town, south over the stony ground and down to the sea where he ran along the ocean shore, yelling to bright infinity, "I pay homage to you, ocean, o mirror of the free man!" It was Midsummer's Eve, flies were swinging on the stalks, a ringed plover piped, and the rays of the midnight sun barred the grass.

In those days the capital was small enough that a sound-limbed man could walk around it in half an hour, so Fridrik was soon back where his evening stroll had started; on the track behind the house of the old, gray tutor, Mr G——. The cook's son came out of the back door, taking care not to drop a tray bearing a tin cup, potato peelings, trout skin, and a hunk of bread; leftovers from the feast earlier in the evening.

Fridrik paused when he saw the boy take this to a tumble-down shed which leaned against another slightly larger out-house in the backyard. There the boy opened a hatch and eased the tray inside. From the lean-to came a scrambling and snorting, a clatter and grunting. The boy snatched back his hand, slammed the hatch, and hurried away—bumping straight into Fridrik, who had entered through the gate.

—What have you got there, a Danish merchant?

He said this in a mock-serious tone to soften its severity. The youth gaped at Fridrik as if he were one of Baron Munchhausen's moon men, then answered grumpily:

—Oh, I reckon it's that hussy what did away with her child last week.

—You don't say?

—Yes, the one what was taken in the graveyard, burying the child's corpse in Olafur "Student" Jonsson's grave.

—And why is she here?

—I 'spect the bailiff asked his cousin to hold her. They hardly dare put her in the jail with the men. Says Mother.

—And what's to be done with her?

—Oh, I 'spect she'll be sent to Copenhagen for punishment, and sold to the lowest bidder when she comes back. If she comes back.

The lad darted a shifty glance around and pulled a small snuff horn from his pocket:

—Anyhow, I'm not s'posed to talk about what I hear in the house...

He raised the horn to one nostril and sniffed with all his might. With that the conversation was at an end. While the cook's son struggled with his sneeze, Fridrik went over to the lean-to. Squatting down, he pulled the cover from the hatch and peered inside. It was dim but the summer night cast enough blue light through the roof slats for his eyes to grow accustomed to the gloom, and he made out the figure of a woman in one corner. It was the prisoner.

She sat on the earthen floor with her legs straight out, hunched over the tray like a rag doll. In one small hand she held a strip of potato peel that she was using to push together fish skin and bread, which she then pinched, raised to her mouth, and chewed conscientiously. She took a sip from the tin cup and heaved a sigh. At that point Fridrik felt he had seen more than enough of the unhappy creature. He fumbled for the cover to close the hatch, bumping his hand on the wall with a loud knock. The figure in the corner became aware of him. She looked up and met his eyes; she smiled and her smile doubled the happiness of the world.

But before he could nod in return, the smile vanished from her face and was at once replaced by mask so tragic that Fridrik burst into tears.

Fridrik unties the knot, winds the string round the fingers of his left hand, slides the coil over his fingertips, and slips it into his waistcoat pocket. He unwraps the canvas from the bundle. Two packages of equal size come to light, wrapped in waxed brown paper. He lays them side by side and opens them. The contents of each appear to be the same: black wooden tablets, twenty-four in each pile. He turns over the tablets like cards from a pack, and notes that they are painted black on one side, white on the other; but not all of them, however, because in one pile some of the tablets are black and green, while in the other they are black and blue. He scratches his beard.

—Well, Abba-di, it's quite something, this picture puzzle that you've carried through life…

And now a strange and intricate spectacle unfolds in the little parlor at Brekka in the Dale. The master of the house handles each piece of the puzzle with care, examining it from every angle; the green and blue faces have lettering on them—a sentence in Latin—which simplifies the game.

He begins the jigsaw.
Starting with the blue tablets.

Fridrik B. Fridjonsson studied natural history at the
University of Copenhagen from 1862 to 1865. Like so many
of his countrymen, he did not finish his degree, and for his
last three years in Denmark he was a regular employee of the
Elefant Pharmacy, then under the management of the pharmacist Ørnstrup, in Store Kongsgade. There Fridrik worked
his way up to the position of medical assistant, helping with
the pharmacist's catalog of inebriants: ether, opium, laughing
gas, fly agaric, belladonna, chloroform, mandragora, hashish,
and coca. In addition to being used for various cures, these
substances were greatly favored by the lotus-eaters of
Copenhagen.

The lotus-eaters were a group who modeled their way of
life on the poetry of French writers such as Baudelaire, de
Nerval, Gautier, and de Musset. They threw parties—which
gave birth to many rumors, but few attended—at which nar-
cotic plants bore the guests away swiftly and sweetly to new
worlds, both in flesh and in spirit. Fridrik was a frequent
guest at these gatherings, and once, when they stood up from
their ether-driven rollercoasters, he announced to his travelling companions:

—I have seen the universe! It is made of poems!

Spoken like "en rigtig Islaending," a true Icelander, said
the Danes.

Fridrik's trip to Iceland in the summer of 1868 was, on
the other hand, a far more earthbound affair. He had come to
sell his parents' farm following their deaths from pneumonia,
nine days apart, that spring. There were no assets to speak of:
the remote croft of Brekka, the cow Crooked-horn, a few
scrawny ewes, a fiddle, a chessboard, a bookcase, his mother's
spinning wheel, and the tomcat "little Frikki." So the plan
was to make his stay brief; it wouldn't take long to sell the

livestock to the neighbors, pay off the debts, pack up the fur-
nishings, hang the cat, and burn the farm buildings, which
were crumbling into the hillside, to the best of Fridrik's
knowledge.

This is what he would have done if the universe had not
thrown up an unexpected riddle in a filthy outhouse one
sunny night in June.

The wooden tablets play in Fridrik's hands; what had looked
like an incomprehensible puzzle now guides his fingers. It's as
if the riddle is solving itself by magic. Without conscious
intent the man lays one tablet against another and the
moment their edges touch, one slides into the other's groove
and then will not be budged; and so on and on, until the blue
tablets have formed a base, while the others are the walls and
gable-ends of what resembles a long, quite deep, trough—
white-walled within, black without.

And the sentence on the base resolves itself: "Omnia
mutantur—nihil interit." Fridrik laughs scornfully: "All
things change—nothing perishes." He can't imagine what
cunning craftsman could have given Hafdis this object, choosing for her a quotation from Ovid, none other.

There is a lowing from the back of the house.

The riddle-solver wakes from his thoughts. Crooked-horn
the Second is demanding attention. Fridrik puts down the
creation and hurries to the byre. He hasn't yet got the hang of
the new household arrangements at Brekka; the animals used
to be Abba's concern.

Twenty-riksdaler stipends to students at the university were
encumbered with the task of accompanying friendless folk to
the grave. Fridrik performed this dreary duty like anyone else,
but as he was a hopeless bibliomaniac and forever in debt to
Høst the bookseller, he welcomed the chance to take the

nightwatch at the city mortuary. While there he took on yet another job, that of translating articles from foreign medical journals for a thick-witted but well-to-do autopsy student from Christiania. Fridrik sat many a night by a smoking lamp, turning descriptions of the latest methods of keeping us poor humans alive into Danish, while on pallets around him lay the corpses, beyond any aid, despite the encouraging news of advances in electrical cures.

In the third volume of *London Hospital Reports*, 1866, Fridrik read an article on the classification of idiots by J. Langdon H. Down, a London doctor. The article was an attempt to explain a phenomenon that had long puzzled people: the fact that white women sometimes gave birth to defective children of Asiatic stock. The doctor conjectured that the mother's illness or a shock during pregnancy might cause the child to be born prematurely. This could happen anywhere on the well-documented developmental stages of the fetus: fish–lizard–bird–dog–ape–Negro–yellow man–Indian–white man, but seemed most common at the seventh stage.

Down's mongoloid children had therefore not attained full development; they were doomed to be childish and timid all their lives. But like other members of inferior races, with kind treatment and patience they could be taught many useful skills.

In Iceland they were destroyed at birth.

Unlike other types of cretins, where it cannot be seen until too late that they do not have their full wits, no one could fail to see that a Down's child was made according to a different recipe from the rest of us, even of different, alien ingredients: It had coarser hair, a yellowish complexion, stumpy body, flabby skin, and eyes slanted like slits in a canvas.

No witnesses were needed. Before the child could utter its first wail, the midwife would close its nose and mouth, thereby returning its breath to the great cauldron of souls from which all mankind is served.

The child was said to have been stillborn and its body was consigned to the nearest priest. He confirmed its nature, buried the poor creature, and that was the end of the story.

But there were always some such unfortunate infants that managed to survive. It happened in godforsaken out-of-the-way places where there was no one to talk sense into the mothers who thought they could cope with the children, strange though they were. Then of course they got lost, wandering off in their ignorance, leaving their bones on mountain paths, turning up half-dead in the summer pastures, or simply stumbling into the lives of strangers.

And as the poor wretches didn't know who they were or where they had blown in from, the authorities would settle them on whichever farm they happened to have ended up.

The farmers were greatly annoyed by these "gifts from heaven," and the household found it degrading to have to share their sleeping quarters with a defective.

There was no question that the unfortunate girl imprisoned in the bailiff of Reykjavík's kinsman's backyard was one of those Asiatic innocents who owned nothing but the breath in her lungs.

Wiping the food off her hands, she embraced the young man's head as he wept in the chicken-hatch, comforting him with the following words:

—Furru amh-amh, furru amh-amh…

Twilight deepens in the valley; the afternoon night begins its journey up the slopes. The darkness seems to flow from the open grave in the western corner of the churchyard at Botn, as if the shadow grows there first, before darkening the whole world. It's a near thing with the light: Four men appear in the church doorway with a coffin on their shoulders, the parson hard on their heels, followed by several of those black-clad crones who are never ill when there's someone to be seen to the grave. The funeral cortège proceeds rapidly, as if in a dance, their short steps breaking into quick variations, for the churchyard path is as slippery as glass, although Halfdan Atlason had been sent to break up the surface while they sang over his ladyfriend in church. Now he stands by the lych-gate, tolling the funeral bell.

A gust carries the copper song down the valley into Fridrik's parlor where he hears its echo—no, it's the knowledge that Abba's funeral is taking place at this moment that has rung the tiniest bell in his mind.

He's putting the finishing touches on the puzzle's companion piece; it's the exact image of the other, except that its base is green with a different Latin tag. This is also by the author of *Metamorphoses*, translating as "The burden which is well borne becomes light." In the moment that Rev. Baldur's pallbearers lower the coffin into the black grave at Botn, it not only becomes pitch-black in the valley but light is shed on the contents of the parcel that Hafdis Jonsdottir brought with her north to the Dale, when Fridrik B. Fridjonsson, favorite student of a close kinsman of the bailiff, got her absolved from the charge of exposing her child, on the grounds of ignorance, and on condition that she would remain in his care for as long as she lived.

Yes, if the two halves of the puzzle were laid together they would form an artfully crafted, highly polished coffin.

When Fridrik B. Fridjonsson rode north with his peculiar maid-servant and settled on his father's estate at Brekka, the parish of Dale was served by a burnt-out priest popularly known as "Rev. Jakob with the pupil" Hallsson, who as a child had taken out one of his eyes with a fishhook.

This incompetent minister was so used to his parishioners' boorishness—scuffles, belches, farts, and heckling—that he affected not to hear when Abba chimed in with his altar service, which she did both loud and clear and never in tune. He was more worried that the precentor would drown in his neighbors' spittle. This man, a farmer by the name of Gilli Sigurgillason, from Barnahamrar, possessed a powerful voice and sang in fits and starts, gaping so wide at the high notes that you could see right down his gullet, and the members of the congregation used to amuse themselves by lobbing wet plugs of tobacco into his mouth—many of them had become quite good shots.

Four years later Rev. Jakob died, greatly regretted by his flock; he was remembered as ugly and tedious, but good with children.

His successor was Rev. Baldur Skuggason, who introduced a new era in church manners to the Dale. Men sat quietly on the benches, holding their tongues while the parson preached the sermon, having learnt how he dealt with rowdies: he summoned them to meet him after the service, took them around the back of the church, and beat the living daylights out of them. The women, meanwhile, turned holy from the first day and behaved as if they had never taken part in teasing "the reverend with the pupil." They said it served the louts to whom they were married or betrothed right, they should have been thrashed long ago; for the new parson was a childless widower.

Gilli from Barnahamrar now sang louder than ever, at the speed of a piston, with mouth gaping wide. But Fridrik was asked to leave Abba at home: the word of God must reach the ears of the congregation "untroubled by the ravings of an idiot," as Rev. Baldur put it after the first and only time Abba attended one of his services.

There was no shifting him from this position; he would not have her anywhere near him. And not one of the newly civilized and well-thrashed parishioners would speak up for a simple woman who knew no greater happiness than to dress up in her Sunday best and attend church with other people.

After this, Fridrik and Hafdis had few dealings with the

folk of Dale. Halfdan Atlason sneaked a visit to Abba when he could. But the parson of Botn took a wide detour when he met them on the road.

The churchyard at Botn stands on the banks of the river Botnsa. This is a middling-sized, smooth stream, of a good depth and high-banked, bordered by spongy patches of marsh, with plenty of good peat land and enough of that deceptive surface rust. After a winter of heavy snow the river runs wild, bursting its banks with such demonic force that the dirty-gray melt water surges out of its course, flooding the marshes and forming lakes in the graveyard, leaving the church stranded on an island in its midst. The water-ringed house of God remains cut off until the graveyard has swallowed enough of the mountain milk for the water to just cover a maiden's ankle; by then the sanctified ground is drunk and wobbles underfoot until well into summer.

After such fits in the Botnsa, the riverbank gives way and the churchyard crumbles into the river. Then it is clear that nature has treated the dead with so little respect that all is reduced to a mush: teeth and coccyx, fingers and toes, adults and children, lower jawbones and scalps, buttocks here, a woman's pelvis there, a vertebra from this century, a man's paunch from the last but one.

No, one couldn't exactly say that "the Lord's garden" here in the Dale was cultivated, and men had to be true neighbors to be willing to revisit their neighbors in such a condition.

So it was that on Monday, January 8, 1883, Rev. Baldur performed the funeral rites for the company that Herb-Fridrik considered worthy of those who could not bring themselves to allow a simpleton to sing out of key with her parish priest: a quilt cover stuffed with sixty-six pounds of cow muck, the skeleton of a decrepit ewe, an empty aquavit cask, some rotten barrel staves, and a mouldy urine tub.

Abba deserved different soulmates, fairer earth.

* * *

Ghost-sun is a name given by poets to their friend the moon, and it is fitting tonight when its ashen light bathes the grove of trees that stand in the dip above the farmhouse at Brekka. This little copse was the loving creation of Abba and Fridrik, and few things made them more of a laughingstock in the Dale than its cultivation, though most of their endeavors met with ridicule.

The rowan draws shadow pictures on the snow crust; there's a low soughing in the naked branches and the odd twig still bears a cluster of dried berries that the birds overlooked last year.

Fridrik toils slowly up the slope; he has a woman's body in his arms. In the middle of the grove is a freshly dug grave; on the edge of the grave stands an open coffin. The man approaches the coffin and lays the body inside. Then he hurries back, but the moon remains.

Hafdis is well equipped for her final journey. She's dressed in her Sunday best and great care has been taken with the whole costume: on her head sits a cap with a long tassel and an oft-twisted silver tube; around her neck is a violet silk scarf; her jacket is of English cloth and the embroidered borders of her bodice are visible beneath; her apron is sewn from rose damask and the buttons, cast in white silver, bear an elaborate "A"; her skirt is striped with cross-stitched velvet bands and her legs are encased in red socks and high black stockings; her shoes are of heather-colored calfskin with white stitching; and on her hands she wears black mittens, with roses in four colors knitted on the backs.

Abba bought these rich clothes for herself, paying out of the wages she received for assisting with the unusual farming that is practiced at Brekka: on the one hand the collecting of plants, on the other the creation of small books on Icelandic flora—"with fifty-seven samples, dried and authentic," as was said of them in the article about Iceland in the *Illustrierte Zeitung*; these were the sort of books romantic young men gave to their future brides, and the last pages were left empty for the composition of pretty poems.

Fridrik kneels beside the coffin, holding a different sort of book. The book is thick and psalter-like, with the odd bird's feather sticking out from between the pages. This is Abba's bird book, in which she collected feathers with passion and exactitude. She glued them to the pages, and under her instruction Fridrik recorded the names and gender of the birds, and the provenance of the feathers. He had often wondered where Abba had picked up all her wisdom about birds, but there were no answers to be had from her, and when he tried to teach her more natural history, she thanked him politely, saying she was interested in birds.

On the title page she herself had written:

"BiRds of tHE WOrld—AbbA fRom BreKKa."

Fridrik places the book on Abba's breast and lays her hands to rest in a cross on top. He accidentally holds them tighter than intended and feels the small fingers through the mittens. This cheers him a little; these are the hands that comforted him after he lost his parents.

He kisses her brow.

He closes the coffin.

Fridrik finishes filling in the grave. He takes off his woollen cap, folds it, and puts it in his jacket pocket. He pulls off his gloves and shoves them in his armpits.

He falls to his knees.

He bows his head.

He sighs sorrowfully.

Straightening up, he gazes down through the earth to where he pictures Abba's face, and recites two verses for her. The first is an optimistic poem, a little bird rhyme of his own making:

A summer bird sang
On a sunny day:
Happiness led me,
O'er the airy way
My friend for to see.
The little bird sang
of its rowan tree.

The second is the introduction to a lost ballad. It tells of the equality that all living beings are ensured in the end, with no need for any revolution:

Earth fails,
All grows old and worn.
Flesh is dust—however it's adorned.

Rising to his feet, he puts on his cap, reaches into his pocket for a little pipe made from a sheep's leg bone, and plays a tune from "The Death of the Nightingale" by the late Franz Schubert, thus linking the two poetic fragments.

Then at last Fridrik's eyes fill with tears. They set off down his cheeks but dry up halfway; it's cold out. He bids farewell to Hafdis Jonsdottir with the same words as she took her leave of him:

—Abba-ibo!

Between the peaks to the west there is a glimpse of the universe where three stars of the constellation Cygnus glitter.

Heavy banks of cloud overshadow the valley.

It snows until late in the morning.

The sky is clear and the first blush of day at its winter blackest. Fridrik B. Fridjonsson stands out in the yard at Brekka, hidden by the farmhouse door, smoking opium-moistened tobacco in his pipe.

Something brushes against his foot: the oldest tomcat in Northern Europe, Little Frikki. He's cold after his feline "Winterreise" and wants to be let in. His namesake obliges him.

Shortly afterward Fridrik sees a man emerge from the farmhouse at Dalbotn. It's Rev. Baldur Skuggason, like a little bump in the landscape. A tiny stick juts up from his left shoulder: his gun.

He slides down over the homefields, then sets a course north over the Asar for the cliffs at Bjarg.

Herb-Fridrik knocks out his pipe on the heel of his shoe.

And goes inside to sleep.

Translation by Victoria Cribb

SEVEN STORIES

by GYRÐIR ELÍASSON

THE ATTIC

UP UNDER THE ROOF in the house over there, the one with the climbing plants winding round it, lies a young man in a gray iron bed suspecting that he is going to die soon. Night after night he has dreamt about tarred coffins, ruffled ravens, Austrian striking clocks, and white horses that jump down into the peat pits.

There's nothing wrong with him as far as he knows, yet he has hardly raised his head from the pillow for days on end and is becoming quite sure that he is dying. But he wishes something would happen so that the dreams don't come true.

In the mornings, the birds sing in the trees outside the windows. But the window in the roof is closed and the song is faint after being filtered through the glass, the sound of life gone from it. Actually, the song most recalls a worm that the birds catch with the same beak as they sing with, and

From *Yellow House* and *Tregahorni*ð, two collections of short stories.

worms evoke thoughts of earth—are connected in that way with the dreams.

He knows no woman anymore. He knows no woman who could take his head in her arms and make the soil behind his eyes disappear. He could die in peace if he knew a woman who could make the soil disappear.

"You can die in peace," she would say to him. "I shall join you in fifty years' time." That's how he feels a woman ought to be, and he would say the same to the woman if it were she who had to die and not he. "You can die in peace. I shall join you in fifty years' time."

The house is old. More than fifty years old, and more than a hundred years old. Many people have died there. But no one has died in peace. Most die without having time to become peaceful. Many dream about clocks, peat pits, ravens, white horses. Then comes death. Others dream about gray flowers in clay pots, white twine, frayed hall mats, and aging refrigerators—and when they open their eyes it is clear where it's leading.

Evening, and the birds that sang in the trees in the morning are long silent. He hasn't the strength to think about life, not for long enough at a time. He becomes fearful, feels that death is just about to come; the ceiling and walls darken. Death comes over the wall—it is not enough to put a roof on the walls, he just comes through the roof window. And if there isn't a roof window when he comes, then he makes a roof window in an instant. Hammering and sawing, and he whistles a snatch of a tune that resembles birdsong. One might think that morning had come when he whistles like that. But he comes bringing dark mist through the window with him, and the dark mist fills the room and glides out under the eaves. No whistling is heard any longer.

Horses, peat pits, clocks, coffins, ravens.

The climbing plants wind around the house. Under another roof far away is a woman who could have said, "You can die in peace. I shall join you in fifty years' time." But to do that, she would have had to know the young man who is in the attic, and she doesn't. In her attic there are bright new lightbulbs in the lamps, lightbulbs that last a long time. But the dark mist is filling the other bedroom.

RAIN

He walks past a basement window with green flannel curtains drawn and there is a big moth sitting inside on the window-pane, an old and wise Large Convolvulus Hawkmoth looking out at the dull weather. But then he sees that it isn't a moth, but a patch of paint.

"Interesting that a patch of paint should be able to grow wings," he thinks. Then he notices something on the pave-ment; a small fish is lying there and one of its eyes squints toward the sky as if it is awaiting a deluge so that it can use its gills again. He thought at first that the fish was made of silver. Sometimes—perhaps too often—one hears of the silver of the sea, and so the fish is silver. Perhaps it had last flapped its tail in the green undersea twilight only yesterday evening. He can see it comes from no aquarium.

As things are, it makes no difference if the heavens open and rain plunges like a waterfall onto the street. The silver fish will never swim again; no more will it use its gills. Its dead eye stares out and soon a cat comes along and swallows it whole with a look of surprise that it should be the first cat on the scene, then ambles across the street, black with white patches on its chest, and disappears into a red-currant bush. But the man who is going to the library with Elias Canetti unread under his arm and who stopped to look at the paint moth and silver fish, this man carries on in his gray dustcoat, which should have been a raincoat because drops have now begun to fall. Elias Canetti, with thick glasses in black frames, is on the front of the book and looks out from under the transparent plastic wrapper at the street and cars and bushes, and drops fall on the plastic so that he can't see very well even though he wears glasses. He is carried by the man in the dust coat, who is sunburnt and tall and sometimes has to bend forward when the tree branches hang down over the garden walls along the pavement.

From a window in an old-looking house, a short distance from the library, comes the sound of a two-man saw. Someone is playing a two-man saw, and not doing it very well. Then a woman leans out of the window and calls to a vicious-looking dog the color of darkness. The dog is in the garden and twitches his ears all the time as if he is shaking off the noise of the two-man saw. In the garden there is also a child, although the dog looks dangerous.

The child has a ball, which is black like the dog. It has begun to rain in earnest on the dog and the child and on the man who is passing and carries Elias Canetti under his arm. The trees and bushes take on a deep green luster in the rain. The woman calls something to the dog—she could be warning him not to snarl at the child—but she says nothing at all to the child. Having thus spoken she closes the window and the saw is heard no longer.

Now it is raining on all the roofs.

Two rather intelligent-looking eyes stare through thick glasses and a plastic film. Elias Canetti is thinking about the sea and aquariums, and the silver fish that he saw before and which the cat has now swallowed. The man carrying him is thinking about the difference between a dustcoat and a raincoat. He takes Elias Canetti from under his arm and slips him into the breast pocket inside his coat. It's a very short distance to the library now. So short that it's hardly worth putting Elias Canetti in the breast pocket.

On the steps of the library sits a man, bowed by age and wisdom like the Large Convolvulus Hawkmoth, and he reads a thick book. The pages of the book have become sodden with rainwater, and the book is getting thicker and thicker all the time. It is becoming one of the biggest of books, and was big enough before. The lettering on the pages is small and there are a lot of lines, but the man peers at it without glasses, though the years that have tested his eyes have also been many. The man carrying Elias Canetti brushes against the man on the steps and tries with a quick glance to see what book it could be that is being read with so much deep attention out in the rain. But in no way can he see what it is. The reader continues to sit immersed on the steps and doesn't look up from the water-swollen pages. He turns the pages slowly. His movements are so slow that it is as if he were poling a barge over a calm wide river in Russia.

"That's what it is," thinks the man who is carrying Elias Canetti. "It's a Russian book. A big book like that must be from Russia. Probably wide rivers have an influence on writing and there are big wide rivers in Russia. Hopefully it's not *Quiet Flows the Don*, though."

He opens the door of the library and disappears inside.

THE HOUSE AT THE BOTTOM OF THE FIELD

Two of us are sleeping in this cottage, but we don't sleep together. Between us is a partition. And I have just awoken and am listening to her breathing on the other side of the partition. The sun is shining through the window on my side of the partition, and a breeze stirs the leaves of the trees outside. The trees are beside the gable-end and lean against one another and have been here a long time and are old friends. Such trees ought to grow on the graves of folk who have not lived to be old.

In the field are many little calves. I hear their wretched lowing and then I get up and put my clothes on. The calves here are withdrawn and suspicious, not at all like the calves in the country where I was when I was a child. Those calves would let themselves be patted and they looked around and were interested in life. But these poor creatures here hardly look up from the grass and despise patting and I have tried going up to the fence with an ancient accordion and pulling and pushing it wretchedly to waken them to some kind of consciousness of their surroundings, but with no success. The only thing that happened was that the farmer came out onto the steps of the farm, looking pretty grim-faced.

The summer cottage stands on the edge of his field.

And I am in the cottage with this girl and we don't sleep together and she is still asleep and I am awake and longing for morning coffee but the coffee machine is in the room where she is sleeping which is also the kitchen.

Outside by the wall are wings, cut from brown canvas. She cut out the wings with the woodman's shears yesterday evening as the dusk fell and painted them white and laid them on a bench by the wall. She said she intended to fasten them onto the accordion.

But inside is a silvered arrow, on the table in the room where I am staying—I don't know what the arrow is for because I have seen no bow. Wings and an arrow—I'll think no more about that. Though I was worried about the newly painted wings outside in the night and thought that perhaps it would rain. But those worries were groundless, that's obvious now.

Fully clothed I listen out for a moment for her on the other side of the partition, the girl with the long hair on the other side of the partition, but she doesn't stir. I go outside, to where the sun reigns, bid the trees good morning and touch their trunks for a moment. They have begun to draw warmth from its rays.

The white cottage with the red roof, that's how a house ought to be in this country, a traditional cottage with an attic and clad with corrugated iron. Under the eaves is a very big spider. I find her unnecessarily big. She has a strong net and fishes well and is industrious about preparing the catch. One day, when I lay sunbathing and looked up at the eaves, the spider suddenly disappeared. It occurred to me that she had perhaps missed her footing on her transparent thread and thudded down into the grass right next to me and I became very concerned and got up in great haste and went in. But when I came out again she was back in her web and absorbed in enshrouding a fly. If I had the canvas wings on my back and flew sometimes, I would avoid that roof—without question. The accordion ought not to fly around there either when it has acquired the wing; it is safer for accordions to fly over unheeding bull calves in the blazing sunshine.

It was yesterday that we went up the slope here north of the cottage and picked thyme and lady's mantle in a hollow for making tea and made the tea in the evening before sleeping and talked about moons and harmoniums and galaxies and hand-colored photographs of active volcanoes and dragon-decorated tea-cups. It had begun to get dark and a faint lamp-light shone in the kitchen while we talked and the wings were painted and spread out to dry. Then we went out onto the steps before we went to bed and there was a smell of hay in the dusk. It was borne on the mild breeze and made me wakeful but the girl sleepy. The wings glittered on the shadowy bench. We went inside again and I lay down in the larger room which we call the sitting room but she went into the smaller room which is also the kitchen. Then we chatted a bit through the partition about Indians, much like the good children in cautionary tales, and both wanted to be Indians and didn't speak well of cowboys.

The accordion in its black box is on the table not far away from me. I looked at the box after we had turned off the light. It was not unlike a coffin, coal black like that, and the twilight dark as earth.

As the dreams slowly engulfed me I thought that I would like to have an accordion played at my funeral. Very robust tunes that would confuse Death.

"It shouldn't be like this," he would mutter to himself. "Things should be dismal and hopeless when I'm around." That's how the playing should be, and the coffin shaped like an accordion case.

I am still under the trees that are old friends. The sun

lights up leaves and trunks. Smoke comes from the chimney of the farmhouse above. The calves guzzle the grass. They must be about to finish all the grass in the field and they have monstrously large appetites in the good weather, and never look up. How many grass stalks would there be in one field?

In the east one can see the glaciers, and nearby a waterfall plunges down from the rock. Light glints on the windows of the farms. There is also light glinting on her window in the summer cottage, but the curtains are closed and she sleeps on until I bang on the window and say I wouldn't say no to morning coffee.

Far, far below is the sea. The way to get there is over broad sands with quicksands here and there and merciless skuas, and walking sticks are necessary because of the quicksands and the birds. Possibly it doesn't matter whether one lands, in black sand or a black box, yet I was relieved to get back to the summerhouse the day before yesterday after wandering around there, and have not thought of having the box made in the near future.

I look up into the canopies of the trees, which should be growing on the graves of folk who never lived to be old.

SUMMER

A brilliant butterfly morning and a man is walking toward the gorge with all the grasses and the murmuring river. In his pocket is a mouth organ and on his feet white canvas shoes, which gradually take on a greenish hue from the grass that still has dew on it.

The sun shines and in the ravine are sheep. Then the mouth organ is taken out and played badly and the sheep look up from the grass and get frightened and run and jump almost to the edge of the ravine. I have seated myself in the grass while I play dismally and look at the sheep. But then along comes a little ram lamb that is unlike the other sheep and he comes nearer and nearer the longer I play, and is downwind of me and pricks up his ears. And I stop playing the tune I have heard somewhere and begin to blow and suck something that the moment brings in the brightness. The mouth organ gleams in the sun and the lamb listens with sensitivity. Then he shakes his head with its little horns, looking displeased, and turns away. He skips down to the bottom of the ravine and is alone there because the sheep are still grazing up on the edge and taking no chances by moving farther down. I am halfway between the edge and the river and slip the mouth organ into my pocket after this audience, and walk on up the ravine. Farther on is a waterfall, where the mountains begin. There is grass all along the river, and I see gentians; two tiny deep-blue plants side by side—they must be man and wife.

At the mouth of the gorge I come to a hut, and around the hut broken glass lies strewn and rusty iron and decaying bits of wood. There is also a half-burnt book. It is the novel *Pan* by Knut Hamsun. The top part of the cover and pages are burnt, but the lower half intact and readable. I don't look through the book, though, because I have read it many times unburnt. I have seen books burn on a low hill in a deep dark valley, and the tales and poems wound upward with the smoke in the rainy sky. It was long ago.

But while I am standing inside the ravine the sun's rays stream over the broken glass at its mouth. And the glass fragments heat up and send the rays back up to the sun. Long ago the fragments were a whole and complete window in a gray stone house farther out in the district. And the window was in the bedroom and young folk lived there and spent a lot of time in the bedroom. Then the sun often shone in through this window, onto the bed of the young people. It shone often, although the region is rainy. And they were completely awake and completely alive and now they are both under the earth. Still side by side, but each in his own coffin, and there are no embraces any more. The glass fragments are that old.

Two low trees fumble out of the earth over the coffins and

intertwine their branches. The young folk never became old folk. Now the sunlight blazes down on what is left of the bedroom window. The gray stone house is deserted and the fragments are so far from the house. I don't know how they got to the hut at the mouth of the gorge.

I have nearly reached the waterfall and I take out the mouth organ again. Then I begin to play a tune that the west wind carries like a drowsy moth over rocky slopes and grasslands, long roads to the east—into the sheer and black mountain that rises from the plain in the gray valley. And I want the distorted notes to last a long time in the mountain. There comes to me a feeling of loss, but I don't know what it is that I am missing. I wish I knew what I had lost.

I throw the mouth organ into the deep pool below the waterfall.

THE NIGHT LIGHT

Together they carried their belongings into the house on the cliff top. It was a cold day at the beginning of September. The wind blew in from the ocean. Clouds shrouded the mountains inland. The island out in the bay was invisible.

The lighthouse stood on the edge of the cliff top.

They had permission to be in the house for three weeks. It was unoccupied for most of the year now, there being no lighthouse keeper any more. They could have stayed there over the summer but then there was a continual stream of tourists who sauntered out to the cliff, stared down at the sea, and watched the puffins glide majestically in front of the cliff face.

That would have been intolerable.

Now there were no tourists and they carried the painting easel between them from the removal van into the house. Then they took the roll of canvas, box of paints, and turpentine container. Last of all, they brought in the large computer and took it up to the attic. She was going to write there while he painted downstairs.

He spent the evening stretching canvas onto frames and listening to the radio while she connected the computer upstairs, sat at the table, and looked out of the attic window over the foggy gray sea.

Before they fell asleep he said, "I think this is a good place to paint."

"I think it is a good place to write," she said.

"I think it is *better* to paint here," he said.

"I am sure it is not," she retorted decisively.

He shut his eyes.

The next morning they woke early and drank coffee together. Then he went into the living room, where he had set up the easel, while she climbed the stairs. The weather had improved. The sky had cleared but it was still cold. There were ships out at sea—not the white type in search of adventure, but rather enormous black vessels without any sails.

The days passed. They were all similar, apart from the weather.

Sometimes they went for a walk in the evening, hand in hand, though they could start quarrelling over who was getting on better. Then they let go of each other's hand and walked separately out to the cliff edge by the lighthouse with its red painted roof. It resembled medieval towers in the south of Europe.

He was always fitting canvas to larger frames and raising the easel until it nearly touched the low ceiling. He was a landscape painter and brought the countryside into the living room, while she brought the city into the attic and peered into the screen in search of people. She printed out her writing every day. The pile of papers on the table was always getting higher. When she had the window open, an occasional gust of wind blew in and stirred up the pages.

"What are you writing, my dear?" the wind murmured.

"None of your business," she replied and shut the window.

At the beginning of the third week he began to find it difficult to paint. He could not concentrate. But she continued to go upstairs and work.

He went out for walks alone, and the paint dried up on his brushes in the meantime.

One evening while they were eating and listening to the news on the radio, he said out of the blue, "We should have brought the television with us."

She turned the volume down. "Whatever for?" she asked. "You never watch television. Say it disturbs you. And I think it is stupid to take the television to another house."

"Is it any better taking a computer to *another house?*" he asked. She looked at him, and he lowered his eyes, stirring his food round and round like a child.

They did not talk to each other any more that evening. He took the radio into the living room, lay on the sofa, and listened to the programs until well past midnight. She went upstairs and wrote.

The following days were identical. The house had become colder, although all the heaters were switched on. The fog returned and one could hardly make out the sea. The lighthouse cast its beam out into the darkness in the evenings. No more painting was done in the living room. On the easel stood a half-finished painting of Thought Mountain. Other paintings, in more advanced stages, were propped up against the heaters but not one was completed. There were no pictures on the walls, just prints that had been there when they arrived.

The evening before their intended departure, she was still upstairs writing. He climbed a few stairs and called up to her, "I am going out!" His voice sounded hopeful. But she did not reply. Her fingers tapped away at the keyboard. The window was half open and the wind played gently with the papers. He retraced his steps ponderously, put on a coat, and went out. It was dark outside. He looked up at the attic window and saw the glow from the lamp. Out on the cliff edge the beacon flashed. Down below, the tide sucked relentlessly. He walked right to the edge of the cliff, and sat there a long time staring out into the darkness.

When he began to feel cold, he took a Fisherman's Friend out of his coat pocket. The lozenge was strong. He screwed up his face while he crunched it. "No need of them on Lake Galilee," he thought. The beam from the lighthouse passed over him like a flash of lightning. Suddenly he felt as if there was a boat at the foot of the cliffs. As he stood up his foot slipped.

Back at the house she sat bent over the computer, which could have been an avant-garde weaving loom. The light from the screen merged with the glow from the lamp. All at once she looked up, stretched toward the window, and opened it wide.

She called out into the night several times but no one answered. She closed the window and went downstairs into the living room. There was a faint smell of turpentine. She looked at the painting on the easel, at the mountain. There was a cliff face at the summit of the mountain. The sky had not been painted.

She left the light on in the living room when she went out.

BORDERLINE

Late one evening I am in my little sitting room slurping tea and peering at *The Mysteries of Paris*, which I had dug up from a box in the storeroom. Then the telephone rings. I answer, and shadows stir in my head when I hear the voice on the other end of the line. It is my friend and contemporary who died last year. Everything goes nearly as black before my eyes now as it did when I heard about his death.

"Hello," he says. The voice is hollow and faint.

"Hello," I answer, trying to overcome the forboding that is creeping toward me over the line.

"Everything all right?" he asks.

"Everything's all right." I answer. "And you?"

"Not too bad."

"Where are you?" I ask cautiously.

Actually I don't want to know anything about that, but

ask all the same. The first volume of *The Mysteries of Paris* has fallen onto the floor, and lies there open.

"Where am I? What do you mean?"

"Well, there are so many places," I say uncertainly.

"Rubbish. There is only one place."

"That's good," I answer, and don't know why I say it.

Underneath, I have been hoping that this was someone so gruesomely waggish that he allowed himself to imitate my dead friend on the telephone. But in this voice from the grave there are particular nuances that I recognized from when it was based in his body. Nuances that others can't achieve. There is no doubt about it—I am connected to the world of the dead.

"I'm just ringing to say I'll meet you when you get here," he says.

"Very kind of you," I say. But now my voice is getting faint.

"It'll be soon."

I can hear that it's all decided.

"It's good of you to let me know," I say softly. But my heart isn't in it. At that moment, I wished that we hadn't been friends, nor even acquaintances.

Yet to avoid a silence I ask dully about the prospective journey.

"What are the roads like now?"

"Magic" he says. Magic. He said that so often. Magic. Not a good word.

"What about transport?" I ask.

"None of that fuss. Just a good-quality coat, a good wooden overcoat." His voice is not so hollow and faint when he says that but I find him quite gloomy enough.

"Just walk all the way, in the dark?"

"What dark? Why do people always go on about the dark? There is no dark."

"That's what you say," I say. I am beginning to get annoyed.

"All right."

I cough, swallow a few words, then say with self-control, "Richard?"

"Yes?"

"Do you ever see Grandfather?"

"I don't listen to that sort of thing," he says. "And carry on reading *The Mysteries of Paris*. You haven't got much time left."

"How do you know what I'm reading?"

"Aren't you feeling well?" he asks quickly.

"I'm okay," I say.

"Then you're coming soon," he says.

"I suppose it's settled."

"Magic."

"You're going to come and meet me?"

"You heard what I said before. Bye."

"Goodbye," I say. And before I know it I have added, "Thank you for ringing." I hadn't intended to say that.

"Not at all," he says with his hollow, faint voice, and hangs up. For a moment I listen to the silence on the line, then I too hang up. The tea has gone cold in the cup, a sort of iced tea. I go and pour it into the sink, and then refill the cup from the teapot; it is still moderately lukewarm. I pick up *The Mysteries of Paris* from the floor.

Light from one of the lamps in the sitting room falls on the gray-looking pages covered with letters.

I have disconnected the telephone. I don't want to talk to anyone else so late in the evening. And what would I talk about? I'm off soon. I'm going on a long journey, alone in a tarred wooden overcoat. But at the journey's end I will be met. In the end, friends last beyond the grave and death, though perhaps they sound distant and faint-voiced over the telephone, over the borderline.

Soon I will set off, soon I shall be gone, and will not even pay the phone bill. I switch off the lamp and continue reading in the dark. I can read in the dark.

A noise of traffic comes from outside. Then a door is closed on the upper floor here, and the woman there storms out in her white coat to a car, which is also white. My over-coat will be black, and the car black as well, but that car won't go far, just to the grave. Then I shall travel immense shadowy heathlands alone in the heavy wooden overcoat under a sky that is like a vault in a coal mine. I don't care what deceased friends say about the dark, I know that it exists. That is all I know.

I am reading in the dark now.

NIGHT

The Pleiades and northern lights are still above the mountain. The mountain is in the east, and on its slopes there are rein-deer. Reindeer always remind me of trees that have taken to moving. They remind me even more of trees than people do. In the distant past, reindeer were trees as people were, but they haven't come such a long way from their origins, and the branches can be seen although they no longer bear leaves.

I have my bedtime book in my hand and my pocket light and walk toward the mountain over the edges of the moorland in rubber boots. The book is a relative of mine, I feel; it is made out of trees and human thought, and thus the relation-ship becomes twofold. These are ancient poems that I am tak-ing to the mountains and the reindeer.

On the way, I pass a building that was originally a stable. But the man who owned the horses was very lazy about clean-ing out the building and the floor got steadily higher until the horses' heads touched the rafters. Then he exchanged them for sheep but continued to be lazy about cleaning out the animals, and the sheep soon began to hit their horns on the roof tim-bers. After that, he turned the sheepshed into a hen house. Thus it remained until the cockerel cut its comb where the sheets of corrugated iron overlapped at the top. Since then it has stood empty, but those that pass by remember that it was stable, sheepshed, and henhouse and find it a strange and lone-ly house at night under the northern lights and blinking stars.

The edge of the mountain stands out tar-black against the starry vault. I wish I could see the reindeer standing on the edge, and their antlers—the branches—would spread out against the firmament. That I would like to see. But I am not sure whether they stay high up in the mountain during the night; they might be near its foot. In general I don't know how animals live at night. It has been said that people don't know the darkness though it has existed on earth for such a long time. But animals know the dark. They have unhesitatingly brushed against its dread-black omnipresent fur.

I, on the other hand, have got a pocket light and intend to go and read next to a stone by the mountain to illuminate myself within. Yet in that way I will also get to know the darkness, for there are animals in the old poems.

Northern lights and Pleiades above the mountain. Reindeer on the slopes, and I am on my way to the mountain with pocket light and book and have passed the stable, sheepshed, and henhouse. I hope that the batteries last until morning, like the stars and northern lights.

The sodden marshland squelches and my boots sink into it. In many places there are deep waterholes where the water beetles are sleeping. I thread my way past and avoid waking them. It is not out of consideration that I don't want to wake them, but rather from a vague fear. Water beetles remind me of black holes out in space beyond the Pleiades, tiny coal-black points—concentrated darkness. Though the waterholes twinkle nicely. The rubber boots shine too and I enjoy splashing in them over the wetlands that the wading birds claim for themselves in springtime. But I don't know where the birds are this autumn night.

THE BOOK COLLECTION

On the windowsill here in the basement I have made a little collection of books. They stand and look out, close together like friends—and are friends. Windowsill book collections have long had a special atmosphere in my mind, right from the time I read a Japanese story that began, "In my youth I had a little windowsill book collection, and on rainy days I sat in my room and read."

I never actually read any more than this opening to the story. It was in a bookshop, I didn't buy the book then, and it was sold when I came back afterward wanting to get it so that I could read all about the windowsill library.

But now I have put some books in the basement window myself.

There are the plays of Chekhov, Sherwood Anderson's short stories, *Pastime* by Gröndal, among others. The books stand together, and all of them are my friends.

Evening now, actually night has fallen, rain. Earlier I had intended to go for a walk, but didn't because it was raining so much. I look out of the basement window, over the books, and see the trees in the garden against the streetlights. A wet and dark green leaf glitters.

A lamp lights up the spines of the books, which compensates for not being able to go out for a walk. This evening I content myself with running my eyes over them, and don't take any of the books off the sill to read. I am feeling comfortable this evening. Yesterday evening I didn't feel as good, but then neither had I made a place there for the books. I did that this morning.

In the sitting room a centenarian clock strikes. It was brought to me unexpectedly a few days ago; my friend moved to New York and said he would like to know it had a good home. In the evening, the bell rang and I went to the door and he was in the twilight with the clock nearly in pieces in his arms and handed it to me.

"I want to know it has a good home," he said.

"Its home is here," I said and showed him through. We fastened it on the wall together in the little sitting room here, between the watercolor of a low mountain in the mist and a wood carving of a giant fly.

I think the clock had been striking one. The night is about to lull everything and everyone to sleep. I stretch myself at the window and open it so that the books can breathe fresh damp air. I suspect that books need to breathe like people, and I think they tolerate damp better than people say. There is no doubt that they stare rather sadly at the trees out in the garden, as if they have a vague recollection of relationship with them, and sighs are borne from the pages to the damp trunks and branches.

I begin to sigh too, for I feel that people are like trees that move, trees that have lost their roots and are always in search of the soil. I have a hazy idea that humans have come from trees that broke off from their roots in a wild whirlwind eons ago—that is my theory of evolution.

And because of that, I understand the books in the window when they sigh so that mist forms on the glass, and I feel even closer to them. All the same I shall soon draw the curtains, turn off the lamp, and let them rest on the sill. I could rearrange the opening of the Japanese story and keep it just for myself: "When I was about thirty I made a little windowsill library in the basement, and on many rainy nights I lay in my bedroom and slept."

Now the lamp is going out.

Translation by Susan Pitts, except "The Night Light," by Janice Balfour

MY ROOM

by BRAGI ÓLAFSSON

ON THE FENCE by my old house on Hagamelur Street someone has written in black marker: "The tidemark of loneliness." I can't help smiling and ask myself: Is that the name of a band or the title of a poetry collection? How does the tidemark of loneliness manifest itself? Have I ever been there and looked out to sea? At least it seems likely that you'd find the sea somewhere in the vicinity of a tidemark. And although Hagamelur is not exactly tidal, I don't suppose loneliness is an entirely unknown phenomenon there, any more than on other streets.

The reason why I've come here to the house where I used to live with my parents, brother, and sister when I was young is that I saw our old apartment advertised and decided to take the chance to go and see it, although of course I've no interest in buying it. Especially not if living here these days you run the risk of being washed up on the dreaded tidemark of loneliness! I simply wanted to revisit my old room, where I evolved from a child into a teenager—to put it rather grandly—and where I made many of my most far-reaching decisions, either to the soundtrack of the stereo (a confirmation gift) or wreathed in soft veils of fragrant pipe smoke, though usually with both on the go at once, that's to say both music and pipe smoke.

"Come in," says a weary but friendly woman's voice over the entry-phone, once I've explained that I'm the person who was coming round to view the property.

"Thanks," I say and push open the door.

So it was here, I think, as I look up the communal staircase to the second and third floors; this is where it all happened.

We lived on the third floor. At a rough estimate I've walked up these stairs maybe eight to nine thousand times. And been down them just as often, I expect. Random memories stir in my mind as I climb the stairs for the first time in twenty-four years, and when the present owner of the apartment opens the door and invites me in, these memories awaken and leap up like a living person. I think I can smell the same old smell. But when I enter the hall, this gives way before a heavy odor of cooking, an odor that instead of whetting my appetite puts me off the thought of food altogether.

Where there used to be a mirror between the kitchen door and the door that opened into the dining room—a mirror that always held the image of my cousin after he made a face in it a few days before he died—there's now a watercolor of a row of houses that seems familiar from here in town. The people who live here now probably don't make a point of checking out their faces before leaving the house.

"I suppose I should begin by showing you the master bedroom and the bathroom," says the woman who let me in. At a guess she's around fifty, with attractive features marred by a look of exhaustion; she clearly hasn't been getting enough sleep. I suddenly feel really bad that she should be making something in the kitchen that smells so horrible. Before I follow her down the corridor to the master bedroom I notice that my old room, which is beside the door to the stairwell, directly opposite where the mirror used to be, is shut, and so is the door to the living room.

"Then there's a child's room here next to the bedroom," says the woman, but when she opens the door I see that what used to be my brother's orderly abode—he was always at great pains to keep it clean—is now a rather dirty storeroom; there are piles of smelly old newspapers, a jumble of videotapes, plastic bags full of Coke bottles and beer cans, and all kinds of junk that no one seemed to have a use for any longer.

"It's really more of a storeroom," says the woman and shuts the door, obviously unwilling for me to get a better look. Then she shows me the bathroom, which is more or less unchanged since my family lived here and reasonably clean, and when I enter the bedroom I get the impression that it's been tidied and the bed's been made specially for my visit. Though the woman doesn't look the house-proud type, she must have felt it right to have the bedroom unobjectionable in this respect. I have the feeling that something happened there last night that she wanted to obliterate all sign of. Despite having used the word *unobjectionable* about the room, in fact I do object to just about everything in it. Both the furniture and ornaments are so hideous and tasteless that I feel in a flash that our aesthetic sense is the element of our minds that forms the deepest gulf between us and our fellow men.

"I'm afraid I can't show you the living room at the moment," says the woman when we return to the hall. She looks at me, her expression turning sad. "You'll have to excuse me," she adds.

"Is it being...?" I ask, meaning is work being done on the living room—redecoration, something of that kind.

"It's simply not possible at the moment," repeats the woman.

"Well, then there's just this room here," I say cheerfully, with a light tap on the door of my old room.

"Actually, that'll just have to wait as well," says the

woman. "But there's the kitchen left—you'll have to excuse the fact that I'm in the middle of cooking. Then there's a storeroom in the attic; you can take a look at that."

"So you're saying it's not possible to see the room?" I ask, aware that my tone is overly astonished. Which of course I am, quite apart from being disappointed: seeing this room was the whole purpose of my visit.

"I'm sorry, it's just not possible at the moment," says the woman, without seeming particularly sorry.

"But the apartment *is* for sale, isn't it?" Now I don't try to hide that fact that I find it a bit odd not being allowed to see the property in its entirety.

"We wouldn't be advertising otherwise," answers the woman, quite directly. "Don't you want to look at the kitchen?" she asks, with such weariness and indifference that my thoughts go involuntarily to what she's cooking in there; it must be pretty unexciting fare, not just for the taste buds and sense of smell but for the eye as well; I picture a defunct stew, sort of dark brown with a greenish film, with watery potatoes and vegetables.

As I turn down the chance to refresh my memory of the kitchen, I summon up a picture of my old room as it was before we moved. Black ceiling, dark-brown walls, a black square on one wall with another smaller square inside, brown like the wall. A wood-veneer sofa bed and desk in the same dark color under the window, a black stereo, worn dark-red cushion, battered old office chair with arms, piles of records here and there about the room, and Keith Emerson on the wall above the sofa bed, sitting in black leather astride a black motorbike with one hand on a black helmet that rested on the gas tank. Keith Emerson, that great magician who made nothing of writing piano concertos, at least one piano concerto, in between hitting the road on his Harley Davidson and getting his picture taken for English and German teen magazines. It was from one of these that I had cut out the picture that hung on my wall.

"Did you talk to them at the real-estate agent's?" asks the woman and I look at her, unsure whether to answer at random or tell her whom I spoke to at the real-estate agent's; there's no telling what kind of answer she's fishing for. Then all at once there's the sound of glass from the living room, as if someone had put down a glass and it had clinked against another glass, something like that. The woman coughs and looks around at nothing; she's waiting for me to leave. I can't say I want to stay any longer either; I thank her and turn to the door to the landing. Then there's a noise from inside my room, as if someone's banged on a table or closet door, and as I take hold of the doorknob, someone shouts:

"Tell him to go!"

I jump and pause with my hand on the doorknob. The voice on the other side of the door is audibly young but strangely deep. I imagine that the light's off in the room. When I look the woman in the eyes, I can see that they too are telling me to go; she's doing as she's told. I nod to her apologetically, turn the knob—it's the same knob as a quarter of a century ago—and when I open it on to the landing the same voice as before shouts:

"I need to come out!"

Trying to avoid meeting the woman's eyes again, I step over the threshold, but before I close the door I hear him call even louder:

"Mum!"

I don't know what exactly I am leaving behind as I close the door, but it's a relief to be alone on the landing. Before going down the stairs—probably for the last time—I look up the steep narrow steps to the attic, where I could have had a look around, if I'd wanted.

On the way down, I notice two pictures hanging on the wall by the door to the downstairs apartment that are the same as when we lived here. I should remember, I tell myself, having walked past them nearly twenty thousand times, if my calculations are anything to go by.

I recall the family who used to live below us. The son was a good friend of mine and suddenly I find it quite absurd that I haven't heard from them since. Could they possibly still live here? When I rang the doorbell of the woman upstairs I couldn't see any names, either by the bell or on the front door, but as the same pictures are still on the wall it's not unlikely that they're still here—at least the parents, who must be getting on by now. But it doesn't have to be that way; I myself left behind the black square with the little brown square inside it on the wall of my room; actually, it was painted on the wall. And the poster of Keith Emerson— I don't remember taking that with me either when we moved.

Translation by Victoria Cribb

UNINVITED

by EINAR MÁR GUÐMUNDSSON

MY FATHER'S HAMMER

AS I RUN down the freshly polished stairs with father's hammer in one hand, Oli is sitting on the oil tank outside the house.

Before I know it, I've hit Oli over the head with the hammer.

Oli shrieks.

Oli quivers.

Oli's head breaks into lots of heads. Oli has four heads.

Then bloop. From Oli's crewcut head a lump sprouts forth, a little white egg, and the tears seem to run in front of him and in through the door to the basement.

I stand on my own in front of the half-buried oil tank.

Alone with the hammer in my hand. With my eyes I blow up the tank. Fiery yellow sparks, sparklers out of the earth.

Bugger and balls.

From *Knights of the Spiral Stair*, a novel.

I curse the hammer.

I curse my father who owns the hammer.

I curse Oli for getting his head in the way.

I curse the shop that sells hammers.

I curse. I curse.

Down with the hammer!

My hands. Me and the clawhammer.

I'm nowhere.

I've thrown my hands up on to the balcony.

I've buried the hammer.

I'm nowhere.

The oil tank doesn't move, even though I've blown it up with my eyes. No strains of violin music from the gutter of the roof, just creaking.

When I hear the impatient rattling of the balcony window I know that my mother has been told over the phone. Through my head I hear what Jona, Oli's mother, has said. Oli, I can hear our mothers talking on the phone through my head.

I don't exist.

I'm nowhere.

Hunched up behind a dustbin lid in the rubbish yard, I think my wish is coming true; in a dream the dustmen take me away. Away away with the other rubbish.

I don't exist.

A green bottle drifts toward the island; when the veiled princess removes the cork I am a cloud of smoke. In an instant I am transformed into a giant. The dustbin lid is a magic carpet.

My mother is out on the steps now. From the rubbish yard I feel her looking all around. She scouts all around with all her weight in her eyes.

—It's useless, Mum, I want to shout. Behind a dustbin lid I have abnegated my existence.

I don't exist.

I'm nowhere.

The only evidence against me is the hammer. Which I've

buried. Now the worms are working all out to erase my fingerprints. Oli, you're just lying. With the salt of your tears you have told on me; yes I just ask you, since when has a crying child's testimony been admissible evidence? I shall send the courts a copy of my soul.

I don't exist.

I'm nowhere.

—Johann Johann, calls my mother, alright Johann in you come this minute. Yes, it's me, Johann Petursson, whose name is Johann. My mother is calling me.

Her voice reverberates against the windows of the houses, crawls down the steps into the rubbish yard toward me as I sit hunched up behind a dustbin lid.

No, Mum, you'll have to play chorus to your voice by yourself.

I can't hear you.

I'm soaring above the planet on the dustbin lid.

After my mother has been calling me for some time, her flip-flops set off down the steps.

—Johann!

I can hear.

And soon afterward she's prodding at me with a yellow carpet beater. I crawl from beneath the dustbin lid and up the freshly polished stairs, a one-hundred-percent-living being.

I exist.

Shut up in my room.

The wait for my father.

I exist.

BALLOONS IN A SAUCER

I can hear when my father parks the car outside the garage, opens the door and closes it. Now he's standing with a bunch of keys in his hand. I can hear; he walks up the freshly polished stairs and takes hold of the shiny silver handle.

I can hear when my father enters the apartment. He

coughs a dry Camel cough in the hall. Walks over to the window and checks whether the car isn't where he left it.

Yes, and since the car hasn't gone, he makes his presence heard by clearing his throat. I hear him clear his throat.

Hi here I am.

He sees himself in the mirror, full-size. He's just on the other side of himself.

Hi here I am.

And locked in my room I hear my mother walk up on her flip-flops with do-you-know-what-he-did on her lips.

Low whispers in the hall.

I'm contemplating whether I should drown myself in my big brother's fish tank or disappear into one of the desk drawers. I look up to the window, should the mysterious sorceress from the fairy tale by any chance want to contact me.

Low whispers in the hall.

No I'll hide in the wardrobe.

—You really mean to say he, I hear my father say.

He laughs. A moment later my father laughs.

Of course it was a relief of sorts for my father to have found it funny, but when he opens the door to my room where I'm hiding in the linen box in the wardrobe, I can see straight away that he didn't find it funny in the least.

—Right out you come, says my father. You'd better not think...

I crawl out of the linen box.

Instead of saying that's my boy like fathers should always do when their sons engage in confrontations, my father glares at me and asks firmly:

—Who said you could take the hammer?

—I've told you time and again not to...

I feel my father only has himself to blame, because if hammers are that dangerous they ought to be kept out of the reach of children. Who knows if I won't fill my pockets with razor blades tomorrow. But before I have the chance to publish my apologia for Johann Petursson, yes, before I can say anything, my father plucks the words out of the air as if he's catching flies.

He thrusts the hand he wears his wedding ring on up to my face and hisses: Alright where did you go and put the hammer?

—I-I-I buried it. In the banal realism of the words I stammer: I-I-I buried it.

—Buried it! Well I'll be… Now you just go and fetch… I tell you I'm not going to lose my hammer because of one of your stupid games.

As I run down the freshly polished stairs there's no one sitting on the oil tank outside the house. I dig up the hammer. My fingerprints press onto the handle. Now I'm holding the evidence against myself. Run back up the freshly polished stairs with my father's hammer in one hand.

I feel there's a whole execution squad inside the apartment when I see my father standing in the doorway. I hand him the dirty hammer.

—And you'd better tell Oli you're sorry, my father says.

Then he takes hold of the collar of my check shirt. I feel myself dangling in the air as he pushes me into the kitchen.

My mother's sitting at the kitchen table and looks at me with big bovine eyes:

—You could have smashed Oli's head to pieces.

—I-I only meant to do it softly.

—Yes, but it's not the first time, Johann. Just yesterday you threw all your brother's schoolbooks into the rubbish. Luckily he'd just put covers on them all. Just what's this supposed to mean?

—I don't know.

Head bowed, I fidget with the dangling end of my brown belt. Since my mother doesn't understand my rebellion against the educational system I probably don't understand it either, because I've never been to school. But I'll soon be starting preschool with the Reverend Daniel.

I bow my head.

—I don't know.

But I've always felt that Tryggvi's exercise books enjoy far too much popularity at home. Yes, you'd think they were a collection of sea shanties…

—Alright go and give these to Oli, says my father. He takes four rubber balloons out of a large saucer that someone or other has given him. Yes give these to Oli. And remember to say you're sorry.

On my way down the freshly polished stairs, along the dark steps to the basement, past the boiler room that flickers fiery yellow around my face, I blow up one of the balloons. It's a giant pink rabbit that wags its ears with a carrot in its mouth.

While the air blows back out of the balloon into my face I'm so afraid that I don't dare make a sound. I don't dare knock. I become metamorphosed into the shadows on the walls. Fiery yellow I flicker.

Perhaps they're all dead, because there's not a sound to be heard from Oli's apartment. I put my head round the door and peek with one eye.

At the kitchen table Oli's mother, Jona, is sitting blowing cigarette smoke through her nose as though she's the last person left in the world, alone with a Chesterfield at the kitchen table.

The moment she sees me she throws her eyeballs straight at me. Like a concertina being played in mid-air, I crumple up completely.

Jona jumps to her feet, ties on her apron in a flash, and heads toward me. She's like a dragon with tobacco smoke blazing out of her nostrils. She's not alone in the world any more.

—Johann, you just don't go around doing that sort of thing.

—I-I've got some balloons.

—Balloons?

—Yes I'm going to give Oli some balloons.

Oli is lying half-asleep in bed with a damp flannel on his forehead. There's a plastic-jointed Red Indian sitting in the lotus position in the window and an orange netfloat in the corner of the room.

When I walk in with the four balloons, Oli looks at me from an indeterminate distance. The thought that he's turned into a cretin crosses my mind.

His head wobbles from side to side until his eyes latch on to me. I know that if Oli's turned into a cretin, I, Johann Petursson, will be sent to the boy's reformatory and be made to tie scoutmasters' shoelaces all day long.

No no, Oli, you know it'll get better. You remember Rebbi got hit over the head by a sledge and was out again hanging onto the backs of buses a week later.

Such are the comforting hints I want to drop into Oli's white bedclothes when he suddenly realizes I'm standing there, I in the third-person singular, just as God made me except for the clothes I'm wearing.

Oli points at me.

—I-I-sh-sh-should-say-s-s-owwy.

Oli points at me:

—You're not coming to my birthday party the day after tomorrow and that's definite, he says and clutches the flannel on his forehead.

—D'y'hear? You're not…

What no…

When I pretend not to have heard he repeats it three times. He repeats it three times, both to let me know that I'm not invited to his birthday party and to make sure that his important message does not go ignored by the readers of this story.

I, Johann Petursson, am in other words not invited to the birthday party, Oli, which you have invited me to all the same.

I raise no protest as I stand there with four balloons between my fingers. I drop the balloons onto the white bedclothes. I raise no protest.

Not being invited to Oli's birthday party is comparable to an entire country being expelled from the United Nations.

Inside my head countless doors slam shut.

Through the fiery-yellow flickering boiler room, every single nerve in my body wields a hammer, up the dark steps from the basement, the freshly polished stairs and into my room.

That evening I go around wearing a balaclava helmet which I put on back-to-front, pretending that I have eyes in the back of my head. I walk back and forth across the floor, back and forth until a flowerpot stand rolls across the floor in front of me with a breaking sound. My mother comes running over from the sewing machine with a pin in her mouth: Isn't hitting Oli over the head with a hammer enough? Do you need to kill my flowers too? she asks and looks me in the face, which isn't a face but rather a balaclava…

Not inviting me to…

I crawl into my striped pajamas. I had a dream this afternoon; I just hope the feathery quilt swallows me, that no Johann wakes up in this bed tomorrow.

I FEEL MYSELF SNUFFLING

Oli.

I thought a gift of balloons was sufficient recompense for hitting you with a hammer, which I contemplated hitting you over the head with again when you didn't want to invite me to your birthday party.

It felt more unjust than all the wars in the newspapers combined, since I didn't get any of the balloons in the saucer myself, but was told I ought to be ashamed of myself.

Ashamed of myself—me!

No. Of course I couldn't feel ashamed because it was you, Oli, with your lump and that damp flannel on your forehead who ought to be ashamed of yourself, for not inviting me to your birthday party.

Yes you and whose army?

I had abnegated my existence behind the dustbin lid when I was roused to life again with a yellow carpet beater.

Yes and my journey through the boiler room is a match for the longest journey ever made through Purgatory. And without having my sins forgiven me either.

Just think, Oli!

When it was your birthday last year I gave you a monkey in check trousers playing a guitar, and the year before a Chaseside digger. Now I've decided to give you a Jaguar, a little white matchbox Jaguar. From the famous matchbox series, as the radio announcer says.

And what do you go and do, Oli, when I've decided that?

Refuse to invite me to your birthday, retract your formal invitation to your party. Actually it's illegal. I should really talk to the Committee for the Protection of Minors. Yes or get myself a lawyer. I contest that you, lying there in bed with a damp flannel on your forehead, were not responsible for the words you uttered. The hammer has thrown your senses into such disarray that your thoughts are no longer organized, or perhaps the lump has started thinking with your head.

On these and many other grounds, I know that by far the best thing would of course be for me, Johann Petursson, to stamp my feet and shout with my fists aloft:

—Oli is a stinking shitbag!

I don't want to go to his birthday party anyway.

But it's not by far the best thing to do as I sit on my brother Tryggvi's bed watching the guppies swimming in the tank, because I want to go to your party, Oli, just as much as the guppies want their fish food.

You surely understand me, dear reader, when I start racking my brain about how to do the dirty on birthday boy.

Oli.

I could creep down the stairs and through the boiler room and fill your shoes with gravel.

I could throw a rubber mouse on a string through your window, make you shriek, and pull it back out the moment someone comes.

And I'm sure I could slip cigarette butts into your anorak pocket unnoticed.

And, Oli, I know the man who drives the dustcart on our street. He'd drive you off to the dump and tip you out with the city's rubbish if I just had a word with him.

Ha ha ha, I laugh to myself.

All this and much more I could do, because by definition I ought to be feeling sorry for myself and in no condition to do anything. Nobody will believe I've done anything, as long as everybody thinks I'm stooping in prayer asking God to forgive me for hitting you with a hammer. You know that God forgives everything. Even though prayers are being said nineteen to the dozen and nobody knows whether God understands Icelandic, he still forgives everything all the same.

As I sit thinking all this up, Oli's birthday party last year runs through my mind. Yes my head is a motorway where time goes in reverse:

Popcorn pours over the floors and your strong uncle in the police lifts five of us up all at once.

I hide in the wardrobe. For a quarter of an hour I sit in the poplin-coated darkness surrounded by shoes of all descriptions.

It's fun.

I sip coke through a green straw.

I walk around with the glitter of red sausages in my eyes.

Your strong uncle in the police tests whether we've got soft centers or hard crusts.

White nylon shirts with boys' heads fly all over the place.

I feel my face beginning to laugh. But as soon as I feel it beginning to laugh it stops laughing. There's actually nothing funny, given that tomorrow this laughter will be at birthday party to which I haven't been invited.

Look.

It's a fact, Oli, that your birthday parties are the best on our street, and not being invited to the best birthday party on our street is tantamount to being the biggest creep on our street. Just like two times two is four or the president's name is Whatsisname.

I'm in a twist.

I've neither been declared war upon nor invited to negotiate a ceasefire.

I simply haven't been invited to your birthday party.

So I'm in a twist.

I can't do what we did on Gylfi's birthday, organize a mass truancy. No I can't do that. I can't get the boys to boycott Oli's party. It would have to be a concerted move.

And it's completely unrealistic to dream of piling up barricades outside the basement door to block everyone's entrance. I might just as well usher everybody off the street and down into the drains. No your birthday party won't be stopped, Oli, because it's your birthday. But we definitely thought it was clever—and so did you, Oli—when we didn't turn up at Gylfi's party at three o'clock. Yes we thought it was clever when we went into town in our best clothes with twenty-five-crown notes in white envelopes, and imagined Gylfi crouching over his fourteen ancient aunties. We thought it was clever.

As I sit here on the bed thinking things over, I have to admit that I do not command the mass support on our street to have a whole troop of boys stage a march-past in protest against the insult of me not being invited to your birthday party. Even if I were to metamorphose my soul into a flysheet and campaign in every house it wouldn't mean a thing, because no one wants to miss Oli's birthday party on any account. Boys even sneak in there with a raging temperature and scarlet fever.

Oli, for a few days afterward you're the hero of our street.

I feel the ends of my hair stiffening.

I clench my fists and beat on the wall.

At the most I could badger Gunni, the freckled fisherman's son from number thirteen, and Rebbi Bigears, who's reputedly a close relative of Dumbo the Elephant, into joining me to smoke king-size filter cigarettes among the sallowing leaves in the park.

But would you, dear reader, enjoy smoking king-size filters (or Lark perhaps) in the park, sad as the autumn leaves in Icelandic poetry, my hands blue with cold in my anorak pockets, on a gray bench with Rebbi and Gunni as the candlelight from the cakes burns in my head, the boys' laughing faces like a nightmare coughing with each drag; all because I hit you over the head with a hammer, Oli?

In my mind's eye I scan the birthday party.

My seat is empty.

Nobody asks: Where's Johann?

I feel myself snuffling.

YOUR UNCLE IN THE POLICE

Oli.

If you hadn't got an uncle in the police, you could be a shitbag and a turd. Yes you could be stuffed with all the abuse in the world. But because you've got an uncle in the police you're forgiven everything.

Quite right.

Everyone's got an uncle in the police. Yes at least everyone who's got roots in the same family tree. And quite right too, not everyone is forgiven everything.

But not everyone has an uncle like yours who, in addition to his police force duties, always turns up at your birthday party.

And not just that:

Your uncle in the police is not just your uncle in the police. He's also an honorary member of the Viking soccer club and a timekeeper at the Neptune swimming club championships. Yes and every other day he throws the discus on the sports page of the paper.

He bends down in his leotard and puffs out his cheeks, or stands on the prizewinners' podium with a smile that stretches three times around the world, on the grayish sports page photographs that you, Oli, cut out and conscientiously paste into an exercise book.

Oli, you might perhaps not be forgiven everything. But most things though, when your birthday draws near and you walk around with your exercise book full of sports photographs, showing everybody your uncle whom you imagine leading you by the hand up on to the prizewinners' podium; yes you show the whole street your uncle in the police. I, Johann Petursson, have reacted by systematically collecting boxing-glove pictures of Sonny Liston. But I am quite aware that even if I were to fill my room with pictures of Sonny Liston, Sonny would never turn up at my birthday party as your uncle in the police does at yours, Oli.

Yes your uncle in the police always comes along at four o'clock when he finishes work—or simply takes time off to turn up punctually with his present, en route into your heart.

Oli.

Sometimes your uncle takes you with him to the police gymkhana. You've seen all-in wrestling there and tug-of-war; yes and even cod-liver-oil-drinking contests and ludo leagues.

But your uncle doesn't just let you watch sports.

At home he's got a set of weights and some time later he's going to build a whole sports hall where you can swing around on the ropes.

Your uncle in the police can do anything.

He can light a fire by rubbing stones together, and can untie the Gordian knot.

In the winter he sometimes runs three laps around the city and rolls around in the snow.

And he beats all comers at old-time dancing at the policemen's masked ball.

Your uncle in the police is also an amateur artist. He's painted countless villages that adorn all the walls in the city, because he knows everyone and everywhere in Iceland, ever since he was a travelling hair-oil salesman before joining the police.

Down at the station he's sometimes known as 007 because his room is number 7.

Oli.

When you told me your uncle could throw the discus out of Laugardalur football stadium and into the shallow end of the old swimming pool, I was flabbergasted. I badgered my father for a whole week to start practicing the discus and, if he didn't want to join the police force, he could at least become a bus driver and let me sit up front.

—Go on, Dad!

But, Oli, I also got one up on you when I asked you how your uncle in the police is related to you. You couldn't answer. Your uncle in the police is in fact married to your mother's sister and thereby your mother's brother-in-law. In other words, he's not your real uncle but only related to you through your aunt.

There you see what a dab hand I am at genealogy. But when I told you, you attacked me with your fingernails that are so long anyone would think you wanted to be an actress and wear nail varnish, yes you attacked me and scratched long marks down my cheeks, tried to rip my lips apart and told me, grimacing, that sure he was your uncle, he was still your uncle all the same.

—No, I groaned, he's not related to you.

Then you clambered on top of me and jammed my elbows under your kneecaps, bent over and aimed a spit, a slippery green blob of snot slightly diluted with saliva.

I looked up into your face, the blob of snot bobbed up and down and your eyes were afloat in rage:

—Is he or is he not my uncle?

—Yes yes, he's your uncle, I groaned.

After that, he was your uncle, yes he was your uncle in the police.

I reconciled myself to the fact that it had just been jealousy, because it was nothing but jealousy. I, Johann Petursson, wanted an uncle in the police too.

Oli.

At night you dream about your uncle. He walks out of the sea swinging the islands in the bay around his head. If he's thirsty he swallows the sea in a single gulp, and he pushes over houses with his fingertips. And what's more: reality begins only two steps from the bed where you dream, because if you see a bird at dawn you never rule out the possibility it might be a discus your uncle has tossed up into the sky.

Yes if Jesus fed all those people with five fishes, your uncle could surely knock them all flat with a single punch, because the world's changed since then. He can do anything. If anyone's father is strong, your uncle's always twenty times stronger. He's got a set of weights in his muscles and has the key to all the handcuffs in the world.

But to recap, your uncle who is both a policeman and discus record holder always turns up at your birthday party. He was probably even present when you were born and had the police choir sing you into the world. He's the mirror you travel with through the years. Because when you grow up, Oli, you're going to be a policeman and discus-record holder too. Yes and somewhere in town there'll be a little nephew who you'll always visit on his birthday.

Oli, when you see your uncle's figure through the frosted glass in the door to your flat in the basement, all the children in our street crowd around. Oli, you open the door and, shush, in he walks with a parcel under his arm.

Over the years he's given you a football game with players on springs and a shiny police car with uniformed American cops inside. Yes he's already started to prepare you for your career. Later you hope to sit in a police car yourself and drive through the city.

Thanks to your uncle in the police who laughs with his horse's teeth as he walks in through the door and rocks like a giant, your birthday parties are the favorite in our street, because who doesn't want to meet the sports page in the flesh?

I, Johann Petursson, I do, for one.

And the climax of every birthday party invariably arrives when your uncle stands up from the table and plonks himself down with a plate of cake on the soft sofa, and we crewcut boys in our nylon shirts queue up (you first, Oli) and take turns at feeling his muscles.

So you can just imagine…

THE RECORDER AND THE ANORAK

…that in some way or another, the presence of me, Johann Petursson, will be announced at Oli's birthday party.

Yes tomorrow either I will be among the guests at the birthday party or they will be among me. I intend to see the sports page in the flesh. I intend to witness the discus thrower walking in through the door. Yes I really think there should be a clause in the police oath allowing me to feel your uncle's muscles once a year.

I watch the guppies in the fish tank. They support my cause. At some time I shall extend their territorial waters too, by buying a larger fish tank. Hey guppies, the Convention on the Law of the Sea and all that. I turn on the light inside the plastic globe that my brother keeps on his desk. I reach over for the recorder that my Aunt Sigga gave me last Christmas.

My name's Johann.

I've got it all worked out.

I put the recorder to my lips and play two flat notes. Aw, recorder, you never hear what I'm saying. All you ever want is "The Bells of St. Clement's" or that sort of thing. Why should I waste my breath on that kind of kid's stuff?

All the notes are flat.

No, locking yourself away in your room is sheer isolationism, an old trick from the fairy tales. Yes, diametrically opposed to my strategies. With a few absurd notes on the recorder, princes attracted dogs and women. I'd rather put some exploding caps in my pocket.

Bugger the recorder.

I want neither dogs nor women.

I want to go to Oli's birthday party.

If I wanted to use music to underline my demand, which is Oli's birthday party period finito and amen, I'd rather play Danny Kaye on a wind-up gramophone than have an entire recorder ensemble backing me.

I contemplate the recorder; perhaps the notes seeped out along the walls in the timber houses of the middle ages. But in the four-story sanded concrete building where I live two floors above Oli, I can scarcely be heard outside the window.

Yes, Oli, while you're lying in bed with a flannel on your forehead I'm playing the recorder. Even with all the windows open you can't hear, because the recorder doesn't outplay the clunking of Ranka's wooden clogs on the floor above you but below me, the clunking that we always wake up to in the mornings. Yes and even if the birds carried flat recorder notes down to you in the basement, you'd just stick your fingers in your ears so the message of the music would go right over your head. I tell you once and I tell you again: on the third floor the recorder player is always alone.

The walls lock up the magic.

So I, Johann Petursson, say unto you kids heading off to buy recorders at Sigrid Helgadottir's Music Shop, you ought to spend your money on a speckled Dairy Queen ice cream instead or take a bus ride around the city!

Yes if, like the princes of old, I wanted to contact a fair-tressled princess I wouldn't play the recorder for her; I'd send in a record request to *Teenagers' Choice*, fiery burning words of love or that sort of thing. Today, broadcasting one's thoughts is the done thing; that some people do so with recorders in their mouths just goes to show how far they are behind the times.

I don't want any princess.

My name is Johann and I want to go to Oli's birthday party, not flying through a recorder but walking down the steps to the basement instead, with a matchbox car in one hand.

I've worked it all out down to the very last detail.

Number one two and five: the recorder cannot break the isolation of a boy who has not been invited to a birthday party.

Bugger the recorder.

Recorder, I shall break you in two. You're only the mediator of suffering. Plimp. Yes broken on the floor you will console no one further and the wind will not inspire you when I've thrown you in the wastepaper basket. Ha ha ha—I just hope my mother doesn't catch on…

Sorry, Aunt Sigga, I'll never be a recorder virtuoso.

I know what I'll do.

Tomorrow on your birthday, Oli, I'll ring the bell on the steps to the basement… ding-dong… and pretend there's nothing wrong. If I'm not invited to your birthday I'll just invite myself. Oli, I pay no heed to your message in the story.

I know what I'll do.

If Oli throws me out I won't start crying. At my age tears need to be used sparingly if they're to be believed. Preferably only cry once a month.

No, I do not flirt with rebellious instincts. Like the yogis in the Himalayas I shall achieve my aims by peaceful means. In the manner of Gandhi I shall reveal my sorrow to the world without a single windowpane being broken. And there will be no riots anywhere on Earth.

If, for example, I were to burn the whole birthday party alive with Bengal matches, I wouldn't have any friends left the day afterward. And later, on the grounds of such an act of arson, I would be prevented from joining the fire brigade, which would be a major setback if I am not accepted anywhere as a barber.

Oli, if you throw me out I won't lie down in the pit in my father's garage either. I reserve that for when I want to talk to myself alone. When I want to flick through my thoughts like pages in a philosophical treatise. It would be an act of sheer surrender to lie down on top of the darkness in the pit, on top of the speechless darkness with its million voices. Although talking to the darkness can be fun, it's just as futile as playing the recorder when a whole birthday party is at stake…

No listen to this: really I hope Oli throws me out. I know you don't believe me. But I really hope Oli lump-head throws me out.

If Oli threw me out it would be tantamount to an invitation to the party. You see, I, Johann Petursson, would then walk up the freshly polished stairs, this time to fetch not my father's hammer but my anorak.

My anorak.

My strategy is wrapped up in my anorak. It's as important to me as Kennedy's hairstyle is to him. If medieval princes had had anoraks, the idea of using recorders would never have entered their minds. Yes while the recorder reconciles the young instrumentalist in his room to loneliness, the anorak underlines it in a tragic fashion. Underlines it zipped right up to the neck. Each time I go out in my anorak I see myself as a protest march. I present invisible demands. And the pinnacle of all the injustice in this world, that's when you, Oli, revoke my invitation to your birthday party. Argol: I shall protest in my anorak.

Yes listen to this. If Oli throws me out I'll go up and fetch my anorak. Then I'll put it on, go behind the house, and stand in front of Oli's sitting-room window to stress my exclusion. I just hope it will be raining, because few things give the invisible protest march of the anorak more evocative power than big, heavy raindrops.

I can see it all.

Going behind the house in my anorak zipped right up and tied tight at the neck, going behind the house in the rain, alone in front of the sitting room window and waiting for Oli's mother to see me. When she sees me, Oli, she'll come to the window and say:

—Johann, what are you doing out there on your own, love, why don't you come in?

I see the guppies in the fish tank smiling at my designs.

They swim up to the glass with their fishy mouths to remind me of the extension of territorial waters.

I can see it all.

I curl up my lower lip. A tear, one tear false as a raindrop, rolls down my cheek. I feel as sorry for myself as your mother does. Snuffling, I walk around the house. Down to the steps to the basement. In the hall I take off my anorak. I remove the protest banner of the mind. Underneath I'm wearing my best clothes.

It's like me, Johann Petursson, having my own birthday tomorrow, sitting here on my bed looking at the pieces of the recorder that stand up out of the wastepaper basket as the guppies swim through my mind.

THE TOYSELLER IN THE ROCKING CHAIR

So with the perfect balance of a violin that has never been played I walk, a minor political party confident of triumph, into the kitchen ready to protest against all the injustice of the world in my anorak and ask my mother to give me some money to buy a matchbox car for Oli's birthday present.

Mother is good.

Mother is kind.

—Yes of course you need to buy something nice for him, she says and reaches out for a jam jar on the kitchen shelf. In the jam jar are a few rolled-up notes.

Mother fishes out a blue twenty-five-crown note with a picture of National Governor Magnus Stephensen on the front, bends down and kisses me. My mother seems to have tossed all hammers away into oblivion.

Mother: Yes do buy something nice for Oli and if there's any change you can keep it. You've been keeping yourself amused in your room so nicely today.

Yes Mother is good, Mother is kind. I can keep the change which of course immediately prompts the thought of whether there isn't something cheaper than a matchbox car to find for

Oli, since measured in terms of chocolate-coated nuts or licorice straws, the change can have a great deal to say. There you see that I, Johann Petursson, am an economically conscious young man.

I walk along the street with the twenty-five-crown note in my pocket, my face screwed up and my head crewcut in the brightness. The note crumples in my hand. I feel the smell of money infusing my palm.

The street is pitted with holes.

The brightness is gray.

The odd beam of light dropping through the clouds straight into my face, the clouds like countless men in overcoats rushing off to work.

I walk along the street. In expectation, before I've made it halfway to the shop, my head changes into a whole toyshop; I feel the toys squirming in my stomach too. Tractors roll out of boxes and heaps of children's books with cover illustrations of freckled girls in the sun pile up in my head. Perhaps I should spend the change before I buy something or other for Oli.

Fortunately I don't meet anyone on the way. It's such a good feeling to be alone with money in your pocket.

When I enter the toyshop, which is really a bookshop, I see the toyseller, an old man in a gray cardigan, asleep in the rocking chair where he is accustomed to sit when business is slack.

An upturned Danish women's magazine is lying on his lap. It's warm and sultry inside the toyshop with the fan off. In proportion to the silence that in other respects reigns, the toyseller is breathing noisily. Asleep, he's a little like a man who has been sentenced to blow up the same balloon for life.

I look around.

When the toyseller snores, the rocking chair creaks. Perhaps I ought to take all the metronomes off the shelf and set them going, tick-tock, tick-tock. Yes and maybe wind up the bells that play Christmas carols, the bells over there in the corner and go and tell the butchers in the co-op shop that the toyseller's gone mad. Yes don't you reckon it'd be fun watching the porters come in from the yellow lunatic asylum with straightjackets, with bare-legged nurses leading the procession.

Yes don't you reckon—the toyseller in his gray cardigan might think the butchers in their white coats were white-clad angels and deduce that he'd fallen asleep reading the Danish women's magazine to wake up in another world, yes in heaven where everything is so white-clad and pure.

Ha ha—no.

I look around again.

Is it better if the toyseller is asleep or awake when I'm going to give Oli a matchbox car for his birthday?

In the emptiness I feel the shop filling up with people.

But there's no one.

Not a soul.

Outdoors, a woman in a poplin coat says that regular bread is the healthiest.

I look around again. Nothing. Not even a clockwork mouse. Not even a jumping rubber frog. Mentally I arrange myself on the shelf in case anyone wanted to buy me.

The toyseller sneezes in his sleep.

Ah, now I know: there's a stepladder under the counter there, the little stepladder the toyseller uses to reach things placed high up.

Then he turns his back on the world and the patches on the elbows of his gray cardigan shine as he reaches out for, let's say, the bald-headed dolls up there.

The stepladder.

I take the little stepladder and put it in front of the shelf of cars. I want to fetch the little white matchbox Jaguar. Maybe I ought to empty all the matchboxes so the toyseller can start selling emptiness in boxes. I want to...

When my left hand stretches out toward the matchbox car my eyeballs roll to the right. Quite involuntarily. They roll to the right. On the shelf above, I see the red fire engine I decided to get before I was born.

The red fire engine has a hose that sprays water when you

press a rubber button behind the handle for winding the hose in. When you push it along the floor the sirens flash.

Gardar's got a red fire engine like that.

I want a fire engine like that.

—You can't have everything that Gardar's got, I hear my father say through my memory.

And holy Moses.

Beside the fire engine there's Mickey Mouse on a scooter with a key in his belly and beside him are Huey, Dewey, and Louie as a trio on double bass, drums, and piano. And endless toys and more toys.

My eyes pop in and out of my head like a yo-yo.

And behind me the old toyseller's asleep in his rocking chair, sleeping as if he intended me to come in while he dreamed his way into a Danish women's magazine.

If he wakes up.

If he wakes up.

My heart bounces like a man wearing springs on his feet.

I can hear it.

It's bouncing.

Hesitating on the stepladder, wobbly-kneed, I stretch out my left hand for the matchbox car. I stretch out. The matchbox car slips into my pocket at forty-five degrees, like a rat. I can keep the change. I move the stepladder a little and stretch my right hand out for the fire engine.

Aw that's enough… enough… No, Mickey Mouse insists on coming with me on his scooter, and Huey, Dewey, and Louie follow hard on his heels.

I put the toys on the counter.

I feel… Now my heart's ticking like a time bomb.

If anyone comes in I'll explode.

The butcher's shop can keep all the shreds.

But no one comes. It was yesterday that the housewives came to get the women's magazines. The shop was packed right out into the car park and the toyseller fussed around under his gray cardigan until his red forehead began to sweat.

Yes if there weren't any women's magazines, bookshops would probably disappear. But no one comes. The burglar alarm's still being invented abroad so it only goes off in the heads of class-conscious shopkeepers. The toyseller in the rocking chair will surely be expelled from the retailers' association for lack of feeling for his goods. He's asleep while I take his toys. Maybe I should order a van and open a toyshop on the other side of the estate. If the cash register weren't so heavy and I weren't so small I'd throw a sweet-feast for the whole street, yes the Sodom and Gomorrah of confectionery.

If anyone…

I stand at the counter. I'm like a toy among the toys. I feel Mickey pricking me the moment I take hold of his black ears and Huey, Dewey, and Louie press their beaks right up against me. The only difference is that I'm breathing.

Now the toyseller smacks his lips in his sleep. My God, if he wakes up, if he wakes up, because I've undone the buttons of my check shirt and now I'm stuffing the fire engine, Mickey, and Huey, Dewey, and Louie inside.

Ow, my woollen vest pricks me.

I'll make the toys look like a paunch.

If the toyseller wakes up now, smacking his lips with the Danish women's magazine on his lap, he'll go stark raving bonkers. He'll take all the toys off me and send me up to his son who does weight training at the sports club.

I don't care if I get the buttons in the wrong holes.

I tuck my V-neck pullover back down, stretch it over the paunch. My white-soled gumboots rush out through the door with me.

Outside it has started to rain.

The street is pitted with holes.

The clouds gray.

The twenty-five-crown note still lies rolled up in my pocket. I can keep the change. I listen to the raindrops take a drum solo. I can keep the change.

LICORICE ARITHMETIC

It takes the toyshop door a long time to close behind me. I hear the door click shut in the raindrops. I turn around. No I'm so frightened I don't look around. I feel warm water flowing around my crotch and down my thighs. I-I've wet myself. Up in the sky the clouds circle in grayish puffs. They're like tobacco smoke exhaled by giants and the raindrops leak down the neck of my check shirt.

Up in the clouds the toyseller's sitting in his rocking chair. His son rushes by holding his weights in a chariot of fire with the whole sports club in the back seat. Beneath my pullover the fire engine's blue siren is flashing.

I don't walk along the street, but run along the alley between the back-to-back houses, run as fast as my gumbooted feet can carry me. Yes I run between the houses so no one can see my toy paunch wobbling in front of me. Sometimes I can feel the toyseller rocking at my heels.

I know exactly where I'm going, past the slippery scaffolding, past sitting-room windows with flowers in them, with dark-brown mud beneath the soles of my gumboots and a gang of bandits out of the *Tales from Hoffman* in my head.

I know exactly where I'm going. Yes I'm heading under the steps behind our garage. I'm going to hide the toys there.

They tumble out from my check shirt. I cover them with sticks.

I was lucky.

The moment I get home my mother asks me to go down to the basement to fetch some potatoes. I was lucky, because a better hiding place than our basement storeroom with its smell of string sacks and old apples could hardly be imagined.

I walk down the freshly polished stairs and the dim steps to the basement. For a moment I feel I'm on my way to see Oli and four balloons grow out of my fingertips. I go into reverse by one day. But I'm going to fetch some potatoes since I'm holding the storeroom key in one hand.

I open the door.

A bare-bummed light bulb hangs from the ceiling. The moment I turn it on the whole storeroom lights up. It's full of toilet rolls now, which my father has bought wholesale. There are enough toilet rolls to keep your arse wiped this side of the next war.

With the door still open I pop along the corridor to where the other storerooms are, through the laundry room and out by the back door. I crawl under the steps and get the toys.

The toys don't look as though they miss the toyseller. It can't be any fun hanging around on a shop shelf all day long. While I'm sorting out the potatoes I drive the flashing fire engine along the wooden shelf where my mother keeps her homemade rhubarb jam.

Mickey Mouse cycles in clockwork along the gray fusebox and I can almost hear Huey, Dewey, and Louie playing cool jazz with a soft piano solo and unobtrusive bass, like I sometimes hear on the radio.

When I've finished gathering all the potatoes I hide the fire engine behind the jam jars. Mickey and Huey, Dewey, and Louie go into an Egill Skallagrimsson beer crate. I hide all the toys. Except the matchbox car of course, which I take up with me along with the potatoes.

Of course I'd forgotten to work out all the technicalities, since when I get back upstairs my mother asks, as if it's somehow connected with the potatoes:

—Well, Joey, what did you find for Oli?

—A sort of matchbox car.

—And how much did it cost?

—Co-co-cost.

—Yes how much did it cost. You hardly got it for nothing.

I put my hands in my pockets. I feel the rolled-up twenty-five-crown note. I don't know what to say; it's as if mother can see right through me… the toyseller is sitting behind her and laughing. Yes how could my mother think I got the matchbox car for nothing when she gave me the money for it herself?

—Yes but you said I could keep the change.

I'm just trying to change the subject while I look for numbers in my head. You can't really say I got the toys for nothing if you count the desperate thumping of my heart in the toyshop.

—Yes, yes, says my mother, you can keep the change, but the car must have cost something. You don't always have to get so worked up, Johann.

Now it came in useful that the painter who was a wizard and painted the attic had taught me a few snatches of multiplication tables while we were listening to dance music on the radio for a few rainy days last summer and he rolled magic letters onto the wall, in his speckled painter's overalls with a cap made out of old newspapers. I used to lean up against the damp walls while various parts of multiplication tables stuck like a chant into my head. But somehow here in the kitchen with my mother I can't get the numbers to rhyme in my mind, not until I re-establish spiritual contact with the painter. In this instance I estimate the equivalent of eight licorice sticks to be a reasonable amount for the change I was allowed to keep. To work out the result I have to visualize the equation in a couple of microseconds; that's to say I have to imagine I've spent the whole twenty-five crowns on licorice, there's no other way I can subtract eight licorice sticks from the total. But when I've managed this, pronto, with flashes of lightning coming out of my head, when I've subtracted eight licorice sticks from the total I'm left with the matchbox car costing twenty-three crowns both in numbers and letters, while to allow for Iceland's permanent inflation I allocate an indeterminate size to each individual straw of licorice.

So on the basis of the wizard painter's applied mathematics I tell my mother:

—Tw-tw-twenty-three, the car cost twenty-three. I'm gonna put the change in my money box.

In fact this is the first arithmetic test I have ever taken, using neither paper nor pencil, in the kitchen doorway with my mother. But if the toyseller goes on sleeping in his rock-ing chair every day there are clearly more futile things I could learn than arithmetic.

I clutch the twenty-five-crown note as I go into my room. I take hold of the money box on the windowsill. The money box is shaped like a pocket notebook with gilt pages. But the difference is that the money box cannot be opened like a book. It's locked with a secret key that only the cashiers at the banks have access to. The money box is engraved with the col-lective slogan of all banks in town—a penny saved is a penny earned—like the title on the cover of a book. Down in the corner the name of the bank is engraved with gilt lettering.

In the middle of the money box there's a slit with gilt metal teeth. When I push the twenty-five-crown note in, the metal teeth lift back and the box opens its mouth, somewhat reminiscent of a cat yawning: Goodbye Magnus Stephensen, farewell through the prison bars of money, see you at the cashier's. I just hope the factories go on making licorice.

I stand here empty-handed, smelling acrid with money. I go to the toilet and turn on the taps. The moment the soap begins frothing between my hands I feel the toyseller episode is over, although of course I, Johann Petursson, have no say in the matter. Now he's sure to be waking up in his rocking chair; he rubs the sleep out of his eyes as soon as he sees the stepladder's not where it's usually kept. His eyes perk up since someone's clearly tidied up the toys on the shelf. He's like a man going nuts. He vaguely recalls a dream full of bare-legged nurses.

My hands are no longer acrid with the smell of money, but scented with soap. Isn't smelling like soap a sign of alle-giance to the Constitution? Anyway, my heart's beating differ-ently. I look at my face in the mirror, in a few seconds I feel the earth revolving around me.

Down in the basement Oli's started counting the minutes that tick away on the kitchen clock. He looks up at the ceil-ing with a lump on his crewcut head and hopes that the floor two floors above him will give way beneath my feet because I, who stand in front of the bathroom mirror travelling around the earth with the earth revolving around me, I hit him over the head with a hammer once.

Tomorrow I will pursue my strategy to the limit. Yes Johann Petursson's spiritual conscription will be launched. On the basement steps, facing you, Oli, I will see whether I need to resort to my anorak or whether the matchbox car will suffice as an admission ticket. I at least want to be present to see your uncle in the police's annual muscle show. I just hope it will be classical in form, even though a modern undercurrent is none the worse, at least from a literary point of view.

CROSSING YOUR TOES TO TELL A LIE

Here I am now at my destination.

Two days after the blow on the head beside the oil tank I'm standing here facing the door to the basement where Oli ran in crying. Yes I'm standing here two days later with a matchbox car in one hand. It could be the devil going to church on a Sunday because I haven't been invited.

Smartly dressed.

Yes who isn't smart when he's on the verge of realizing a yearning that's lasted two days. Yes two days that have taken as long to pass as a whole era in the history of Man. Yes in spite of my milk teeth I'm really ninety.

I'm standing here.

Like a fireman, I'm prepared for everything.

My eyes are as big as the drain in the corner.

Here I stand. I can do no more.

Someone empties a washtub over my head and a water pistol is thrust between my buttocks. Up with your hands down with your trousers says a voice out of the air. Behind me stands the world with a red neckerchief tied across its mouth.

On the steps to the basement, prepared for anything, me:

Yes as predicted the bell goes ding-dong when I press it.

Ding-dong. It's me, Johann Petursson, standing here with a matchbox car outside the door. It's me...

If only Oli's birthday were tomorrow... Or I were standing here wizened with age with a walking stick, seventy years on.

Ding-dong.

I'm ready to take to my heels if Oli appears in the doorway. I bow my head. I look the drain in the eye. I'm not ready to take to my heels. The broken recorder stands up out of the wastepaper basket of the mind. My thoughts turn to my anorak.

Oli.

Luckily enough it's your mother who answers the door, and not you, Oli, with that lump on your head, not you but your mother with flour in her hair, untying a white apron.

—Well Johann, nice to see you.

I bow my head. I wish I were invisible. I don't think it's nice to see me.

Your mother looks hammers at me.

As I go into the hall a mixer stops in the kitchen. Your sister Birna is helping with the cakes.

Otherwise the flat's silent.

Perhaps it was Oli's birthday yesterday. Or perhaps it's all prearranged and you, Oli, are standing behind your mother with a lump on your head, ready to pinch and scratch me. You can't tear my hair out, since Anton the barber has shaved it all away. I'm almost bald.

But behind your mother there's no Oli.

What—what, isn't there any birthday party?

Oli, did you disappear in a puff of smoke with the magic power of the hammer to hold your party up in the clouds?

I take my shoes off in the hall. Your mother silently shows me the door to your room. Yes if I'm not the first one at the party then everyone's left.

Oli.

You must have sensed I was coming, since when I walk into your room you're sitting there with your legs folded, contemplating the world with a lump sticking out of your head;

yes it's as if the doorbell I just rang didn't affect you in the slightest. Don't children usually stand guard by the doorbell on their birthdays? I almost jump back out of the room.

You must have sensed it, because the moment you notice me standing in the doorway with my feet on the threshold you start rummaging in a toolbag full of plastic tools.

I stand in the doorway and look you over; I haven't seen you since I dropped the balloons onto your white bedclothes where you lay with a damp flannel on your forehead.

Now, two days later, the lump's grown.

It's standing up out of your head like a mountain. When you turn round to see me, the first guest at your birthday party, it looks at me too.

The lump's a mountain.

Out of your crewcut head, an eye watches from a mountain.

When I try to smile I'm met by big deep eyes that roll round in circles. I think you might turn into a dog and start barking. No you turn back round with your legs folded and begin rummaging again in the toolbag that your grandfather gave you for Christmas.

Just as if I'm invisible. Just as if I don't exist. I feel like going into the toilet and flushing myself away. I don't know what to do with myself.

I'm wearing a white nylon shirt and black terylene trousers. I shove my hands at forty-five degrees into my pockets. I look down my shirt and count the buttons—one, two, three, four...

I feel my lips moving. Happy birthday, I want to say. But it's just like someone's tugging at my vocal chords. I can't hear the words I say myself.

Oli looks up. He looks at me. Oli, you don't say anything.

—Here you are. I hand him the parcel tied up with a ribbon.

Oli.

Now it was in many respects fortunate that I hit you over

the head with a hammer, because before doing so I was set on giving you a parcel which you in your greed would have torn undone with hands like lightning and then... then a spring would have shot out and up your nose. Now I can see you would have exploded. I would have had to scrape your heart off the light switch.

Oli opens the parcel painstakingly as if he wants to keep the ribbon, or lazily as if he doesn't really want it at all. I don't know which. But when the parcel's lying there undone in front of him he takes the matchbox car, puts it to one side, and goes on rummaging in the toolbag.

Oli.

I'll tell you one thing, if you go on rummaging in tool-bags you'll be sent to work for the council and dig trenches all day long. For a moment I regret not giving you all the toys I took from the toyshop. Yes I could even have wrapped the sleeping toyseller up in his rocking chair and posted him to you in a parcel.

I lean up against the doorpost, let my eyes roam around the room hoping that little white carrier pigeons will come gliding in through the open window with an offer of concilia-tion. Or perhaps I should phone and order the Industrial Arbitrator from the government. There's a man who works for the state, you see, who reconciles all enemies.

I go on making conciliatory overtures, ready to sign my name to any ultimatum that Oli presents, even to stand on my hands or wiggle my ears in leapfrog position if he asks me. Yes I inch my way forward and ask whether he's blown up the balloons.

Oli says nothing.

Then one of the most brilliant tactics in the entire history of the world clicks like fingers inside my head, not entirely divorced from the wily Machiavellian tricks of the modern age although tracing its pedigree all the way back to Jesus:

—Hey, Oli, I say, if we make friends again you can hit me over the head tomorrow. I'll take the hammer again.

I ask Oli just as if I'm in control of all the peace talks in the world, chairman, vice president, and all the rest. It's as if an invisible hand pinches Oli's bum. He leaps to his feet and says:

—Can I really?

—Yeah tomorrow—n-n-not today.

—Tomorrow. Promise?

—Promise.

Of course I make sure to do what all politicians always do in all important negotiations, in all peace talks. I make sure to cross my toes to tell a lie. I'm also lucky that Oli neither asks me to put up ten fingers to God nor cross my heart and hope to die. Tomorrow—bah tomorrow, there'll be no problem wriggling my way out of this one then. Yes, easier at least than here in this room, where you, Oli, are the center of the world.

Translation by Bernard Scudder

AMERICA

by Hallgrímur Helgason

Alðalbjörg Ketilsdóttir in all her clothes. On the shore at Tangi in the autumn of 1889. A Saturday, with a silent sea. The woman young and red-cheeked. In all her skirts, long and heavy. The parents dead and four siblings on the way to the sea. The boat waits at the foremost rock. She and her three brothers climb aboard. With a look of fear in her eyes. And the coal-black ship out in the fjord: four sails. Four white sails like giant empty sheets of paper in an unwritten biography. And above them, far in the distance, away in the highlands, just as many ash-gray clouds like smoke signals, a message from the volcanoes of Iceland. Farewell? Don't go? Fifty people on the shore, with bag and baggage. Iron-ore-red faces in black shawls and jackets. America written on every brow. The great country, the great word, the great promise. And a half-grown, homespun boy following on. A shambling country lad with a hungry look.

From *The Author of Iceland*, a novel.

Þórður from Bakki. On a trip to town with his father. Drawn to the shore by curiosity.

"I forgot my shawl," says the girl all at once, and clambers back off the boat, getting her feet wet. Moving heavily, wearing all her dresses, she waddles through the crowd; the people on their way to board. Her brothers surprised, one of them picks up a garment, some kind of shawl, a large thing, with a bottle in his other hand. "Alla! It's here!" She turns round on the boulder and thinks for a lifelong moment. Then turns back and continues her way up the shore. Her brothers: "Alla! Alla!" Then they sit down again and had a drink.

"Will you marry me?"

The lump of candy nearly went down the wrong way. She stood before him like a heap of clothes with a large nose and two round eyes. After all, he'd only intended to buy a bridle, not a wife. He knew who she was. She was from the folk at Langanes. The youngest of Ketill's children. She'd stayed the night with them on the way back from the trading station. She had been fourteen then. Now she was seventeen. He was twenty. The second-youngest lad in Bakki. He was skillful with wood. Had made the famous chest. She'd seen him earlier in the store. Trying on a bridle. She thought him silly but possibly clever: she wasn't sure—smiled when the others laughed. He had seen her earlier in the store. She was with her brothers. They were buying *brennivín* and dried cod for the journey. Icelanders on their way abroad. He saw she was watching him, so he put the bridle over his head, thought it clever, but felt a fool. "Have the colts at Bakki started buying their own bridles?" one of her brothers had said. Then they laughed. His father: "Yes, the boy must be tamed. You're going to America?" "Aye, this country's going to hell. You can't even get a woman round here any more. There's been no fucking at Langanes for two years now." They laughed again. They looked each other in the eye. "It's bad for the country to be seeing the back of men like you," said Þórður the elder. "But it's worse for us to have to see the back of this Arctic asshole! Ha ha! The holes in them bitches got frozen up last winter. We had to re-christen the ram and call him Icebreaker! Ha ha ha!" they all laughed together. "Well, America! They say that over there a man can't chop wood for all the trees! And the grass comes up to your chin! You have to cut it down before you can even cut it! Ha ha ha!" said one of them. "And you don't have to fuck to keep warm!" added another. "Ha ha ha." Great brothers all, and drunk as lords after their visit to the duty-free store in Tangi, three hours before departure. "Yes, America," said the farmer from Bakki slowly and thoughtfully. "I have always considered Leif Ericsson a fortunate man for coming home again, but I wish you every blessing—watch out for the red-skins. May Iceland be with you, lads." "Yes sir!" they said gal-lantly, in English, and that was probably the first time this expression was heard in our land. She watched the old man leave the store with his son. And then her brothers continued their patter. "I have always considered old Leif Ericsson a for-tunate man, ha ha ha! The old windbag. May Iceland be with you, indeed! May this damned iceblock land sink to hell and dissolve down there in Old Nick's cauldron! Skol!" She looked horror-struck at the horror-stricken storekeeper. At least some-one was glad to be getting them out of the country.

She stood facing him on the shore. Transfixed. Stared at him.

"Hurry up. The boat's leaving."

"For America?"

"Yes. They're going to America. I don't want to go to America."

"Oh? Why not? Why don't you want to go to America?"

"I don't know. My brothers, maybe. They're halfwits."

"Halfwits, eh? No, they're just drunk."

"They're always drunk. And when they're drunk, then… Will you marry me? Please do."

"I… eh… how should I… Can you spin yarn?"

"Yes. I can do everything. I can sew sheeps' stomachs, dye clothes, gut fish and full wool and… I can also mow."

"Mow?"

"Yes, I can mow."

"Well, I've never seen a girl mow. Girls are no good at mowing."

"I'll show you. If you'll... marry..."

She could hear her brother calling from the shore behind her. Her name was carried close: he was coming to fetch her.

"Quick, you must..."

Decide. In the boy's mind an ocean surged, the entire Atlantic. On one side was Iceland, on the other America. He was in love with the storekeeper's daughter. Sigríður Soebech. Why hadn't she been in the store earlier? She was always serving in the store. He'd prepared a whole dramatic spectacle for her. Putting on the bridle and staging a show. A horse staging a horse show. She would fall for it completely. But then she wasn't working. Why wasn't she working? He'd been hanging around the store for a whole two hours while his father went to talk to Gestur in the Quiet House. Then on the way down to the shore he had met her, she was with Jón. Jón Grímsen! The fellow didn't even know how to use a knife. The good-for-nothing from Gunna's house. Were they together? She hadn't even looked at him when they met.

He saw the girl's brother approaching, turning heads as he plodded unsteadily through the crowd of emigrants. People had started to look. Perhaps here a final memory of the old country was being born. A boy and a girl. A boy and a girl and a whole ocean between those two words: yes and no. Iceland and America. He had her life in his hands. His father was getting the train of packhorses ready up at Slakki. They were about to set off. They had no saddle with them. Of course there were four horses, but what would his father say if he arrived from the shore with a whole woman?

"I'll bear you ten children."

Þórður looked at her, that face. Not a bad-looking face, though the nose was rather thickset. He had had a different nose in mind. She stared fixedly at him.

"Eleven."

He looked away from her, out at the crowd of people who had now formed a semi-circle around them. Sigrídur was nowhere to be seen. The brother was now coming up to them, red in the face, weary with drink:

"Alla, what are you thinking of, you silly girl?" he said, pulling at her wrist, but she stood firm, tried one last time:

"Twelve children."

The lad moved away. He did not like the look of this.

"Aye, it's all the same to him, so come on, I say," said the brother. There were twelve of them, the brothers and sisters from Langanes.

"Thirteen! Thirteen children!" said the woman, now with such great determination that the homespun boy from Bakki had had enough. And all those eyes staring at him! He had to bring this to an end, looked at her dead-drunk brother, down at the gravel of the shore, then up at her, riveted his gaze on her nose, that large and determined nose, and said:

"All right, then."

Translation by David McDuff

A RUSH OF WINGS

by Þórarinn Eldjárn

SHE HAD OFTEN heard stories about eagles taking lambs and even children, but she did not see it as it arrived and had no time to be afraid, let alone to try to escape or shoo it away. She only heard a strange shuffling sound that she thought at first was the wind where she sat from morning to night at the edge of a field below the coastal farm and looked out at the sea. That heavy cold shuffling that she has never since been able to forget, the rush of eagles' wings.

There was quite a wind, too, and it seemed to be rising. Dark strands ruffled on the surface of the sea and the sun picked out patch upon patch of white surf. Then this shadow appeared that surrounded her and sent a shudder through her. At first she thought a cloud had passed across the tentative spring sun and adumbrated exactly the spot on which she sat that morning. She was going to shift her position, but as she moved it locked her in its talons and the only sensation she registered was a swift upheaval into the sky. Her mother had dressed her in several layers of knitted sweaters until she looked almost like a ball of yarn. After her little brother drowned in the river, her mother wanted to protect her from everything all the time. She was hardly allowed to leave the farm. No climbing, no wading, no going too close to the sea, no allowing herself to become cold—and she always had to have that red woollen bonnet so that it was easy to see her.

It made no difference how short a distance she moved away from the farm, her mother would immediately start calling and searching and reminding her. And she was so preoccupied with the little baby now who was always sick and was proba- bly not going to survive much longer than all the others. It was the new baby's fault that her brother had fallen into the river. Her mother could not keep a close enough eye on him, and he slipped out of the house and waded into the water.

She saw those terrifying wings that battled the air on either side of her and wondered whether she was dead, too, and had become an angel. But that could not be because then she would have been blue and cold and placed in the ground. Instead she was rising high in the air. And now she had for- gotten everything except what she could see. She saw the farm become a tiny bulge and the mountains spread out and disappeared and new valleys and rifts appeared everywhere between them and there was all the snow that had fallen that winter, still there. Halfway across the mountains, she saw into the valley where she would come to live when she was a grown woman.

As they flew, she felt herself overcome by an inexpressible sense of joy that came from being lifted up, a sense of elation. She felt separate to herself, in a luxurious sense of happiness that she would always remember and by which she would judge all other sensations. She wished with all her soul that this feeling would never diminish but this wish was not to be because the bird seemed to her to be descending. They were directly above the island and she saw how the ground approached at great speed, as if she were being pulled toward it, and suddenly her happiness turned to fear. The bird dropped her just before they landed and she fell against some stones and grazed her knees and her hands a little and began to cry out so loudly that the bird flew away from her and perched farther up on the scree-covered slopes and waited to see what was in store. It was as if he had been drawn there.

She realized that she was alone there now, out on the island, and could not scale the cliff face to call to the people on the island for help. Moreover, the farms were on the far side and no one ever ventured to this end. When the eagle took off again with a loud clapping sound, she ran after it a short distance and spread her arms before falling, as if she were bidding it to take her again, not to leave her behind.

"See the eagle," shouted the boatswain who had lain down in the hull to take a nap. "Isn't that a lamb it has in its damned talons?"

The fishermen lifted their oars and looked over their shoulders just in time to see where the bird landed high up on the cliffs with its burden. It soared high above them, but they could no longer see what it had been carrying. They were just north of the island, rowing their way home along the coast west of the fjord.

"Lamb? It looked to me as if it had a red bonnet," said the youngest man, who had the best vision.

"Probably blood," said the boatswain. "They're merciless, those birds."

It was getting more and more blustery and they were not going to risk taking a detour to the island to save a solitary lamb. It was also highly unlikely that it was still alive. But the man who had seen the bonnet was not to be persuaded otherwise and, besides, the prey was unusually large if it was a lamb. They had to investigate this, whatever the cost. He was insistent and persuasive and had his way in the end.

As they rowed their way toward the island, they shouted out continually and the boatswain fired a round from his gun. That scared the eagle and it flew, its talons empty, west across the fjord and quickly disappeared from view.

They reached the island and two of the strongest men were sent ashore. They reached the place where the girl lay unconscious and, yes, she did have a red bonnet.

She did not stir before they brought her down to the boat. No one knew who she was, but they knew for certain that she was not from the island and not from the west coast. On the other hand, they did not know the farms on the other side very well, and when she began to come to they quickly realized that she was from Nes. Even though the wind was blowing up threateningly, they felt there was no other course to be taken than to row east without delay and bring the child to its home.

The weather worsened, and as they reached the landing place at Nes, they thought it sufficient to have the strongest of them wade the short distance to shore while the others waited. They did not want the boat to become marooned or be smashed against the rocks and they had to make speed before the waves became to dangerous.

As soon as she appeared above the crest of the shoreline alone, her mother came running toward her, angry and welcoming at the same time and cross-examined her:

"Where have you been child? You don't know how hard we've been looking for you. Your father is up in the mountains and the boys have walked along the riverbank. Everyone's left off work to search. Where have you been? Answer me, child," she said and shook her. But the shaking soon turned to hugging. "How did you get those scratches and scrapes? Have you been climbing? I was so frightened. You mustn't frighten me like that. I thought I was going to lose you too, just as your little sister was beginning to recover."

She was about to tell her the whole story and was indeed beginning:

"You see, I…"

But she realized at the same time how absurd it was to think that anyone would believe her. The fishermen were far out of sight at sea, too. She did not want to be scolded for lying and making up tales on top of all this, so she continued:

"You see, I got all sleepy… so sleepy that I fell asleep right there at the edge of the field and I began to dream. Then when I woke up I found myself down on the beach."

Now the years have passed, and she almost believes herself that it had been as she said—until she got a view of the valley when she came over the slope and knew all the farms anew, just like the eagle had shown her when she was a child. As a housewife in the dales, she met again the sharp-eyed fisherman who first saw her red bonnet and then waded ashore with her. He was now a well-to-do farmer in that part of the country, and they quietly remembered the events between them. The rest of the crew had decided at the time to keep quiet about the incident in order not be admonished for not alerting the people at Nes. Nevertheless, she never mentioned the incident to man or child, in order to protect the men who saved her.

When she was very old, she finally began to tell her great-grandchildren about what happened, but they all thought it pure nonsense, that she was half-senile, and that is why the story has never been recorded.

Translation by Victoria Cribb

A ROOM UNDERGROUND

by GUÐBERGUR BERGSSON

IT HAD TAKEN me a considerable time to find a suitable room where we could meet inconspicuously, because it had to be a basement flat where you could walk straight in off the street. It was supposed to look as if you just happened to be passing by on the pavement but could suddenly turn around and vanish as if the earth had swallowed you. No other tenants could be there, because people who live in basement flats are curious rather than sympathetic about the business of other people who live in the same circumstances as they do, and deep down they despise them for not getting on in life and owning a house. Such people tend to listen out for the slightest sound, but do not make others suffer the consequences of anything improper that is revealed: theft, homebrew, prostitution, adultery, or contraband. The reason is not that such people are tolerant, but rather that they think to themselves

From *The Tormented Love That Lives in the Depths of the Soul*, a novel.

that by disapproving or interfering they would risk not finding out something else, something much worse, because scum can always sink lower. In this respect they show more understanding than healthy, well-off people. People who live in basement flats could be imagined as the last descendants of cave-dwellers who had their good and evil earth-spirits before we became civilized and acquired what is called the spirit of man. It is not only bad circumstances that drive people down into darkened holes to live; a particular type of character is motivated to live in apartments that are either in basements or on the ground floor.

I knew this from my own experience, having found out about it during my student years, when I arrived as a stranger in the city. I rented rooms in basements then, not only because I had little money and the rent was low, but also because I was still almost an earth-dweller in the full sense of the phrase. Since then I have always had warm feelings toward people who live in basements and sensed an affinity with them in my soul, even though I have gradually been advancing on the surface of a society that I despise in my heart, especially the embellishments on its smooth, neat coating. All the same, I have set up what is called a solid home with large, bright, and tasteful sitting rooms, four bedrooms, and a dream kitchen. This is not completely true—no one gets on in life by his own means alone—for in my case it is my connection with a childhood friend and his success or misfortune that have made me prosper or brought about my bad luck. So everything is tied up in a single whole and everything in a person's life can perish at one stroke.

While I was looking for a suitable place, I felt as if I had inspected almost every basement flat in the city and not been impressed by any of them. In the end I decided to advertise for a spacious storage room in a basement, imagining there had to be an old, wealthy widow hidden away somewhere, whose eyesight was failing and who had decided to rent out the children's old playroom that had long stood empty next to the laundry room. Probably my thoughts were turning back to the fine woman who had been my landlady once: she was a half-blind widow who did not care about her appearance and smelled of old food but was warm and sympathetic in the way that such women can be. They lift themselves above prejudice because of their futile experience of marriage, their children's misfortunes, and their blind eyes, and they love life from lack of interest rather than because they demand something for themselves. Far from it, they have long since given up expecting anything from existence and want younger people to enjoy the life which is inherently nothing—if anything can be described as inherently nothing—but which can accept countless things from others, and thereby become desirable to man.

I received one written offer after placing two advertisements in the newspapers. When I entered the house the old woman gave me a sardonic and suspicious look and either she did not entirely believe me or was amused that I was looking for a storage room; she asked:

—Isn't it really a little flat for your own needs that you want? They're easy to come by these days. That's because of the depression, which isn't a depression at all for us who knew the Depression—but at least I hope you're not like the young man I rented a room to once last year.

—What was he like? I asked in order to say something to this kindly woman. I had taken a liking to her the moment I saw her standing in front of me, slightly pot-bellied and unconsciously smoothing down the sides of her dress with her thumbs.

—No, how I ramble on, she answered, apparently realizing it. It wasn't now, it was at the time when there was almost no way of getting somewhere to live no matter how much money you offered. He took the room in the basement here but had his own notions about what a household involved, which were rather peculiar, because he rented the kitchen in one part of town, the bedroom in another, and the bath in a third, and rented the corridor in the city center.

She paused to regain her breath, because she was short-winded.

—Can you imagine such a combination? she asked.

—Yes, I replied, trying to fathom something about this labyrinth that the man was obviously putting together, and feeling convinced that its construction had to signify something special, perhaps even for me and my own life.

—Well, I was surprised, the woman continued, and I asked about that sort of living arrangement and he said, "I piece the household together in the Icelandic fashion: everything's a complete mess but it's all there in its place, and even though nothing fits together properly with anything else it might just hang together all the same." That was the way things were with him. Every bit of everything was there but nothing fitted together because each part was separate.

The old woman laughed the laugh of a female chain-smoker, ending with a strange rumbling noise and a yearning for tobacco, which she denied herself while she spoke. She was amused, not by what she was saying but probably by an associated memory from her own life within the four walls that she was renting to me.

—Let's hope he managed to fit in somehow with his own fragmentary lifestyle, I said, trying to express myself well, but not too well.

Then she answered cryptically:

—You must never take anything at face value. Some people live spread out and their lives follow that pattern. But it could be a reasonable life. And to tell you the truth I thought the young man had found a good way of joining up time as it passes with the time that has usually stood still while we live with other people and is lying smashed to pieces in the kitchen, maybe in the bedroom, the bathroom, the corridor, or the most unlikely places.

—Yes, I said. Maybe his marriage had worn thin and spread over the place.

—Could well be, she agreed. Of course he was being

unfaithful to his wife and he admitted that the most difficult part was getting the man who rented him the corridor to understand that he wanted a corridor that did not lead to a flat. "What bloody house has corridors like that?" the man shouted angrily, the way old people do when they are completely stumped. The young man explained to him that since the home he had set up was broken anyway, it was logical for him to rent a flat that was broken up all over town. That calmed the old man down and he realized how things stood and let the lad rent the corridor, but I said, "The women who wanted to rent you the bedroom didn't understand the logic of it in the same way, my dear." And he said, "It's their right to understand nothing more than suits them at any time."

—So what did you say? I asked.

—I just said, "Well then, where's your wife supposed to be in a strange setup like this? Is she supposed to chase you all over town?"

"No," he answered, "we're separated but live together in our own separate ways, so our renting arrangements have to follow suit. When I'm in the bathroom in one part of town she'll be in the kitchen in another, then in the bedroom while I'm in the room you're going to rent me here in the basement. But we'll meet with our hearts in the center of town, on the corridor that doesn't lead to any room, if we ever meet at all for fear of the old landlord who uses the corridor to stomp around in his fury at how bad the radio reception is."

She sighed distractedly, moved slightly and said:

—All this goes to show that the room here brings great luck in certain ways. They were queuing up outside for him.

—Hopefully it'll be the same for me, but not in the same way, I said.

That moment she opened a door inside the room and showed me a little bath and toilet there, then opened another door that led to a kitchenette, adding as she softly smacked her lips:

—You get both doors into the bargain. You can live here

and act as you please. I'm half-blind anyway, so I can't see anything, and I'm deaf as a post so I can't hear a thing unless you yell it into my earhole.

To prove it, she looked at me and spread her vacant eyes wide open without looking or scrutinizing, smacked her lips a few times, and went on:

—At a certain age, all men want to live life, and it's about time they did, too: you're that age. But my husband was too normal and proper to take his desires and fantasies any further than furnishing this little closet here to have to himself when he felt bad and was grumpy. He had his own private grumping room right up until he died, but I never set foot inside it and now I rent it out to other people who need the same sort of hideaway. What did you say you were going to do with it?

I told her the idea was to use it for writing or meditating.

—Yes, that's a healthy modern activity, she said. I can see now that you've got a lot of energy centers inside you.

—Actually I'm a teacher, I said.

She said "yes" and I thought she was going to add, "It's healthy because all teachers have countless energy centers inside them," but she suddenly turned vacant and seemed to have lost interest, just like someone who feels convinced he no longer needs to believe a word of what other people say, that it's all untrue and he knows better.

The old woman had the style of days gone by about her, not the incongruities and pretentiousness of the modern age that erases all kinds of time with endless hustling and bustling. Later it would turn out that she didn't spend all her time snooping around in the basement, although of course she did go there to take the occasional look into some boxes. That's the way things will be on earth for as long as bric-a-brac and old people exist. I would later discover the joy of making love while an old woman is rummaging around in bric-a-brac on the other side of the wall of pleasures; it is like sinning sweetly against female nature and defying the establishment. Old women have a vague notion of what's going on behind the wall paneling; their nature informs them of it and they rejoice that duty is being denied at last. That is why it is a delight to end up in such rare and difficult circumstances at the instigation of old women.

I could tell that her greatest wish was for me to throw my wife down a deep well and let her watch me and my partner making love on the wall around it as I bent over pretending to rescue her from the water. I thought to myself: The old woman wants my wife to think my screams are screams of fear about her being stuck in the cold water, that I'm afraid she'll give up splashing around and drown, but the old woman is amused because despite her blindness and deafness she can see and hear that the screams are caused by something different. I'm drowning my sorrows while I drown my wife. That amuses the old woman. But I'm not a murderer, except perhaps a murderer of souls. No, I'm a man who does his duties according to the rules, though I might bend them and not be able to keep myself completely in orbit in the solar system of morality.

—God bless the nature that forgets its solar system, the old woman would say at the end.

When I chance upon that old hag of a landlady she pretends not to see me and does not reply if I greet her. However, she does accept payment on the last day of each month, firmly but uninterestedly. I fear it every time, thinking she will scold me or tell me to move out, which she never does. Yet my heart starts pounding when I knock on the door and she seems to be at the end of her tether as she waits for me to pay up, but never opens the door more than just enough to stick one arm through and take the money. Then she hands me a receipt that she has already made out, and slams the door with a considerable rumpus.

Afterward, the slam echoes in time with the beating of my heart and my awful sense of guilt, but the strangest and worst thing of all is that despite her slamming the door—or perhaps because of it—I am seized by an almost irresistible urge to tell the old woman the truth and beg some comfort or understanding from her, even though I know that in such matters there is no comfort or understanding to be found from anyone. Everyone has to live with his emotions, live the life he has chosen for himself, and fall by it if need be or ward off the onslaughts that arise more from within and from doubts than from the outside. After all, few things are too puny to fail to defend themselves against attacks from anything other than themselves.

At first I noticed most of all how terrifying the silence in the house was. When I tried to check whether the old woman was snooping on me and I sat quietly, hardly daring to breathe, I thought the house would be crushed by the weight of the silence and tumble down upon me, crack apart with the sole purpose of breaking the silence indoors and the unease within my heart. I was choked by the suffocating quietness and thought:

What can that old hag be playing at up there? What can an old woman potter around doing all day with a flat and attic all to herself?

The longer I rented the room there, the more I feared she might die, and I thought she was perhaps lying dead as a doornail on the floor up there while we were alive and kicking in the room beneath her bedroom. Some primitive, archetypal fear makes you associate love with disaster, terror, and death, or at least bad tidings. I know this is superstition and recognize it within myself, but no matter how much I try to let reason and common sense prevail, I know that love is connected with death and that we (probably I) will sooner or later have to sacrifice our lives, perhaps not for love but rather because of it.

Of course I expect one or both of us are bound to catch AIDS; that disease fits like a glove into the superstition that passion and love are inextricably linked with tragedy. Ever since the disease was first identified, Christians regarded it as punishment for the way that a specific, corrupt, and ungodly character had turned love and the need for physical closeness into a self-serving closeness. Love became a pleasure and closeness something single and self-contained. By his behavior this particular ill-fated and outcast character freed love from the fetters of the mind and sought release and satisfaction only in the flesh for the flesh's sake, and with his own sex into the bargain.

The disease, the burning sword, was therefore sent into the world by God, who created a special chastising virus to smite the body of the corrupt with a terrible death for not enjoying love in healthy marriage according to the Christian code with the object of propagating mankind in the womb and filling the earth. The illness originated when someone insulted the holy sanctuary of woman, who is the source of life, and this same someone is said to yearn for baser and darker chasms or cavities in the body where no light is born from the darkness, where the seed is exposed to die at birth by the primitive custom, but before any child is even conceived.

Yet it would transpire that life is mechanical and without a spirit. The disease was not an agent serving the wishful thinking of the faith in Christian hearts, but was immune to sorrow and sought out all holes and every type of blood, noble or low, blue or gray, it went its own way obeying nothing but its own laws, and was not sent as a punishment for breaches of God's commandments and his passages of conception. It was one against all in the same way as each and every death.

I have fathered children, but a comical yearning still arose within me to die from the demonic virus. It is well worth dying in a special way for the truth of soul and body. That grants as much appeasement these days as when certain people wanted to die for an ideal in the times of the great enlightenment, die for their opinions, give their life for their faith or something else close to man, like sacrificing oneself for a father, mother, woman, or child, God and society: the whole world, just as the Savior did—the art of imitating him has been considered a great virtue. But it will take a long time before people with AIDS will be counted as saints by anybody; enjoying love and dying on its account from a real and terrifying disease has nothing to do with philosophy or economics or gods, but rather with a vague and uncontrollable longing which Christians call perversion because it dies on its own account the moment it is satisfied.

I had little idea then how scientific studies would later reveal that all men, good or bad, righteous or unrighteous, are equally defenseless and prone to this disease as any other, because diseases hardly discriminate, they have none of the ethical sensibility, intellect, or logic of learned men, have no god, and do not confess any right and true religion.

That was what I was thinking about in the room.

After I got a phone I thought everything was set up and my partner could call me whenever he wanted, but he phoned a few weeks ago and said:

—I'm not coming near you until you've been for an AIDS test and can produce a doctor's certificate to prove you're not infected.

For all my contemplations and need for holy martyrdom I took this as an insult, a slap in the face, and I said:

—I'm not going to such lengths just to please you. I'd sooner die than do that.

—Oh well, it's all over and done with then, he said.

So I went for a test and was able to wave the certificate in his face. He glowed with delight and was proud.

—Really, the things people dare to do, he chirped with joy. What does the certificate say?

—That I'm serum positive, I told him.

—What does that mean?

—I've got positive blood, I told him.

—You've always been positive toward me, he said happily.

—Yes, I said. I've lived a positive life.

—Everything's positive in mine too, he said, growing happier still.

—Good, I said.

—Really, the things people dare to do, he chirped again.

—I was the one who dared, I said emphatically. And I also dare to die for my nature and my disease.

—Don't give me any heroics, he said curtly, provocatively. I was the one who had the idea because I thought I'd caught AIDS and infected you.

Sometimes he would look at the certificate and become so enraptured that he forgot why he had come.

—What would happen if it said something else and you were infected with AIDS? he asked, then answered himself at once: Of course my wife would find out everything and I'd be under a death sentence too.

—This isn't the only thing that puts the death sentence on you, it's in everything from the moment you're born, I said coldly and haughtily.

He didn't even listen to this truth, but just repeated the words:

—What a bloody nerve I had: daring to send you!

—What would happen if I'd got AIDS and I'd caught it from you? I asked, trying to maintain my respect.

—I'd have to commit suicide before it was the talk of the town, just like your childhood friend did. He was tough.

—How? I asked, not liking the look of this type of conversation.

—Daring to kill yourself is the bravest thing there is, that's for sure, he answered.

I didn't understand what could be brave about taking your own life until he said:

—It's braver to kill yourself than to kill other people because you kill off the whole world for yourself at the same time.

—How come? I asked, looking at him, but somehow shrinking back emotionally.

—Because then you feel the pain yourself, of course, he replied, surprised at my stupidity. If you kill someone else no one feels the pain except the person who's killed.

I'd never thought about the game we constantly played

and the delight brought by provoking pain.

Once when my partner came around and was sitting in rapture reading the AIDS test certificate, something seemed to dawn on him and he said half-surprised:

—So condoms are mankind's main hope of survival now!

He started roaring with laughter at his discovery.

—Yes, a condom grants life and murders at the same time, I said curtly.

—No, I don't get it. It doesn't add up, he protested. How?

—The one who wears it lives, but what goes into it dies and never becomes a human being, I said.

—That's how you figure it out, he said perplexedly, adding: I've never wondered about being dead before I was born, but my wife often says, "If anyone ever died to save mankind it wasn't Jesus Christ—it was the rats they use to test drugs in laboratories to heal us sick people. They definitely die for mankind. And it's much more of a riddle to know how you were dead before you were born into the world than to know how you leave it." So I said, "Of course you take your body into the grave while your soul flies up to God." "So what grave were we buried in before we were born and what God were we with?" she asks back.

—And what do you say when she says that? I asked.

—I don't look into the future or the past wondering about what we were or will be. I just want my leg over, he replied.

I didn't like the way he was looking at me.

—I always get my leg over after that kind of conversation, he said arrogantly. And even if we sometimes argue way into the night or until your spirit leaves you completely, the urge just takes its place.

—Where the spirit leaves off, passions take over, I said.

October 13, 1988

I had gone to bed at the appointed time in the afternoon, because he was going to "put in an appearance" between one and two o'clock. I had taken a bath so that I would be clean and he could besmirch me for a while with sacred impurity, defile me with passion, roll me over in his surf and nourish my love upon what is surely just lust on his part, but for me something like tormented, pure love.

I find the body better for engaging in lovemaking if, instead of being freshly washed, it has reclaimed the salts on its skin and is no longer unnaturally clean and scented with soap or perfume. This applies to men at least. It is a different matter when I am with my wife: she is best just after she has taken a suitably warm bath. But I have to take a cold shower or pace the floor before I can go near her, because as she says:

—Sharp contrasts are best for this, like everything else.

I have never seen my friend's latest wife, but she is probably excessively hygienic because he is careful, almost feminine, in the way he handles his body fluids, although in other respects he treats flesh roughly. I have to give way to him in external cleanliness, with a suitable amount of bathing and ablutions. When he announces his arrival over the phone he always says:

—You'll have to be out of the bath and finished getting ready before I put in an appearance.

I want the body to retain its normal scent during lovemaking. I prefer one that has just come from work, has the scent of toil about it, is reasonably tired and needs to find repose in love.

I had eaten lunch and prepared my body for us to devour each other's flesh in a silence broken by the occasional commonplace words, which are always the same yet just as effective in the heat of the moment as they were at the very start, but become embarrassing afterward and jar on the mind, making you feel half-ashamed and astonished that such empty, trite words in the right place and at the right time can seem true and grant pleasure.

Just as I had finished getting myself ready he phoned and said in a low, hoarse, and frightened voice that he could not meet me. His wife was down in the laundry room but could catch him at any moment so he had snatched up the telephone and our conversation was short and abrupt.

Somehow I have the feeling that his wife spends an awful lot of time down in the basement in the evenings, washing and making sure that the beds are clean and everything is tidy around her. Meanwhile he sneaks to the phone to call me and say naughty things before nightfall. If I try to tease him that he only does this to work up his own libido, he denies it and says:

—I always keep my pecker up toward the missus and don't need any special methods.

All the same, it's not unlikely that he works himself up with me and transfers his passion to his wife when she finally comes up from the basement full of bright thoughts, carrying the clean washing, and is baffled by his advances.

—I hardly seem to be able to go downstairs in the evenings without you losing control of yourself when I come back up, she says wearily but aware at the same time of her power over him, and she enjoys giving in to his persuasions.

—I miss you so much, he says with the rasping voice that men get when they are in that kind of mood.

—Just if I go down to the basement? she asks, adding: Well, whatever turns you on.

He often tells me about this, not so much in confidence as innocent astonishment about being compelled to say something when we've finished; he always wants to leave at once. When I hear how heartfelt his words are I think he is showing a special kind of trust in me which surely springs from sincerity. Instinctively, in order to have my wish confirmed, I ask:

—Why are you with me then, if all your wife needs to do is nip downstairs with some dirty washing to make you need to take her to bed afterward?

I hope that he will say something that might suggest warm feelings toward me, but generally he just says either:

—I can't control myself because there's something I resent

about all this, or I meet you to give the missus a rest. Aren't you trying to give yours a rest with this too?

—Is what we do just to give our wives a rest? I ask.

—Of course, he replies, giving me a look of shock at possibly thinking otherwise. That's the good thing about being unfaithful in marriage. Married women and mothers can't stand much pressure from their husbands.

I feel strange inside, grow half-perplexed, not knowing whether to laugh or cry at his childish but natural attitude to our relationship and his opinions about showing consideration for mothers, but I summon up my courage, steel myself against established notions of sin and the possible bearing it has on carnal rights, and say with a sarcasm that is more in my mind than in the words themselves or on my lips:

—As far as I'm concerned I'm not giving my wife a rest. I've taken a liking to you.

Then he glances at me, silent and ill at ease, and I imagine him thinking, "So you're with your wife at night to give me a rest during the day? I thought she was on holiday." He is clearly pleased with the idea, even smug about his stake in my libido, but says straight out:

—Women have to get their leg over too.

When he phoned just now they were going to go into town. She needed to buy some clothes for him; he often says, "The missus chooses everything for me—my socks too."

The ship's sailing to America tomorrow, he whispered down the phone. We won't see each other for three weeks.

Suddenly the blood and juices coagulated in my body. My head ached and I was on the verge of the peculiarly painful weeping that I imagine old people constantly feel in their lives: the dry tears born from sorrow at the dwindling life left in a rapidly debilitating body that has continually less future ahead and a lost lifetime behind it. For someone in that state, not even sorrow can be permanent; nothing remains unfulfilled for an old body except the grand finale. Life has passed and is far away. This is why everything that old people miss out on is only part of a nonexistent future. If an old man is sensible he realizes he can lose his future too and add that loss to everything else that has been mislaid in his lifetime. I felt somehow similar, because I am middle-aged and my libido is waning, but to console myself I thought that even though I had not always had him for a partner I had lived all the same, and I still do not have him for certain yet I manage to survive.

Age brings a special kind of joy alongside sorrow, namely that you stop being afraid of life, the less that is left of it. This kind of love is also courage: it is quite unlike the love that I felt naturally and candidly toward my wife while it lasted, and was called marital bliss. If you become tied by different bonds of love you automatically start living a life that cannot be lived openly or in reality, it turns into a type of fancy and fiction that defies description.

Perhaps that is one explanation why, at my age, I have plunged myself into something with another married man of my own age that I would not even have allowed to sneak up on my longings in a dream when I was younger, and a ladies' man then as well.

For much of my life, ever since I got married, I have been the most respectable of men and never tolerated any mark on my existence. Now, on the other hand, I live largely for that mark, which was probably a birthmark and is only appearing for the first time now, however pure and white my body or soul might have been before that blemish began to emerge in my relations with the world, my wife and children, and especially our youngest daughter. Like anyone who has had a fairly strict Lutheran upbringing and is loyal to its ideas, I would have expected to leave this life as pure, unblemished, and naked as when I was born into the world. Now I have decided to leave it for dead because of a different kind of faith.

So I won't be meeting him this time before he sails away. Judging from the telephone conversation, he has decided to go on with this when he returns in a fortnight, three weeks or longer; who knows when ships seek a way out of the ocean fogs for harbor, even when they are on scheduled sailings?

November 14, 1988

I have been waiting restlessly all morning for my partner to call and say that he could pop ashore or had found an excuse to slip away from work for a moment, but the force of that wish is by no means powerful enough to make it come true. By noon I had given up all hope, I abandoned my wish and mentally watched the ship leaving harbor. I imagined his wife wishing him goodbye. She would do it the way uneducated people do, neutrally and remotely as if unable to apply their feelings, so that they fail to reach the people they are aimed at and seem like a burden to the ones they well up within, and fade out in a muddle.

I could see him clearly, slightly sheepish, leaning over the side of the ship with far-too-large workman's gloves on his hands, relieved that soon he would be out of sight of his wife who didn't know what to do with herself either by the car on the quayside, whether to wave or call out something. She didn't have a clue, since she was no longer able to send him out on some errand or talk to him about the endless trouble with their children, who would probably never manage to stand on their own two feet and always needed to borrow more money from the parents, who were forced to take bank loans with exorbitant rates of interest in order to answer their helpless pestering. He put an index finger to one nostril and snorted out through the other just to do something before he forgot himself and became absorbed in work and exertion, pleased that he was now more aware of his body than his emotions, because there is a lot to do onboard a ship, not just continuous painting and banging rust off the bridge, and there is no time there to think about trivial things ashore, muddling and sentimentality. Once I had asked him:

—Is love more in your head or there…?

He pointed straight away to "there" and asked in surprise:
—Where else should it be?

Perhaps I am making this up, perhaps I have long grown accustomed to him sailing out into the unknown in all kinds of weather, living with uncertainty at sea, never being master of his own time, never knowing for certain when he will come home and when he has to set sail out of harbor, his life spent on the art of living with varying degrees of uncertainty and risk, working for low wages, doing physical labor, seeing the raging weather and crashing waves, enjoying little love on land—but with regular installments of something awaiting him there, and eternal errands to run in his car.

I recall now how bright the blue sky was over the bay that same afternoon when I went up to the storeroom on the second floor in the school, and I knew then, as I looked out of the window, that the sight was more the product of my state of mind, my emotions and longing, than of the sea itself. The following day I went back up to the storeroom early in the winter morning, before the sun came up, and took a bleary-eyed look at the sea and the mountains from the unnatural electric light, in a dusk that was gloomier than real light because the clock said it should have been daytime. I looked out into the darkness below the building, at the crate or little transportation container that lay there on its side and was labelled Seaship Ltd. I did that to remind myself of my friend and be close to him by looking at a tangible, visible object that was connected with his job and his shipping line. Although I could not touch it and only saw it vaguely in the faint glow of morning, the container kept me company in a way while I looked through the shelves and gathered the materials for my lesson.

None of my pupils could have known or suspected how many times I did not go up to the storeroom on the second floor in order to fetch teaching materials for them or to the toilet to relieve myself, but rather to weigh down my mind and magnify my sense of loss by taking a look at the container from the shipping line. In that way I sailed farther and deeper into the torment that love arouses.

Sometimes when I return to the classroom a red glow tints the mountaintop. The glow is weak but full of hope for a bright day or longing for a new one. Later, when I am teaching another class on one of the floors above, the bay comes into sight bright and clear through the big windows, as the daylight opens the sky wider. The light moves slowly, but the dawn spreads resolutely out of the night.

I suddenly started to drift off in class or would watch the ships on their voyages across the bay to the harbor, which I had not paid any particular attention to before. I discovered the view and at the same time its beauty, especially seen from the window of the place that I had considered nothing more than a necessity for the body to relieve itself, where I had always disposed of my bodily waste and hurried back down to my students, or to my fellow teachers to argue about politics and pretend to know everything under the sun. Now it became a garden of fantasies that had more affinity with teens and puberty than with the middle age of a married paterfamilias or the mature emotions of a father of three. But what can be more mature than allowing a fully formed body and mind to fly out of the egg of habit?

My students sit downstairs in the classroom, pleased that I have gone out so they can whisper for a while and attend to their own secrets. Meanwhile, I am exalted in clarity. Once when I went back to the classroom a girl was describing her sadness about her boyfriend, who had gone to sea. It was in a drawing lesson. I'd never taken any particular notice of her before, and even though I remained silent and listened to her candidly recounting her tribulations I realized that we had this in common, because her love and the loss that it caused were natural reactions to a need, a yearning to merge into a sea that flows over you, until the person who is the skerry beneath it appears pure and intact on the shore, like a free and independent individual.

After listening to the girl quacking away to the end of her story, I asked her, more from curiosity than sympathy:

—Is he a merchant seaman?

She seemed to brighten up. She looked at me with grateful eyes, happy that I had taken part in the affairs of her heart instead of telling her to shut up and trying to enrich her soul and the students' hands with learning and knowledge about how to draw forms. In an instant I changed from a boring old drawing teacher into a living human being and she answered with a slightly pretentious sadness:

—No, my boyfriend's on a fishing boat and won't be back ashore for another three days. It's an awfully long time, an eternity. You just don't know what it's like.

What are three days compared with a whole lifetime? I thought, but I said:

—When you're young, three days away from the person you love seems forever, but it's paid back many times over with the joy of meeting again. But with age you become grateful when the people you love go away for a couple of days so you can take a rest from them and their constant, overwhelming presence; this is because you live in the hope that someone will enter your life unexpectedly while the other is away, maybe even more than one. If you're not that lucky, you can always believe that the person who went away will surely return with something to renew you afterward.

The girl gave a gentle smile, the way people do when they pretend to understand but are prevented by their age or lack of experience from doing so, or perhaps she did it to show tolerance toward a teacher who says very little apart from incomprehensible things. Young people do not understand anything except what is tangible or presented as a very simple problem to explain something more complex; but if the teaching works, the pupil will sense something in the teacher's words that may turn out crucial later in life. In the playfulness of youth an ordinary pupil cannot understand the harsh fact that a complex problem demands complex explanations, which really need to be incomprehensible in order to arouse a lasting desire to understand them.

We looked each other in the eye and I thought:

I wonder if you would show understanding and tolerance or would refuse to come near me as my pupil if you knew what no one may know? Would you say the same as I have said to you?

The next day the girl suddenly began showing me unexpected understanding and asked how my wife was getting along. When I answered nonchalantly, "Oh, she's getting along reasonably," she smiled at me for giving an ambiguous answer and trying to conceal my problems, and even nodded to show that she was going to put on a brave face in life and never complain about love—I had taught her to put up with its tribulations. For the first time in my career I heard through the grapevine that I was a fine teacher, one of the few in the school who understood his pupils and young people; the reason was that I was having some kind of trouble in my private life, although I put on a brave face. The pupils asked the headmaster to put me in charge of the school leisure center and be available for discussion and consultation with anyone who wanted, parents as well as the kids who drifted in off the streets on Wednesday evenings for no particular purpose, I had such a knack for dealing with pupils—but I declined the honor.

—Of course you want to spend the evenings at home with your wife, the headmaster said.

—Yes, I said. Our youngest girl has been rather poorly of late.

The girl undoubtedly got word of this, because she began inquiring diplomatically, but with an irritating and cloying sympathy, how my daughter was feeling. When I merely answered with a neutral smile, I heard talk later about my daughter having an incurable disease and the whole class improved their grades in most subjects for the next fortnight. The pupils' dedication was a campaign to show their sympathy and embolden me with a reasonable midterm examination performance. Then everything returned to normal, or worsened if anything, and I began to feel uneasy and was cautious, listening to hear if any untoward stories were going around. When I heard nothing to suggest that, I calmed down and told myself snidely that anyone would think Reykjavík was a city of millions of people: it was a hopeless task trying to pry very deep into other people's affairs, and nobody gave a damn about anybody else except in elections for the local council and parliament every four years, between which the citizens bolstered their sympathy with constant collections for the poor in their affluent society that the recession was undermining as the gross national product dropped.

November 21, 1988

Today when we had been together I lay on top of him and smelled the scent of what we had done. Afterward he had stretched out his arms as he always does, giving the impression that, dumbfounded and satisfied, he is welcoming heaven. I put both my arms onto his and we clenched our hands with our palms together; we are around the same height and of a not dissimilar build, so we fit each other, like two matching pieces of a pawned pledge. When I nestled my face slowly against his neck I could feel the warmth and scent of the pleasure that comes from loving, the sweet aroma of love itself. His flesh was everywhere, both tangible and subjective. We lay like that for a long time, like beings who have been nailed against each other of their own free will in order to die on a shared cross. I lay in a dream, perceiving how our bodies slowly merged, rather like a worm crawling into moist ground. I felt how flesh grew into other flesh and we were glued together with the only glue that can glue all things, and was now outside our bodies but had been inside them before. This position, in a certain sense, depicts our feeling and longing to die into each other.

Then I suddenly thought:

No, this is only wishful thinking.

We slumbered crucified against each other like that, or perhaps I only dreamt it. I think that dreams should be an exploration in the deep void; a dream should follow winding paths through the labyrinth of the only certain thing, which is the body's transience. That alone exists for certain, for as long as we manage to live, and at the moment the only confession of faith I can make is this:

If someone made an eloquent invitation to me to step down from the cross and return to the society of other men in such a way that no spear would ever be thrust into my tormented flesh and belly and no blood or fluid would pour out from there as a symbol of the inner flow, and I was offered heaven with countless mansions, security with my father and constant feasting in his home, and I could live under the sweet protective wing of my mother for time ever after and thereby end up in the bosom of the holy family—I would rather hang crucified upon my friend, though the world considered it a mortal sin and stoned me and cast me out for preferring to die into his dust than to live in harmony with what I married fifteen years ago but had my first child by twenty-five years ago, just turned twenty then.

December 1, 1988
Today he said he does not keep anything from his wife, nothing but this. He told me over the phone when he was lying in bed alone with the flu and said he could not come.

—I've got a cold sore too, he said by way of apology.

When he said he couldn't come, and when I had confided in him that I wanted to lie down ill beside him, I felt to my considerable surprise that in many ways I preferred being with him in my mind than in reality. Yearning is often better than not—better than having.

It is a pleasant, fulfilling, and voluptuous feeling to be alone and wait for the person you love but know will not come. When I started to ruminate on this I reached the conclusion that it is because the person who is absent is always really with us, as we would have them, but by being there he clashes with most aspects of our behavior, and eventually drives himself away for good with his constant presence.

So what is it that came?

If someone is glued to a particular man or woman, so little imagination enters his daily life that what was once special and desirable becomes routine; closeness drives away yearning and leaves someone sitting with us who has nothing but his own selfish image, with a will that encroaches upon us and exterminates what is best in our emotions. That is why, if the presence of the loved one deprives the lover of his imagination, the long-awaited meetings become fervent but dead acts, followed by a need to be free of them. This makes us want to run away from our home and children into a freedom, which is destructive because we are unaccustomed to having no ties and do not know how to handle either freedom or joy.

Instead of disappointment, I was enveloped by a strange and greater calm than I had ever known. But peace has its tormenting side too, which is a taste for emptiness. Nothing remains unpolluted by its antithesis except satisfaction, which consequently is perfect loneliness, but only for the short moment that makes it into nothing.

I left the room and was a good husband and father. In the evening my wife said I could sometimes be so kind that she could die for me.

—Wouldn't it be truer, my dear, to say that we've been playing our marriage rather like a lottery recently? I asked.

—Yes, we have, she admitted hesitantly, not understanding exactly what I was driving at, but she soon realized and said happily:

—So I seem to have won the jackpot tonight?

When I heard her say that and knew how she deluded herself and I deluded her, I was saddened by her simplicity and all that I had been led into, and I wanted to tell her the truth. But I was most saddened of all at myself, for not loving her anymore, and I fervently longed to love her simply because I did not. For a while I felt convinced that people must be capable of such love, pure love that springs from lack of love, but when I considered that she got her satisfaction from daily life although it was not given from love and she was happy all the same, my mind turned away from such trivia that are the exclusive province of the conscience. I grew tired and fell asleep, like her: doubtless we snored together like a true Christian couple, but in our own separate ways while we turned our backs to each other, sleeping.

December 9, 1988

I am somehow permeated by torments and want to escape from the pleasure they bring me. I do not go out of the house for fear that he might phone the very moment I leave, or come round to the room and not find me there. Perhaps I want to be under love's house arrest. Although I know that he is cautious enough only to phone every once in a while, the phone rings endlessly in my mind every time I slip out and, without anyone lifting up the receiver and answering, he says he can drop around now; but then of course I am not in.

He is everywhere in my life but I fear I might never get a proper hold on him and the best thing would be to abandon everything and gain it all at the same time by dying. Death is sure, but still no solution, I know that, because when the body dies it is neither tormented nor released from torment. From the viewpoint of human consciousness it is nothing. Nonetheless I regard death as a panacea in the old-fashioned way.

Does love find itself only love itself, which is self-destructive, and was it originally of a single sex, just as life came into being when a single cell split into the whole realm of life, which constantly searches for its origin by killing itself?

We meet up and often share our bodies without being together mentally. Still, what is in the mind could well be something physical that we have yet to identify. We only know each other at this one level, which is a small and isolated part of our routine lives and doings. For this reason I hunch expectantly over this hole in the ice of my life like a hunter, or like a curious eavesdropper at the door of my own unfamiliar traits, asking: Does man make do with relations with others if they are only physical? Can touch satisfy us indefinitely, rolling around like newborn babies without language or any other forms of expression than groping at flesh, even though we know that this will surely deliver us from the belly's hot passion and into the cold within man and the cold of our surroundings?

Most or all of what I know about my partner I have imagined or guessed for myself. Perhaps this is the most wholesome way to treat others: silent physical proximity to the products of your own imagination. Above all we get to know each other when he phones and can speak quite frankly because we are not looking each other in the eye then, and this makes us bolder when his wife goes out to the shop or down to the laundry room. For some reason or other I think she exists much more in his words than at the washing machine and dryer. It has crossed my mind that he only has an imaginary wife whom he uses to protect himself against me or my conceivable encroachments upon him. His wife could be a figment of his imagination, not unlike the way he lingers in my fantasies. I know neither for certain. Perhaps he thinks the same about me, that my wife and children are a figment of my imagination or a means of protection if he ever thought of taking advantage of the weakness he senses in me and bursting in to deliver an ultimatum, to demand money from me or endless loans on the strength of our acquaintance and friendship, as men do to other men, although they use different methods to vanquish women.

Now that he has left the ship for the time being and has started working on land—for a change—and we should presumably have more frequent and better chances to meet up, he begins sidestepping the issue and our relationship has switched to the telephone. His wife is continually sending him on some errand or another, he is endlessly paying bills, doing favors for his mother-in-law, sorting things out for his children, or something unexpected happens, his car gets scratched, so he cannot meet me. Despite being so busy he always somehow manages to spend hours on the phone, and then he explains that his wife has popped out to the shop or gone down into the basement, so he can talk dirty to me in the meantime. Those long conversations and intimate words seem to have no impact on his telephone bill.

—Next time you'll claim you have to pay the telephone bill and can't come round, I said.

—Don't worry, he answered resourcefully. I have it charged to my Visa card.

I don't know where he calls from. Sometimes he is apparently visiting a deaf aunt or mother (maybe deafness runs in his family); they have retired and live by themselves, and are therefore given a free telephone, which he uses while his wife is doing the women's laundry down in the basement. Once I asked him why deaf mothers would ever need a telephone.

—It gives them security, he replied. My mother can always phone someone if she has some errand that needs running for her.

—But she can't hear the phone when it rings, I said.

—No, he said. That's even better for her. Telephones can be a nuisance, and then it's an advantage to be deaf.

In our telephone relationship, the conversations are more a physical presence in words than dialogue in the normal sense, but I do not treat him as a him confidant, even though I act in a way that encourages him to be frank, try to gain his trust and make him tell me a little about himself, by striving to assure him that he is the only person I can confide in. As a result our talk becomes a continuous act of avoidance, whereby he dodges every question and tries to cloud the issue if something is said in earnest that he does not want to get around. But I don't let him confuse me, not yet. I have suggested that if he finds it difficult or impossible to meet me, the best thing would be to change our acquaintance into pure friendship. He doesn't want that.

—Sometimes I need to meet when I feel that way, you can never tell when, he says, hesitantly gripping the bottom of one of his nostrils between his thumb and index finger, which he always does when he feels unsure of himself and thinks he ought to say something different to someone with all my learning, though none of it might be of any practical use.

I feel a premonition that I think must be akin to mysticism and he convinces me that his need for me is greater than the body and its higher needs.

Our telephone relationship has made me start hoping he will never find a permanent job on land and will no longer be able to keep up this new arrangement, but be forced to go back to sea where he charges himself up with a salty force, which he brings ashore and divides up fraternally between his wife and me. And on the way between us he becomes charged with new energy. Then everything will be cut and dried again, the lines clearly drawn, our meetings rare but all the more vehement. Our relationship would be divided into set periods of closeness and distance which would not be organized by us at all, but rather by the random sailing schedules of Seaship Ltd. between Iceland and continental Europe, and occasionally to America and even Africa.

I am not a religious man in the normal sense, because

I lack a hypocritical streak, but I have come close to praying to God not to let Seaship Ltd. go bankrupt, which would disrupt its schedules and thereby his visits to me.

The longer he works on land and takes on all kinds of odd jobs, the more I yearn for absence, loss, and then suddenly being struck by closeness, which lasts for as long as we seek gratification and then slowly changes into distance again, like the sea and the land meeting at high tide and moving apart at ebb tide, without ever becoming completely separated. That would grant me respite from my quest for what fortunately is never gained completely, merely over with for the time being, but will come back.

All of a sudden he said:

—I can't drop in again on Thursday.

I was lying with my back on his left arm, which he did not put around me because his body had become neutral.

The body of an ordinary man who has little sense of love but all the more need for making it can be tormentingly distant or neutral, impotent I might almost say, like an empty sack, after it has been coupled with another body.

—I'm completely knackered, he said, and he lapsed into what I call the cot state of the newly weaned baby.

I have felt this benumbed state when having sex with women, the way that finding or regaining myself afterward instills in me a distaste for the spirit that had turned me into nothing inside them. I find it natural to give everything in lovemaking and that is something that women like, but they cannot understand how a man who has given his all during the act has nothing left when it is over. I have transported them into the netherworld of the man and the higher world of the woman at the same time, and when the fusion of these two worlds is completed and I have taken enough and given enough, it is up to them to find their footing in their own obligations toward themselves. Oblivious to this, they want to relish the emotions of dusk and oblivion, gain security, even get married. But you don't go to bed with a woman to get married, but rather to rid yourself of the man within you. Once a woman said to me, rather embarrassingly, because I did not want to give her either eternal love or lifelong loyalty:

—Won't you just have your teat and take a nap after you've finished straining to do your jobs in mummy's potty?

I was young and did not understand her sarcasm, but she explained the male nature to me because she claimed to have plenty of experience with men and knew every detail of their makeup.

The female body is different. You often make better contact with it after sex than during it. After sex a satisfied man can become doggishly submissive and gentle, or rather quiet and obedient; a celestial calm descends upon him, while the woman turns confident and commanding and goes off to wash. Having an orgasm is doubtless a triumph for her, but she thinks that giving one to someone else is such a denigrating sacrifice on her part that she has to wash the offering away at once.

My partner's body did not exactly become like a sack of potatoes that a housewife has rummaged in to find a few to put in the pot before it crawls away of its own accord back to its storage place; instead, he was on his guard against my presence and I could tell he was listening out for something about me that would make me feel bad. I thought he was thinking, "I don't want this married bloke to latch onto me like a black, slimy, toadlike pansy."

Yearn for him as I might, I know that if it came to the crunch I wouldn't know what I was supposed to do if ever actually had him to myself. I know that he resembles a wish and its granting, which must never last. He ought to know from experience that I do not like him to stay with me for long. Otherwise he would need to have a heart full of much more than what he has in his blood: something worth talking about and connected with work or what has happened to him in his daily doings. When he brings nothing but his heart and the circulation within his body, it is enough for him to stay there while we open an artery to each other. Then he has to leave. All the same, he isn't the typical visitor who suddenly blurts out in a flow of words the little that he has to say and becomes a pest afterward if he comes back. A disposable guest is like that. Most people realize that they hardly last for more than a visit and a half and do not feel capable of more, which is why they spend all their evenings at home in front of the television. In this way even boring and stupid people have realized their limitations and know that they deserve nothing better than staring at a screen. But because my partner uses his words sparingly and rarely drops in, my expectation lasts, and I hope I provide a little adventure for him in that monotonous life of his in which this is almost the only variety.

—Do you think life here won't be dull and boring enough for you if we keep on having our fun together? he once asked me after I wanted to end it all for his sake.

—We go on meeting because I can't be bothered to read thrillers and detective stories, he said.

Experience alone will show what will become of our adventure if it turns into a routine event.

Of course it will become bothersome, an endless tinkering with ordinary realism!

I turned over to snuggle up to him and feel the warm scent of his body, the scent that envelops me in brightness whenever I do that to him, the aroma of a tired but healthy body, which spreads over me like rest.

After lying like this I looked him in the face and said:

—Why can't you come on Thursday—surely it doesn't take your balls two days to fill up again?

—I can't neglect the missus like that, he replied. It's only good if you do it in between.

He smiled dreamily into the air with a smile that was neither apologetic nor infused with guilt. I have never noticed anything resembling that in his character. There does not seem to be a trace of repentance inside him. Nor is there any passion, nothing painful or charged with emotion. He just comes around for the sole purpose of getting what he wants when nature calls, and he has his urge gratified plainly and willingly in various forms, physical or mental, without anyone knowing. I said to him, trying to show neither generosity nor understanding:

—We can stop this if you want.

—No, he replied.

—Why not? I asked, hoping he would show some sign that I meant something to him, but he said vacantly:

—I don't know that any more than you do.

Translation by Bernard Scudder

NERVE CITY

by Birna Anna Björnsdóttir,
Oddný Sturludóttir, *and* Silja Hauksdóttir

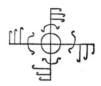

I TAKE A STROLL through the smallest campus in the world. A
slight chill runs down my spine as the walk compels me to
recall my glamorous start at the University of Iceland. My
expectations for upcoming things are usually a bit too high.
I tend to romanticize future projects, jobs, parties, and just
about everything else. And that's how it was with the damned
University.

All summer long I had seen myself in an imaginary music
video that showed comp lit–Dís embracing academia. I had
visions where I vigorously took notes using well-sharpened
pencils, with a loosely tied knot in my hair and an occasional
lock flowing in contemplation down onto my forehead.
Between classes I engaged in passionate debate with my fellow students regarding -isms and currents of thought. They
usually tilted their heads a bit when I spoke and gazed at me
with great admiration. The library was my second home,

From *Dís*, a novel.

I spent hours and hours on end there, my shoulders and back throbbing with pain, but I couldn't stand up, couldn't tear myself away from the literary canon. But when I did, I drank herbal tea at the university café with handsome boys who were tall and broad over the shoulders, dressed in turtlenecks, with a deep and meaningful look in their eyes—directed at me of course. At other times I saw myself lying on the campus lawn under the autumn sun, nibbling on an apple and scribbling in a diary, the turtleneck men never far away.

I was always very trendy, naturally without too much effort, since fashion slavery is beneath the cerebral class. My imaginary university evenings were spent home at my desk analyzing novels for seminars from the perspective of diverse minorities and subaltern groups. I also frequented evening roundtables and cafés where I sipped Portuguese red wine and discussed Soviet puppet theater and the perishing heritage of the Solomon Islands. With the handsome boys in the turtlenecks. The candlelight, which does wonders for me, gave my eyes a turquoise glow and my cheeks were rosy and flushed from wine and the love of knowledge. The nights sometimes got wilder (university parties were supposed to be completely crazy) and we students danced on tabletops to the music Dad and Mom played at parties when I was a kid. We hardly ever went to clubs—they were way too loud and full of people who worked in fashion boutiques.

I was so exhilarated about becoming something, becoming a university student, on student loans and everything. Being a "comp lit student" had a much better ring to it than "high-school girl" or "clerk." I knew that family gatherings would be so much easier now that I was an academic with a bright future. My relatives would no longer consider me an unenlightened chick who was always hungover at Sunday brunches; instead I would become their pride and joy. At long last I would have good grounds to consider everyone else fools, idiots even. Or so I thought.

My first day as a member of the academic community

didn't start out quite the way I had imagined. I spent way too much time making my hair look adequately nonchalant and doing my makeup so that it looked like I wasn't wearing any. I had stopped by at a bar the night before and hadn't had time to wash my favorite jeans which had about a pint of beer on the left leg. So I wore my other cool outfit, which was probably a bit too racy for the first day of school. Glancing into the mirror on my way out I didn't see an intellectual pretty schoolgirl, only a shabby-looking gal that seemed to be the younger sister of Barbara Cartland (may she rest in peace). What the hell, I thought, and promised myself I'd wash the jeans and get a facial. Hoped my future classmates were still traveling abroad and wouldn't make it to school until tomorrow.

My heart was struck with awe as I entered the Main Building of the university. I felt I had done right by choosing comparative literature, since it is categorized with the old disciplines that are so clearly Main. The professors also inspired confidence, even though none of them seemed that exciting at first glance. The men were all wearing vests and corduroy pants, with an occasional free spirit wearing jeans. The women were much more scarce, all of them dressed in black, wearing brooches by Icelandic craftswomen. I reproached myself for my vanity and reminded myself that here in this temple of knowledge, the outer shell has no bearing on the inner self. These were intellectuals.

The first lecture wasn't all that elaborate, more of an introduction to the course. The professors did sometimes say stuff that the other students found devastatingly funny but I never quite grasped. Everyone laughed out loud at something the professors called an "academic quarter of an hour" (aka "cum tempore"). Must have had something to do with deep thought. Maybe a critique of the velocity of modern life? Dís already coming up with interpretations and feeling damned good about herself.

The turtleneck guys weren't there yet and I hoped my theory about them still being abroad would turn out to be correct. They were probably all on Interrail trips or working on kibbutzes in Budapest, and would come to school when their calling descended upon them. I decided to give it a chance, even though I didn't understand the titles of the books I was supposed to buy.

The following days I started having some doubts. I didn't really get to know these alleged soldiers of free thought. Everybody seemed so old and sure of themselves. A bunch of my classmates were middle-aged women who seemed to bond amongst themselves, but weren't the ideal candidates for apple eating or tea drinking, let alone dancing on tables. Most of the boys were a bit like Tom Sawyer and I was certain they had all grown up out in the boonies. They either looked like they had been raised on hay and milk from steel buckets, or in front of a computer screen with a supersized soda can in one hand and a Snickers bar in the other. The adventurous broad-shouldered savants were clearly still in Eastern Europe. During classes this motley crew took notes like they were getting paid per word (which they kind of are—they just have to repay it all). They all seemed to have developed an efficient and advanced note-taking technique, that is everyone but me, for I couldn't decide what was worth writing down and what wasn't. So I just stared into space with decision-anxiety growling in my stomach. I didn't understand shit during lectures anyway, and I seemed to be the only one. Words such as "dystopia," "discourse," "polyphony," "modernity," and "nihilism" were driving me insane because they sounded so simple but were so horribly complicated. I had already begun to worry I wouldn't find a subject for my thesis, it being impossible to write fifty pages about something you're completely clueless about.

Yet I had become fairly skilled in figuring out when to expect roars of laughter and therefore I knew when to laugh along. The recipe was as follows: The vest man or the brooch woman speaks softly for a couple of minutes and then pauses. Looks coyly out into the class, speaks up, smiles with one side of the mouth, and tells the "joke." Everyone laughs hysterically, me included, and all compete in who finds the joke funniest, since that demonstrates that they understood it. This takes about two minutes and then people take a sip of disgusting undrinkable coffee, reach for their pens, and continue taking notes. And I continued wondering what the hell I was doing there and trying to figure out which one was the problem, me or them? The problem had to be them.

Instead of spending time at the library with the "kids in my class," I took to long sessions at cafés with my friends Blaer and Lilja Rós, making use of my analytical skills to interpret the problem. I explained to them how it was all so different from what I had expected. Comparative literature was so dry and somehow not about anything. I had yearned to read the Western canon under the guidance of distinguished educators; instead I was meant to master incomprehensible terms referring to intangible phenomena. To me this kind of knowledge seemed meaningless and its sole purpose to create jobs for overeducated professors. I wanted to learn something real, something that made me more of a person and helped Me understand Me. The girls showed compassion and that was somewhat of a consolation. They did mention something about me giving it a chance, doing a bit of homework, but I didn't see the point since clearly this didn't suit me. The café sessions grew longer and I attended fewer and fewer classes. More and more often I found myself sitting alone reading the paper—the girls had to go school I guess. But why go when I couldn't even take notes? The women's club had also begun to get on my nerves big time, even though I wasn't there, and reliable sources said that eligible male comp lit students hadn't shown up yet. So I decided to check out psychology.

Psychology was taught in Oddi, the Social Sciences Building. Things were far more modern and upbeat there than in the Main Building, with marble floors, computers, and even an ATM. The guys were a lot better-looking, even though they had something of a jock/sportscar thing going.

You could at least look at them without getting depressed. I also had a feeling psychology was a more practical education, since everyone has a psyche. I was sure the studies couldn't be too obscure; after all they were based on scientific facts about us human beings.

And so I attended my first lecture with a positive attitude and took notes like my life depended on it. This time my policy was to note down everything rather than nothing. Slowly I began noticing some dubious personalities. Tape-recorder girls and guys with no sense of humor, all of whom were there to succeed. They all wanted to specialize in the psychology of advertising, marketing, and human resources or something even more ambitious. They weren't too keen on lending their notes and gossiped about people who had cracked from the pressure or lost fifty pounds during last year's exams. They used slang when referring to course titles and told funny stories about the teachers, whom they all claimed to know personally.

"How did Kalli do in the Prince [Principles of Psychology]?"

"He's supposed to have done really well, but he totally screwed up the Person [Psychology of Personality]."

"Yeah, old Óli [professor Ólafur Jóhannsson] is dreadful when it comes to multiple choice. That's what comes from doing your Ph.D. in Germany! hah! hah! hah! hah…!"

"Right. As for me, I'm having some trouble with the Soap [Social Psychology], the Hiss [History of Psychology], the Deev [Developmental Psychology], and the Bi [Biological Psychology]. Maybe I could take a peek at some of your notes?"

"No."

Then there was the training-suit issue. Why psychology students couldn't wear jeans and sweaters like other people was completely beyond me. Did polyester make studying easier? And what was it with the water bottles? All the girls walked around Oddi clutching onto one, gulping water like they were stuck in the middle of the desert. I was somewhat enlightened about this mystery when I overheard a conversation between two thirsty girls in the ladies room.

"Oh, I just love throwing on these old rags when I'm studying. Then you don't get tempted to go to the mall and spend valuable time there…"

Why? Why was it essential for university students to look like aerobic groupies? Does university suck out every last bit of people's desire to look good? Is academia so utterly demanding that you can only do one at a time: a) be cool, or b) go to school. The contradiction in all of this was that psychology students were not wearing "old rags." They wore brand-new and expensive training suits that probably cost more than my whole wardrobe combined. Some also claimed it helped to wear the same clothes all semester. That way you condition the information you absorb with the clothing you wear. One actually went so far as to say the same applies for body odor. Don't think I'll be sleeping with him.

I tried reading at the university library but didn't get anything done since people only seemed to be gathered there to get laid. Really, students prowled around the library like newly divorced middle-aged men at Café Reykjavík. Starved eyes of engineer students, who hadn't had sex since last spring break, almost melted holes in the back of my pants.

This certainly wouldn't have gotten on my nerves so much had the curriculum itself not been so bizarre. I wanted to explore human nature, feelings, the soul, but instead I spent way too many weeks of my life memorizing the structure of cells. The Limbic system, myelin, nucleus, and cerebral cortex. Electric shock, spit, and rats. I felt altogether out of place when the teacher was explaining things that seemed as natural to the average psychology student as a tape recorder. Once again I didn't understand a thing. I had thought that unlike comp lit, psychology was a general field that would suit everyone interested in people. I like people. My friends tell me I'm a good listener. That must be just as important a trait for a psychology student as note-taking strategies and water guzzling. Was I misunderstanding something? Or was I just misunderstood?

Either way, I said goodbye to Nerve City. Sneaked away to a café and never looked back.

Translation by Birna Anna Björnsdottir

INTERFERENCE

by ANDRI SNÆR MAGNASON

ARCTIC TERN / *STERNA PARADISAEA*

WHEN THE ARCTIC terns failed to find their way home one spring, appearing instead like a storm cloud over the center of Paris and pecking at the heads of passersby, many people thought the end of the world was nigh, that this would be the first in a long series of calamities. The city-dwellers stockpiled canned food, hoarded water, and waited for a plague of locusts, for droughts, floods, or earthquakes, but nothing happened, at least not in Paris. The Arctic terns overran public parks and traffic islands, and defended their territory fiercely. But the locals soon grew used to these aggressive creatures and old men were able to sit on benches in peace so long as they carried a bag of sardines or fry as a sop to the birds.

The terns no longer flew from pole to pole. Summer nights in the Arctic were screech-free and peck-free; summer nights in the Antarctic, likewise. The birds' innate sense of

From *LoveStar*, a novel.

direction had become confused; some instinct had informed the terns that their global position was correct, that they were undoubtedly on the right spot north of the Arctic Circle; the city must have grown up while they were away down south. The older terns were irritable and disorientated but the first generations of birds in the city knew nothing other than traffic noise and human crowds. The tern soon became one of the typical sights of Paris. Tourists could buy postcards with pictures of a tern-white Eiffel Tower and street vendors tried to press people into buying bags full of guppy fish. This didn't bother the terns, and as no predator was directly dependent on them it didn't significantly upset the balance of nature either.

A few seasons later, Chicago filled up with bees, literally filled up with bees as if it were covered with nectar, though the city was actually far from being covered with nectar: there was barely a tree or flower to be found there. Yet bees swarmed to it. On weather-satellite pictures a black depression seemed to cling low over the city, a gray swirl twisting counterclockwise around a black epicenter. The bees buzzed and droned and stung and drove the citizens mad. The only answer was to use poison; planes specially designed to extinguish forest fires flew back and forth, poisoning. Yet the bees continued to be drawn to the city and so the poisoning continued until the last citizens finally abandoned the place. The streets were covered with a fifty-centimeter-thick layer of evenly fallen bees, yet the insects continued to flock there, carrying seeds or pollen on their feet. Soon flowers sprang up in every nook and cranny, putting down roots among the dead bees. Vegetation climbed the walls of the skyscrapers and spread over the streets. The largest glass buildings turned into greenhouses, hot and damp, full of reptiles, insects, and tropical plants that sprawled unchecked from their pots, while other buildings resembled huge beehives, full of honey that oozed down the walls, trickled along the streets, and dripped into the drains. Bears got wind of the city from far away in Alaska; they licked the buildings, birds fluttered from flower to flower, and the poor took their lives in their hands and ventured into the city in search of valuables and honey.

In the center of Chicago a golden pond formed of honey that had trickled down the streets, over squares, and between the floors of almost every building in the city. On its way the honey had absorbed every imaginable scent and substance that its path had crossed, and those in search of unusual sensations tried spreading the honey on bread and found that the world and time itself turned golden, viscous, and sweet. At first sight the approach to the pond seemed easy, an endless carpet of wildflowers. But the wildflowers grew in a thin layer of soil, beneath which lay twenty meters of thick-flowing honey that preserved adventurers like formalin. Those who made their way there seldom came back, but if they returned with so much as one jar of golden honey from the pond they would be set up financially for the rest of their lives. So every day young men could be seen hanging jars and bottles about themselves until all that could be seen through the glass was an irregular human shape or distorted face. The jars clinked as they stepped onto the sticky streets and inched away. After a week they were generally still within calling distance and mothers would launch kites with a sandwich or bottle of milk suspended from them, until their sons had passed beyond the reach of the average kite. After that, they were on their own. They couldn't seek shelter in buildings, for these contained nothing but the compartments and vaults of bees. Nor could they flee if spotted by a bear or a swarm of killer bees. Where an ordinary man could travel at a maximum of ten meters an hour, a bear could cover twenty meters. The chase was as gruesome as it was slow. Generally, however, it did not require a bear or killer bees to do away with the men; most died of malnutrition or digestive disorders after being submerged up to their shoulders and eating nothing but honey, flowers, or grubs for a month.

Shortly after the bees had lost their bearings around Chicago, monarch butterflies began to behave oddly as well.

Since the oldest people could remember, the butterflies had flown every year in enormous swarms right across America to Mexico, where they would hibernate over winter. The hibernation forest was red with butterflies that clustered on every trunk, branch, and leaf, and most people saw it as a sacred forest that must not be chopped down or touched in any way. Nor was it ever chopped down or touched in any way. But one autumn the monarch butterflies took themselves up and flew in completely the opposite direction. Instead of heading south to their wintering grounds, they flew north. People tried to point them in the right direction with giant fans or nets; they were trapped from helicopters and taken to the butterfly forest by force. But some instinct was telling them to fly north and that's what they did the moment they were released. They set a course for the North Pole and swarmed around it until they froze in the air and fell to earth like giant snowflakes. They continued to flutter north until the ice cap around the pole was red with monarchs. Viewed from space, the world seemed to have acquired an orange hat. Polar bears, wandering around in the camouflage they had evolved over ten thousand years, could now easily be spotted from a hundred kilometers away. When the white blobs moved over the butterfly-patterned carpet of snow, the seals yawned and slid unhurriedly through holes in the ice. The polar bears almost died of starvation; they didn't have ten thousand years to turn orange. But then they learned to roll in the butterflies when their pelts were wet and if enough monarchs froze to them they became invisible again. Their tracks remained white but the seals didn't have the wits to beware of white tracks with sharp teeth approaching at speed.

THE CORPORATION

People soon began to suspect the reason for all this: the world was so saturated with waves, messages, transmissions, and electric fields that animals were reading all sorts of gibberish from the air. When four jumbo jets crash-landed the same day exactly seven kilometers from their intended destinations, people began in earnest to seek a substitute for all these waves. A monarch butterfly weighing ten grams could find its way a thousand kilometers without the help of a satellite. An Arctic tern could fly year after year by instinct alone from its nest on Melrakkasletta in north Iceland to its favorite rock east of Cape Town in South Africa. Creatures with brains the size of a nut, seed, or piece of fluff could do this, yet humans with their heavy heads would have needed eighteen satellites, a receiver, radar, maps, compasses, a transmitter, twenty years' training, and an atmosphere so thick with waves that it had almost ceased to be transparent.

No one could prove that the waves were harmful to humans, but many were ready to believe so. It was quite enough to believe; the rest was a mere detail. And so an extraordinary industry flourished as never before around wave-defenses. The public had become afraid and paranoid. The world was radioactive. Everyone who got ill, with anything from leukemia to a cold, blamed the waves. Legal proceedings were started weekly against the world's most popular radio and television stations for the most-unrelated problems blamed on wave pollution. "Put on a thick cap!" said mothers. "It'll protect you from the waves. Otherwise your hair will become electric and sap your life force!" "Put on your gloves, son! Bare fingers are like aerials that attract waves." "Keep a stone in your left pocket and a small bottle of water in your right. That'll balance the flow of energy."

If someone rang another person's mobile phone unusually often, suspicions were raised:

"Hi, how are you?"

"Fine. Did you want anything in particular?"

"No, just to hear your voice."

(Coldly) "Right." (Thinks: She's trying to kill me.)

Microwave transmitters and broadcasting towers were blown up daily by fanatical members of radical residents' associations but these incidents were generally hushed up by the media to prevent an epidemic. It was mainly the print media that gave good coverage to such news items, as their sales increased in direct correlation to the number of towers blown up.

Scientists shook their heads over the public's stupidity. Doctors told them it was completely unproven that waves had any effect on the human body, and serious academics did not want to be associated with such a crackpot field.

In an old hangar at Reykjavík airport, however, a small international group of ornithologists, molecular biologists, aerodynamicists, and biochemists had gathered to dabble in waves. Day and night they worked, dissecting and examining terns, pigeons, bees, salmon, and monarch butterflies. They were driven by the unshakable belief that it was possible to unlock the secrets that lay behind the navigation instinct. The outfit was called LoveStar, and the boss himself was never known by any name other than LoveStar. No reasons were given for the name and people soon gave up expecting a sensible explanation, as the employees of LoveStar were regarded by most as crazy. They pretended to be either mad or autistic when journalists tried to obtain interviews with them and ask questions about their work. They did not wish for anything in their research to rouse the interest of the outside world. Outside the hangar there was nothing to be seen but nine-year-old family cars. This was in keeping with the LoveStar dictate: "Nine-year-old Toyotas are invisible."

In the LoveStar laboratory, people pondered such questions as how a shoal of fish could spin round on the spot, every fish at the same split second, as if they had a single body, without it being possible to detect a message passing between them. Or how a flock of birds could fly in perfect unison, as if controlled by one mind.

In the age of ideas it was generally possible to find solutions to problems by making enough men think for long enough at once. That wasn't so complicated. One man was made to split a rock, the next to split the split rock, and so on until the atom was found. The man who split the atom was not available for comment.

At LoveStar, measuring equipment was developed that could detect signals so weak as to be at levels formerly considered supernatural. This is where the firm's strength lay. The research department's motto was simple: "Everything has substance. The complicated exists, the strange exists, the incomprehensible exists, the unexplained and imaginary exist, but the supernatural does not exist, though nothing is ruled out." The LoveStar group was motivated by a deep conviction: It was obvious that birdwaves were neither imaginary nor supernatural.

It was not long before the LoveStar experts were on the trail. They discovered ways of transmitting sounds, images, and messages between human beings using birdwaves that were weak, harmless, and could be picked up by devices as light as a butterfly's brain.

While most companies had Mood Divisions that tried to market the company, talk up its success, and inspire investor confidence with premature press releases, LoveStar took the opposite course. He ran a deliberate anti-mood program. The company's unofficial story, *Vogelmenschen* by Andreas Vollmer, included the following account of "anti-mood":

> LoveStar owned the majority of shares in the company himself and raised a glass with his employees every time rumors got round about the worthlessness of the shares on the gray market. The employees spoke an incomprehensible language in lectures and interviews, never giving a hint of an intelligent idea or optimism for the future. Journalists were only once admitted into the hangar before the company's discoveries were made public. Elena Krüskemper, a journalist from *Der Spiegel*, was among them and described the visit as follows in

her memoirs: "LoveStar insisted that this should be a group of journalists from the most influential newspapers in the world. He welcomed us himself, a tall, handsome man with a shrewd eye, and was amiability itself. When we went to greet him we noticed something in his hands. 'I was preparing lunch,' explained LoveStar apologetically. We saw a live puffin peeping out from between his fingers. He gripped the bird's head and twisted it a few times while the puffin struggled and tried to bite his thumb. 'They've got such a strong grip on life,' said LoveStar when he saw our faces. 'Sometimes you have to wring their necks ten times.' He laid the lifeless bird on the table and held out his hand; it was soiled, as the puffin had defecated in its death throes. Several people had questions but LoveStar wanted us to look round the company first.

He opened the door into the main area and whispered, 'Be very careful not to alarm the staff.' He accompanied us into a gloomy space where the walls were almost covered with birds' wings. Then LoveStar suddenly seemed unsure of himself, as if nervous, and whispered to the employees, 'Stay calm. They're just going to have a look at you.' A woman journalist from the *New York Times* walked up to a red-haired man who was leaning forward over his desk, hiding something under his chest. 'What have you got there?' she asked. 'He doesn't understand English,' answered LoveStar. 'This is Gudjon. He's an unusually tame physicist. He won't move even if you pat him.' LoveStar patted the man on the head, which he seemed neither to like nor dislike. Then LoveStar suddenly became jittery again, turned to us, and said with a stern expression, 'You must take care, not all my employees are this tame, and don't touch anything.' The woman from the *Times* made a face and went to the next table. On it lay a small egg. She made as if to pick up the egg and LoveStar yelled, 'No, that's Yamaguchi's egg!' The woman looked at him bemused and LoveStar yelled even louder, 'Watch out!' Before we knew what was happening a small Japanese girl had run across the room and jumped on to the table. She screeched and stabbed the woman on the head with a pencil. The staff went berserk but LoveStar reprimanded them in incomprehensible Icelandic. The woman journalist ran out into the lobby and kicked and hammered at the security door. When LoveStar reached her she was like a cornered beast. He tried to calm her down; she touched her skull and looked at her bloodied finger: 'Blood! She drew blood! You'll pay for this!' 'There, there,' said LoveStar, 'worse things have happened to journalists.' He opened the door and the woman ran out into the gray light. We had been driven into a corner but LoveStar tried to make things better. He turned to us and apologized: 'I do hope this incident won't spoil your image of the company. Any questions?' (*Vogelmenschen*, pp. 213–235)

The reporters took a savage revenge, as LoveStar had intended. Movie stars took up the cause of the puffin and investors all over the world withdrew their finance from research into birds and butterflies. Capitalists refused to fund universities that carried out research into birdwaves, and politicians were advised by their image consultants not to be associated with cranks. LoveStar found positions for those who lost their research grants.

This was all according to plan. In birdwaves they had found an unexpected and fabulous virgin territory for science, which would eventually free mankind's hands and render copper wires, fiber-optic cables, satellites, and microwave transmitters obsolete. The discoveries of LoveStar's Bird and Butterfly Division transformed the world in a matter of a few years. One could say that birdwaves were a new stage in human evolution. The "hands-free man" arose, with a keener sense of direction than a tern and freer than a monarch butterfly.

A HANDS-FREE MODERN MAN

Indridi Haraldsson was a hands-free modern man. Hands-free people had as little as possible to do with cords and cables—not that they were called cords or cables any more. Cords were known as chains. The old gadgets were not called gadgets, they were known as heaps, weights, or burdens. People looked at the heaps and burdens and thanked their lucky stars. In the old days, said some, we were wire-slaves chained to the office chair, far from birdsong and sunshine. But it wasn't like that anymore. When men in suits talked to themselves out in the street and reeled off figures, no one took them for lunatics; they were probably talking business with some unseen client. The man who sat in rapt concentration on a riverbank, apparently doing Müller's exercises, might be an engineer designing a bridge. When a sunbathing woman piped up out of the blue that she wanted to buy a two-ton saithe quota, bystanders needn't automatically assume this was addressed to them, and when a teenager made strange humming noises on the bus, nodding his head to and fro, far from suffering from severe autism he was probably listening to an invisible radio. The man who breathed rapidly or got an erection at an inappropriate time and place probably had his visual nerve permanently connected to some hard-core material, unless he was listening to the sex line. There was no limit to the filth that flooded through the permanently connected heads of some, but of course it was impossible to ban people from filling their own heads with filth, violence, and obscenity. You might just as well ban thinking. If someone stood beside you and asked: "What's the time?" and you answered straight away: "It's half past nine," the man who asked could answer, even though there was no one else in sight: "Thanks, but I wasn't actually talking to you."

So if a stranger seemed on the point of striking up a conversation, it generally paid not to answer. You might be interrupting.

Indridi Haraldsson was a hands-free modern man, so no ordinary person could see whether he was going mad or not. When he spoke to himself out in the street there might be someone on the other end of the line. When he laughed and laughed it might be for the same reason, unless he was listening to a funny radio station or, of course, he could have some comedy film or joke playing on the lens. In fact, it was impossible to tell what was going on in his head but there was no reason why it should be anything abnormal. If he ran down the street shouting, "The end of the world is nigh! The end of the world is nigh!" most people assumed he was taking part in a game on a radio station for a prize of free hamburgers. When he rode naked up and down the shopping-center escalator seven times in a row people assumed something similar; there was probably a prize being offered for anyone who would ride an escalator naked seven times in a row. It was difficult to tell what prize he was aiming for because he was naked and people could only guess at what target group he belonged to from his hairstyle, age, and physical build. Indridi was thin and pale-skinned with sparse, black bodyhair, while the hair on his head was fair, rough, and unkempt, so he was doubtless not in the target audience of the funky radio station that advertised bodybuilding, sports cars, highlights, and solariums. He neither had a tattoo nor a pierced lip, brow, forehead, or foreskin, so he wasn't in the target audience of the "no-shit" station that played covers of rock and punk and advertised raw beer, unfiltered moonshine, and filterless cigarettes. He was naked and unkempt and definitely didn't belong to any of the more sober target groups. Perhaps he was a performance artist. Artists were always busy performing. Perhaps the escalator scene was worth three points on the College of Art's performance-art course. Or he could, of course, be in an isolated rare target group. There were plenty of them around but generally an attempt was made to direct people into a more popular area where they could be reached more economically.

If Indridi suddenly barked at someone, "IIIIICE-COLD COKE! IIICCCCCE-COLD COKE!!!" for ten seconds without his eyes or body seeming to follow his speech there was nothing abnormal about that. The reason for this behavior was simple: the advertisements he had transmitted to him were directly connected to his speech centers. "IIIIICCCCE-COLD COKE!!!!" So he must be an *advertising howler*, or *howler*, as they were popularly called. He was probably broke enough to fall outside most target groups so it wasn't worth sending him advertisements. But it was possible to send advertisements through him, to others, by connecting them to his speech centers and using his mouth as a sort of loud-speaker. Those who walked past howlers could expect an announcement:

"IIIIICE-COLD COKE!"

This was more effective than conventional reminders on advertising hoardings or the radio. So Indridi squawked when he met a man on his way to the car park:

"FASTEN YOUR SEATBELT! SLOW DOWN!"

The man had been arrested for speeding without a seat-belt. As a punishment he was made to listen to and pay for two thousand edifying reminders from advertising howlers. That was probably the best thing about the new technology. It could be used to improve society.

"LOVE THY NEIGHBOR!" squawked a shady-looking man at half-hourly intervals. A born-again murderer, Indridi correctly assumed, and gave him a wide berth. Prisoners could be released early if they squawked for charities or religious firms.

Howlers were not all broke. Many were simply scroung-ing a discount or perks, and some only became howlers for the first three months of the year while they paid for the latest upgrade of the hands-free operating system. Those who didn't get their system upgraded could have problems with business or communication. Hands-free home appliances and automatic door openers only recognized the latest system and the same applied to the latest car models. They wouldn't automatically slow down if someone with the old system crossed the road, so it was just as well to take to one's heels.

If Indridi came across a group of teenagers he could yell:

"GROOVY SHOES! YOU WERE UNBELIEVABLY COOL TO BUY SUCH GROOVY SHOES!"

Getting people to buy first and then arranging for them to be praised afterward was a completely new strategy. It was believed to strengthen this behavior pattern and bring things into fashion earlier.

The announcements were sometimes absurd, sometimes just one word, slogan, or phrase, unconnected to anything else. In that case it was probably part of a longer campaign, a so-called teaser campaign that encouraged people to think long and hard. On the way down the main street you might meet an old woman who said out of the blue:

"Smoothness!"

Farther down you might meet a teenager who said:

"Smartness!"

And even if you veered round sharply and headed up the next street, you would hear whispered from a basement window:

"Reliability!"

Finally somebody would come racing down a side street on a bike shouting:

"FOOOORD! FORD!"

These campaigns always hit the target; there was no way of escaping them. Everything was measured to within a half a centimeter and the announcement was perfectly tailored to the recipient's target group, which was categorized down to their most minor eccentricity. The howler system was efficient, simple, and convenient, and ordinary members of the public could order a howler for a small fee if they needed a reminder.

"You have a meeting with the minister at three o'clock, and don't forget your wedding anniversary!"

Those who had recently moved to the city liked to order a howler or two to greet them on the street or strike up a conversation.

"Hello Gudmundur! What lovely weather we're having!"

This made the big city less cold and unfriendly. Uprooted farmers who liked to wake up to cockcrow could get their neighbors to crow at six o'clock in the morning if they were lucky enough to live near a howler.

"*Cock-a-doodle-do! Time to wake up!*"

Many entrepreneurs felt it essential to receive a confidence boost first thing in the morning:

"You're the best!" said the Chinese cleaning woman.

"No one can stop you, Magnus!" said the shifty caretaker.

"You're looking good today!" said the taxi driver. "Today's a day to win!"

Passersby were prepared for anything when there were free men around, so no one paid any attention when Indridi sat in a café and wept. He sat in a corner, crying his eyes out, but it crossed very few people's minds to ask him what the matter was. It was probably Greek-tragedy week with his target group. It was simplest to assume this sort of thing. Or he could be an advertising trap.

"Why are you crying?"

"I want a Honda so much—they're such great cars and there's a brilliant offer this week."

Advertising traps or adTRAPS went further than howlers; they hired out not only their speech centers but also their primitive biological and emotional responses. The method was still technologically imperfect, so sometimes traps couldn't stop laughing or crying for days on end. Of course, no one was compelled to become a trap, to laugh, cry, or wet themselves in public and say to a woman with a howling baby:

"Now would have been a good time to have 100 percent absorbent Pampers!"

Many people let themselves be persuaded to become traps, as the hiring out of one's emotions paid as much as ten conventional speech-center connections and was generally more effective, especially if people were made to do something funny, like wet themselves or cry like a baby.

When the hands-free, permanently online modern man

emerged on the scene with his lens and invisible earpieces, most borders were broken down. For example, it was never possible to know where a company's outside parameters really lay. If Indridi met an old school friend in public he could never tell whether the school friend was actually "serving" him. After a bit of a chat (which, on reflection, did begin with the words, "Dear Indridi, can I help?") the conversation generally ended the same way:

"It's clouding over," said Indridi, "best get a move on."

"Oh, that doesn't bother me—I've got an excellent umbrella. Can I offer you an excellent umbrella like this?"

"No thanks. There might be a thunderstorm."

"Oh, I've got such a great insurance policy with LoveLife. I got the umbrella as an extra when I bought this great insurance policy with LoveLife."

It was clear that the old school friend was a *secret host* and his conversation was slanted toward his goal of selling an umbrella or insurance. It didn't matter what was being discussed. The offer was like a magnet, black hole, or drain and every single conversation was doomed to be sucked down that drain, regardless of what was originally being discussed.

Family:

"How's your mother?"

"She's fine—she's got such great life insurance, with LoveLife…"

Art:

"What did you think of Jonas's poem?"

"I wonder what sort of life insurance they had in the nineteenth century? LoveLife hadn't been founded then…"

Sports:

"Good game yesterday."

"Yes, poor Gisli—torn ligament—I wonder if he's covered for that? I'll look him up at LoveLife—you're with them, aren't you?"

It was difficult to distinguish a secret host from anyone else. So people didn't always know whom it was safe to believe and trust. A host could be anyone, even a member of one's own inner circle. Unlike traps and howlers, secret hosts advertised on their own initiative. A good secret host didn't give himself away and alternated products regularly. Some sold nothing directly; they merely advertised and created the right mood.

"I recommend this *film*, you must go and see this *film*, it's supposed to be a really good *film*. I'd go right now."

Secret hosts sometimes worked as *spies*. They sent reports to iSTAR (LoveStar Mood Division's Image, Marketing, and Publicity Department). Only a handful of managers worked in the iSTAR office; the rest were hands-free modern people, scattered around the globe, drawing their information from a database on Svalbard.

iSTAR had no problem collecting basic information about culture consumption, television viewing, radio listening, food bills, musical taste, daily journeys, main interests, and opinions, but more detailed information could come in useful. Hosts and spies twisted their conversations round to the company's interests in search of image, while iSTAR experts got to be a fly on the wall. A discussion among a group of friends about love, death, God, or friendship could abruptly take a U-turn when the spy asked out of the blue, "Did you think the politician's tie was tasteful? What about his opinions? Do you sympathies with them? Do you remember how many civilians were killed eight years ago? Do you remember where? Would you put up with a greater loss of human life if you listened to more pop news? The leader has a cute little cat called Molly. Do you find him more likeable now? What about the disabled? Are they fun? Would you take a cut in your standard of living in order to provide them with more services? What do you really think of Madonna?"

Indridi was on his way home that day but no one said to him encouragingly, "Hello, Indridi! You're looking good today!" as he couldn't afford such luxuries. On the way up through

Rofabaer he began to sing "May Star." All the howlers in town were singing "May Star" at that moment; it was part of a publicity campaign for an international song initiative the following week. The song echoed round the town but it was hard to tell who was singing voluntarily and who wasn't. It wasn't considered cool to be a howler, so many people pretended to be singing voluntarily by doing their best to look as if they were loving it. To most passersby, Indridi appeared a living, lighthearted advertisement. Their lenses showed the notes pouring from his head along with the lyrics, which hovered cheerfully in the air:

"Sing and be happy! International song week starts on Monday!"

When the song was over, Indridi had to fight back tears. Something unbelievably important had been struggling to emerge from his mind but he had lost the thread when "May Star" began. His life was going to the dogs and everything was upside-down; only a few weeks before, life had been as sweet as a strawberry, love as golden as honey, but now he wasn't sure that love was all that would be waiting for him when he got home.

Translation by Victoria Cribb

NOTES ON CONTRIBUTORS

GUÐBERGUR BERGSSON has published nearly twenty books. He has twice been the recipient of the Icelandic Literary Prize, in 1991 for *The Swan* and in 1997 for *Father and Mother and the Mystery of Childhood.* He divides his time between Iceland and Spain.

BIRNA ANNA BJÖRNSDÓTTIR, ODDNÝ STURLUDÓTTIR, and SILJA HAUKSDÓTTIR became friends as teenagers. They collaborated on the novel *Dís.* Besides writing, Silja has worked in filmmaking, Birna Anna as a journalist, and Oddný as a piano teacher. In December of 2004, the feature film *Dís* was released; all three wrote the screenplay and Silja directed the film.

KIARA BRINKMAN is working toward her MFA in creative writing from Goddard College. She lives in San Francisco and is writing her first novel.

JUDY BUDNITZ is the author of the books *Flying Leap* and *If I Told You Once.* Her new story collection, *Nice Big American Baby,* will be published in February.

JIMMY CHEN lives in San Francisco. He enjoys tennis, reading, and writing.

RODDY DOYLE'S latest novel is *Oh, Play That Thing.*

THORARINN ELDJARN is a poet, novelist, short-story writer, playwright and translator. His novel *The Blue Tower* was published in England. Among Thorarinn's translations are works by August Strindberg, Erlend Loe, and Lewis Carroll.

GYRÐIR ELÍASSON has written ten volumes of poetry and five books of prose. *The Yellow House,* a collection of short stories, won the Icelandic Literary Prize in 2000. He lives in Reykjavík.

SETH FRIED is a student at Bowling Green State University in Bowling Green, Ohio, where he majors in Latin and creative writing. He is also an intern at the *Mid-American Review.* This is his first published story.

EINAR MAR GUÐMUNDSSON'S novels, short stories, and poems have been translated into Danish, Swedish, Norwegian, English, and German. He wrote the screenplay for the film *Angels of the Universe*, adapted from his novel of the same name.

HALLGRÍMUR HELGASON is the author of three novels, including the Icelandic Literary Prize–winning *Author of Iceland*, and a collection of poems. The film *101 Reykjavík* is based on his novel of the same name. His comic strip runs in one of Iceland's newspapers, and exhibitions of his art have been held in Reykjavík, New York, and Paris.

ERIC HANSON is a writer and artist who lives in Minneapolis. His art appears occasionally in *The Atlantic, Harper's, The New Yorker,* and other magazines.

ROY KESEY lives in Beijing with his wife and children. This is his third story to appear in *McSweeney's*; other stories of his will soon be appearing in *The Iowa Review, Other Voices* and *Prism International,* among other magazines.

ANDRI SNÆR MAGNASON is the author of a novel, two books of poems, a short-story collection, and *The Story of the*

Blue Planet, the first children's book to win the Icelandic Literary Prize.

STEVEN MILLHAUSER is the author of several collections of short stories and novellas, including *The Knife Thrower, The Barnum Museum,* and *The King in the Tree.* He lives in Saratoga Springs, New York.

BRAGI ÓLAFSSON has written three radio plays, four books of poetry, a short-story collection, and two novels. Bragi is also a founding member of the Sugarcubes; he played bass.

PADGETT POWELL has written six books of fiction and directs MFA@FLA, the writing program at the University of Florida (www.english.ufl. edu/crw/).

BENJAMIN ROSENBAUM lives in Virginia with his wife and two small children. His stories have appeared in *Harper's, Quarterly West, Vestal Review, F&SF, Strange Horizons,* and elsewhere.

SJÓN has published novels, poems, and children's books. He has written lyrics for Björk, and his libretto for Lars Von Trier's musical *Dancer in the Dark* earned him an Oscar nomination in 2001.

NOTES ON SUBSCRIBERS

[chosen at random]

RAQUEL AGUIRRE is a student and a petsitter in Austin, Texas.

LOU ANDERS is the editorial director of Pyr, an science fiction and fantasy imprint from Prometheus Books. He lives in Birmingham, Alabama.

KATIE ARMSTRONG recently traveled around the world. She lives in Fort Collins, Colorado.

CEEBS BAILEY is a writer and copywriter living in West L.A.

DONA BAILEY teaches college-level multimedia courses. She lives in Little Rock, Arkansas.

ED BAINES lives in Edinburgh, Scotland. He writes about Latin American stock markets and is currently learning how to cook.

JIM BALL is cofounder of Alpine Access, the fastest-growing technology company in Colorado. He lives in Arvada, Colorado.

SABRINA BALMICK is a student at NYU's Center for Publishing. She is currently interning for Atria Books and hails from South Florida.

MARK BAXTER edits lame television shows in Toronto, Ontario. He is currently looking for work.

CAMI CARTER is pursuing her Masters of Arts in Teaching at Brown University, after teaching in the Bronx for two years and cofounding a nonprofit organization with her mother.

LEAH HANZLICEK is a social worker and photographer in Eugene, Oregon.

PRUDENCE HOCKLEY is a New Zealander who lives in Seattle, Washington, and teaches high-school English.

VALERIE VADALA HOMER is the director of the Scottsdale Public Art Program. She has written about the work of artist James Turrell and Robert Indiana.

BRIAN JASIORKOWSKI manages a private investment fund in New York.

JACK JOWETT has been traveling the world for the past six

months. He hasn't gotten to read the last issue yet.

J.D. LOWRY lives in Las Vegas, Nevada. She is an attorney who represents hospitals and doctors in medical malpractice cases, and does not know how to ride a bicycle.

SHARAIN SASHEIR NAYLOR works for the United States Navy as a Chinese linguist and lives in Waialua, Hawaii.

DANIEL NEISES works as an infectious disease epidemiologist for the Kansas Department of Health and Environment.

JOSH PETERSON works with historical census data at the Minnesota Population Center at the University of Minnesota. He is also an undergraduate student there, studying history.

ELISE PUGH studies the Restoration and 18th-century theater and church at the University of Virginia. She

also paints and shows her work in her hometown of Memphis, Tennessee.

CELESTE RASMUSSEN is a lawyer. She lives in New Orleans, Louisiana.

BRYAN ROBERTS writes about his experiences as a government mule in Iraq at the on-again, off-again weblog e-rocky-confidential.com. He is from Portland, Oregon.

DEBBIE SCOTT works as a graphic designer in an environmental engineering firm. She is studying 3D imaging and animation at NYU.

BEK SMITH lives in Perth, Western Australia and studies theater and creative writing at the university.

MURRAY STEELE is a first-class-honors computing graduate. He loves movies and music.

CHIP WOODS fixes laptops for middle and high school students. He lives in Georgia.

IF YOU WOULD LIKE TO JOIN THEM:

www.mcsweeneys.net/subscribe